Don't Make Promises

Editing by: Allie Bliss from Blissed Out Editing
Proofreading by Sarah Baker from Word Emporium

Don't Make Promises

BREAKING THE RULES SERIES
BOOK THREE

KA JAMES

KALEIDOSCOPE PUBLISHING LTD

Dedication

To all the girlies who've ever had a thing for their siblings best friend...

This one's for you!

Trigger Warnings

To help you decide if this book is for you, I have included a trope and trigger warning outline below. Rest assured, there is a happy ending but to make it interesting for you, there has to be some turbulence on the journey.

This is a contemporary romance.

Tropes: Brother's Best Friend, Forced Proximity, Billionaire, Protective Alpha

Triggers: Domestic Violence

Playlist

Listen Here
Doesn't Really Matter - Janet Jackson
I'm Real - JLO
Drop It Like It's Hot - Snoop Dogg Ft. Pharrell
Don't Let Go (Love) - En Vogue
Are You That Somebody - Aaliyah
Come & Get It - Selena Gomez
Dress - Taylor Swift
Apartment - Bobi Andonov
All In My Head - Tori Kelly
I Miss You - Beyonce
Lose Control - Teddy Swim
Like I'm Gonna Lose You - Meghan Trainor & John Legend
All of Me - John Legend
I Hate This Part - The Pussycat Dolls
Till There's Nothing Left - Cam

Prologue — Savannah

I'm walking down the corridor, trying to avoid the jocks and cheerleaders who always seem to crowd around after the final bell has rung, when I see him. Even though I'm not one of the popular kids, I still know most people in this school, but I don't know him. He must be new.

My hand comes to rest on the latch of my locker as I stare at him unashamedly. It's like all the air has been ripped from my lungs as I take him in. A fluttering starts in the pit of my stomach as my body heats.

I've never felt anything like this before and I'm not entirely sure what's caused it.

He's the most beautiful boy I've ever seen, but I know I'd never stand a chance with him. Not with my braces, awkwardness, and weird reddish-blonde hair. I reach up and wrap a strand of it around my finger. As soon as I'm old enough to go to the salon alone, I'm going to dye it.

With a shake of my head, I turn my focus back to unlocking my locker and putting away my books so I can head home.

"Sav, come here."

I roll my eyes as I turn to face my brother, hating that he calls me that, but in typical big brother fashion, Jack does it all the time. He's four years older than me, and one of the popular guys in our school. He's the reason I know most of the people here, and why they also call me Sav.

"Come on, Sav, I wanna introduce you to my new friend."

My eyes land on Jack before moving to the boy that stands next to him. I swallow down the moisture that floods my mouth as his gaze connects with mine. The intensity in his green mixed with brown eyes forces me to break eye contact. The current of electricity in that one look is too much for me to handle.

Jack has an innate need to introduce me to people so that his friends become my friends. He hasn't quite grasped the fact that I don't mind doing my own thing. Or that I'm old enough to choose my own friends.

I don't really want to know who the new guy is, why he's here, or what he sounds like. From one look alone I know he'll occupy my thoughts and that he'll haunt my dreams at night.

With my eyes firmly on my feet, my heart hammers in my chest as they approach. Even when they're standing in front of me, I still don't look up. *Jeez, his feet are big.*

"Noah, this is my baby sister, Sav," Jack introduces me as he slings his arm around my shoulder, pulling me into his side.

Noah.

A swift elbow to the ribs makes Jack drop his arm. He laughs at me, a knowing smirk on his face when I lift my eyes to give him a death stare. *God, he can be insufferable.*

"My name's Savannah." I hold my chin up high as I look into the new guy's eyes, fanned by long dark lashes.

His voice is rough and far deeper than any boy I've ever met when he says, "It's nice to meet you, Savannah."

He holds out his hand, and because my mama taught me to have manners, I slip mine into his. His skin is smooth and warm as he envelopes my tiny hand in his far larger one. It feels like an eternity passes between us as we stare at each other. There's something hidden behind his dreamy gaze that tells a story of a lifetime of pain. It's hard to believe he's the same age as Jack.

The sounds of the busy corridor fade away, and I have an overwhelming urge to step into his arms and just hold him.

A frown pulls at my brow, and I drop his hand like it's on fire as I step back. He doesn't seem to mind, because he turns to my brother, an easy smile on his face.

"Should we get going?"

I look to Jack for an answer, unsure of what Noah

means because Jack's supposed to give *me* a ride home, not him.

Sensing where my thoughts have gone, Jack slings his arm around my shoulders again and says, "Don't worry, Sav, Noah's just coming to our house for dinner. Mama already cleared it."

Oh no, that's even worse than not having a ride home. I'd rather they left me here and went somewhere else. Jack turns me in the direction of the parking lot, too busy chatting away to notice my internal panic.

The feelings coursing through me are too much for fourteen-year-old me to handle, so I do what I do best and what I hate most; I retreat into myself.

The car ride home is filled with R'n'B songs as Jack navigates through Montgomery, Alabama as I try in vain to distract myself from the boy in the front passenger seat. I love this city and the familiar streets that pass us by, as the car eats up the miles home. There's so much history here, and when I move—my dream is to live in New York and make it big on Broadway—I'll be sure to come back and visit.

As soon as the car comes to a stop, I throw my door open and bolt for the house. My body is overwhelmed with feelings I've never felt before and I need some time away from Noah to sort through them. How I'm going to make it through dinner is beyond me. Maybe Mama will let me eat in my room.

Yeah, that's wishful thinking.

I race through the house and shut myself in my

bedroom, tossing my bag to the floor. Next off is my jacket and then my shoes, before I dive onto the bed and bury myself under the covers.

Later that night when I'm called for dinner, I drag my feet, wishing my earlier plea to eat in my room hadn't fallen on deaf ears. Especially as at dinner when I quickly realize that isolating myself in my room has done nothing to prepare me for seeing him again. It's been a matter of hours, and yet it's like I'm seeing him for the first time again. My legs feel like jelly as I walk to the table and sink into my chair.

There's no way I'm going to be able to eat, not with the way my tongue feels thick in my mouth.

My mama, always wanting to make people feel welcome, starts the conversation as she sits at the table. She's oblivious to the rushing in my ears when she asks, "So, Noah, how long have you been in Montgomery?"

"We moved right at the end of summer, ma'am."

Mama laughs as she says, "Please, call me Sadie. How are you finding it?"

Noah serves himself some of the salad from the bowl in the middle of the table, and I watch his movements from under my lashes. "It's different from New York, but I'm liking it."

He's from New York?

"You don't sound like you're from New York," I blurt out before I can stop myself. My cheeks flame as all eyes turn to face me.

My dad is the first to speak. "Now, don't be rude, Savannah."

I drop my eyes to the mac and cheese on my plate. "Sorry, I didn't mean to be rude."

When I'm greeted with silence, I look up into his stunning hazel eyes. One side of his mouth is lifted, and it's then that I notice how pillowy his lips are. "It's okay. I grew up all over, so was never in one place long enough to have just one accent."

"Oh, okay," I breathe, as if he's just told me the most fascinating fact.

He doesn't try to hide the smile that lights up his face and I drop my head as my cheeks heat again at being the center of *his* attention.

I spend the rest of dinner focused on eating my food until I can excuse myself to my room on the pretext of doing my homework. The reality is I did it hours ago. I just need to not be near him right now.

When he leaves, I watch through the slats of my blinds in my bedroom window as he walks down the driveway and to a house a couple of doors down. When his front door closes, I finally move and flop down onto my bed as I look up at the ceiling. Everything that happened today plays like a movie in my mind as I scrutinize our every interaction.

Laying in the darkness, unable to sleep, I vow to myself from this day forward I will be brave and bold. I won't hide anymore.

This is how I met Noah, my brother's best friend. It was the first day I fell in love and realized that you can't always have the one you want.

I wish I'd known when we first met what was to come, of all the heartache and pain that would follow.

Would I still have gone through it?

Most definitely.

ONE

Savannah

T his has been both the longest and worst week I've had in a very long time. I've been away for weeks at a workshop with my theatre production. Which wouldn't normally be an issue, especially as we'd nailed the timings and had everything perfected. But then we found out the producer had pulled the funding and the show was canceled.

Just like that.

Four hours ago I was working my ass off upstate, pushing through the pain of my aching feet and now I'm walking down the sidewalk of New York City, ready for a nap.

Despite shows being canceled all the time, it doesn't make it hurt any less. Everyone had worked so hard to get everything perfected and for it to all go to waste is just so frustrating, but unfortunately, it is the nature of the beast when it comes to Broadway.

I love working on Broadway; it's been my dream for as long as I could remember. Get out of Montgomery, Alabama, check. Make it big on Broadway in New York, in progress.

That goal is one that's going to take me years. If you want to 'make it big', you have to perfect your craft and that isn't something you can do overnight or even in five or ten years.

It doesn't help that shows can get canceled at the drop of a hat, cutting off any potential opportunities to be seen and get your name out there. Being a Broadway star isn't for the faint hearted. It's why I work multiple jobs. Because when things like this happen, you lose your whole income stream, and living in New York City is not cheap.

Pulling one of my duffels further onto my shoulder with one hand, I slip my other under my white t-shirt and into the loop of my jeans, tugging them up. I can't wait to get out of them. There aren't many things worse than having your jeans fall down as you're trying to keep up with the pace of a crowded street.

The air conditioning was broken on the bus ride home and when you add in twenty already hot and sweaty people, it's just a recipe for disaster. I get a whiff of my armpits, barely holding back the gag at the stench as I trudge along the pavement. Maybe a long overdue soak in Will's tub wouldn't go amiss.

Our tub?

Will—my boyfriend of six months—and I moved in

together just before I went away. Some may call me impulsive, but I like to think of myself as decisive. *Why hang around when you know what you want?*

Okay, maybe I don't *know* that I want Will, but what I do know is that he's nice enough company, and he does make me laugh... sometimes.

When I told Mama that I was moving in with him, she told me I should wait. Perhaps she's right and I should have. Or I should have at least waited until I came back from the workshop, but his suggestion came at a time when I needed it most. Living with five other girls in a small brownstone mere blocks away from him seemed like a waste.

Especially when, slowly, over the course of a couple of months, there seemed to be this weird tension growing between me and one of my roommates. It was even worse if Will came around. I put it down to the fact that Will can be a bit cocky even if the other girls didn't seem to mind, so I suggested we spend more and more time at his. One night, we were sitting on his couch and he asked me to move in. It didn't sound so bad, so I said yes.

Except for the fact that we've lived together for ten weeks and only seen each other for two of those.

Of course, we've spoken—occasionally—while I've been away, but it's always crazy busy when you're work-shopping a show and priorities change. Because of this, our contact has been brief. Had I been in the city, my focus would have been on building a relationship with him.

Add in all the late nights and early mornings, and it's really hard to maintain a relationship when you're trying to build a career that demands you give it your every waking moment. I'm lucky to have found a guy that also works insane hours—he's a stockbroker—and so doesn't mind that his girlfriend is barely around. It's a comfortable companionship.

On the ride home, I pulled out my phone and typed out a message to him to let him know I would be home early, but something in my gut told me not to press send. Will should be at work, so there should be no reason for this heavy, sinking feeling in the pit of my stomach, like a foreboding of what's to come. But my gut has got me this far in life, so instead, I put my phone away and decided not to tell him.

'Home' is currently a brownstone in Brooklyn. I wouldn't really call it home, not when—aside from my suitcases—there isn't a whole lot of evidence that I live there.

Lost in my own thoughts, I get shoulder checked by a commuter on the sidewalk. My bag slides from my shoulder and I bend to pick it up to a chorus of curses and "get out the way." Hurriedly, I swipe it up, as I move my legs and match the flow of the crowd.

The bus dropped us at the theatre and for some reason, even with the ache of the last two months, I still thought it would be a good idea to walk home. I just want to soak in the tub, get changed, no doubt tidy up Will's mess and make us some dinner before he gets back. An apology of sorts for being gone so long.

My eyes snag on the subway sign on the corner of the block and I pick up the pace. From here, I can be there in fifteen minutes. It seems like a no brainer.

The rest of the journey passes in a blur and before I know it, I'm turning my key in the lock, letting myself into the house. A blast of cool air hits me as I step out of the warm late July air. Thank heavens I'm home, but I don't think this weather warrants the air conditioning being left on while Will's at work.

Throwing my bags on the floor by the door, I toss my keys on the table that sits underneath the coat hooks. Taking a step forward, I still when my eyes land on a bralette that's haphazardly hanging on the bannister. My brow tugs together as my mind runs through my two weeks in this house.

It's right in view of the front door. I haven't done any laundry. Neither have I had a chance to unpack my fancy underwear.

Moving toward it, I pick it up from the dark mahogany post for a closer inspection. It's cute but definitely a few sizes too big for me. A closer look at the label confirms the DD cup bra belongs to someone else.

All of this leads me to the one conclusion I was hoping wasn't true—that bralette is most definitely not mine.

With the bra dangling from my finger, my gaze darts

around the room, finding more discarded clothes. A white men's shirt lays crumpled on the floor, with a bright pink crop top not far from it. I follow the trail of clothes into the living room to the right of the staircase.

In typical brownstone fashion, the entryway is narrow, with the staircase to the upper floors directly in front of you. The first room is the living room, with the kitchen at the back of the house and a half bathroom between the two rooms. It's a nice house, but it's a bachelor pad, all grays and blacks, with no color to break up the boring aesthetic of his furniture.

There's a jacket thrown over the arm of the couch, but other than that, there's no more clothing in the living room. Returning to the hallway, my eyes land on pieces of fabric leading upstairs. It's like I was blind to it all when I first stepped inside.

There's no mistaking that these are hastily discarded. I squint as I try to figure out if the belt buckle glinting at me is the one Will wears. He told me some story or other about how he came to get a belt with his initials, but to be honest, I tuned him out.

Who even wears their initials on things?

It definitely looks like his.

My gaze moves to the flash of red draped over the step above. Last time I checked, my boyfriend doesn't wear G-strings. Or bralettes for that matter.

The sounds of New York draw my attention to the still open front door. Moving to close it, I stand still, listening for any sounds that don't belong.

That's when I hear it.

The unmistakable sound of a woman faking her orgasm. It's all breathy and porno sounding. I should know, I had to do enough of that with Will.

Maybe it's not him.

Who am I kidding? Of course it's him. He's very anal about his space. He wouldn't let just anyone in here and certainly not to screw.

Not one to shy away from confrontation, because I firmly believe that life is too short to cower away from it, I move toward the staircase.

What strikes me in this moment as I sneak up the stairs, trying to be as quiet as possible, is that I'm not hurt by what I've walked in on. Not even a little. If anything, I'm relieved.

Relief that I don't have to give up my time and effort for a man I knew even before I went away, wasn't right for me. I was settling, but in doing so I was playing the greatest role of my life. The doting girlfriend. Heck, I was coming home from an exhausting trip, prepared to clean up after this guy. My meemaw would be furious if she could have heard me.

I reach the top of the stairs, pausing as I plan my approach. One side of me—the one with a flair for the dramatics—wants to make a scene, play the scorned woman. But the other side—the one that's bone tired and just wants to shower and go to bed—wants to get her stuff and leave. I settle for somewhere in the middle.

The noises grow louder with each step I take. Why

does it suddenly feel like he lives in a mansion? The anticipation builds inside of me as I move down the corridor.

It really is a surprise I didn't hear them when I first came in. I can't help the smirk that graces my lips as a thought comes to me.

I'm surprised he's lasted this long.

With me, Will was more of a two pumps and he's done kind of guy. The more and more I think about it, I really am better off. I'd almost go as far as to say, he's done me a favor. Although this is the first time I've ever been cheated on—as far as I know—I can imagine it's never nice, but when you were only half in, it doesn't really hurt at all.

As I navigate down the corridor, I send up a silent prayer that I don't run across a stray, creaky floorboard that gives away my approach. Before moving in, I stayed over countless nights, but never paid much attention to the noises that the house made. I really wish I had, because if my plan is going to work, I need the advantage of a sneak attack.

My approach is halted when my gaze lands on a small bag of white powder laying in the middle of the floor. I'm trying to process everything that I've seen so far but nothing is making any sense.

Is this even Will's house?

I mean, the key worked, so it's got to be the right one, but drugs and people having sex in the middle of the day? *That's not Will.*

Clearly I don't know Will, because there's no denying the moans and grunts are him.

Maybe whoever he has in there brought it with them. Will treats his body like a temple. I'm talking about green juices that taste like ass and protein shakes that aren't much better.

He wouldn't do drugs. But who am I kidding, I don't know what he would and wouldn't do. Especially because he's in there having sex with another woman.

My eyes dart to the slightly ajar door, and if the grunting noises are anything to go by, we're reaching the grand finale.

I pick up the packet and move toward the door with it clutched in my hand. Their voices fill the room, both gasping for breath as if they've run a marathon.

"More, Willy baby. I need more."

Will grunts, his voice coming in breathy gasps as he replies, "God, you feel so good. You've got the most perfect lady garden. It's the best I've ever had."

I think I might be sick.

Pushing the door open soundlessly, I stand and watch as my—ex—boyfriend and a mysterious redhead have sex in our bed. *His bed.* They don't hear me as I wait; they're too engrossed in each other.

As I lean against the doorjamb, watching Will's hips as they piston at a speed I'm unfortunately very familiar with and know happens when he's about to come. Like a lightbulb moment, it hits me and I realize why I'm not hurt by this betrayal.

I'm not going to get into that now. There are more important things to confront than why I was never one hundred percent in this relationship.

With a slow clap, I push away from the doorjamb and move into the room before they can finish. "That was quite a show. Y'all should sell tickets, I'm sure it'll sell out. Personally, I won't attend again. I think once is enough."

Will and the mystery woman separate at high speed. My lips twitch as I watch Will comically leap like a grasshopper away from the woman. He moves so fast I'm surprised they don't sustain any injuries.

Throwing off the covers, he stands next to the bed, his now softening cock slapping around as he tries to get his bearings. *Nice, no condom.* His chest rises and falls with his labored breaths and I watch as he looks from me to the door, licking his lips, as he assesses his options.

Briefly, I wonder how long this has been going on before my gaze moves to the bed and I see my old roommate: Melanie. I should have guessed. She's the reason I felt like I needed to move out of the place I was in before here. If only she'd been woman enough to come to me instead of sleeping with my boyfriend behind my back.

Obviously choosing to stay and try to charm his way out of this, Will says, "Babe, I can explain."

With as much sarcasm as I can inject into my voice, I fold my arms across my chest and reply, "Really? I'd love to hear how *my boyfriend* can explain away the fact that he was just having sex with my old roommate. How long has this been going on for?"

"Well, sh—"

I hold up a hand, because I'm really not interested. No amount of words will ever make this okay. "Actually, I don't really care, Will."

Moving to the closet, I drag out the suitcase I hadn't finished unpacking before I had to leave, and walk to the door. Neither of them move. Melanie's face has a smug smile on it as she sits nestled in the sheets, marking the bed as hers. That alone tells me everything I need to know. Well, she's welcome to him, because there is no way I would ever allow him to touch me again.

Nobody utters a word as I walk across the room, at least not until Will seems to get himself together and says, "Baby, please. I'm sorry. She doesn't mean anything to me. Please don't go."

He moves toward me, but when I turn to face him he comes up short next to the bed with his shriveled cock on display. Melanie lets out an audible gasp, and I shake my head at his audacity. She burrows herself under the covers, hopefully in embarrassment or shame, but I doubt it.

My Southern accent comes out full force the more irritated I get. I've been working so hard to tone it down so I can broaden my range, but I'm so pissed that I can't control it right now. "Save yourself the embarrassment of beggin' for a second chance that ain't ever gonna happen. The moment you slept with her was the second you lost me. How you can stand there tellin' me she don't mean nothin' to ya, when she's in the same room and clearly has feelin's for you, tells me all I need to know. You don't deserve me."

Now that I'm focused on him, I see his glassy eyes, no doubt from whatever drug is in the small plastic bag. I throw the packet I'd forgotten about on the table next to the door. "Y'all dropped that in the hallway."

I have zero interest in getting into an argument with him. My suitcase trails behind me as I walk down the hallway. When I reach the top of the stairs, I turn to find Will—thankfully now dressed—has followed me.

He tries to cajole me into staying but it's just condescending when he says, "Come on, baby. We can talk about this."

"I don't have nothin' else to say to you."

He just can't let it go. *Let me go.* "You don't have to say anything, please just listen. I can explain. You mean the world to me."

It won't make a lick of difference.

Despite turning away to walk down the stairs, Will takes my silence as his cue to go ahead and spout whatever hogwash he's come up with for his reasoning to cheat on me. I try to tune him out as I concentrate on navigating the steps with my suitcase.

"You were never here."

I was working.

"Any time I wanted to hang out you told me you were busy."

What is he, five?

"She showed me attention and I gave in. I'm only human, Savannah. I have needs."

You motherfucker.

I don't swear much, because my mama would wash my mouth out if she could hear me, but this man is testing my last nerve. How dare this pathetic excuse of a man blame *me* for his lack of self control?

When I reach the bottom of the stairs, I set the suitcase down and turn to face him. With an almost deathly calm tone and a serene look on my face, I say matter of factly, "So, let me get this straight. It's my fault for working multiple jobs and not giving you enough attention? That's why you slept with my roommate while high off your face on whatever I found on the floor?"

Will runs a hand over the back of his neck as he looks away sheepishly. He's not as stupid as he looks then. With a shake of my head, I turn and walk toward the door, dragging my suitcase behind me.

I can hear him scurrying behind me, as he replies, "Okay, that came out wrong. Maybe you can take a couple of days to calm down and then we can have a rational talk about this. Put it all behind us."

First of all, I thought I'd been pretty darn calm for a woman that just walked in on her boyfriend cheating on her. Second of all, is he really delusional enough to think I'd ever talk to him again? The moment I walked through that door, he was dead to me.

Much like if I was talking to a child, I face him again

and say as slowly as I can, "Will, this," I motion between us, "is over."

When I turn to continue toward the door, he grabs a hold of my arm, his cold, clammy fingers painfully digging into my flesh. I try to yank my arm free, his grip tightening, his eyes crazed as he bares his teeth at me. "You can't leave me, Savannah."

"I can and I will. Now let go of me."

"No. You can't leave." He tries to be forceful but it comes across more sulky now.

"You're hurtin' me, Will. Let go of my arm."

My words seem to have the opposite effect as his hold tightens and he tugs me in closer. His voice is a dark whisper as he says, "You *can't* leave. I won't allow it, Van."

Most people would be frightened of someone who's nearly twice their size in weight and nearly a foot taller, but many years ago, I made a promise to myself that I wouldn't ever be afraid of anything.

At this point, I just want to get out of here and find somewhere to stay because it's getting late. I'm tired. From the traveling and having this one-sided conversation.

Yanking my arm and putting my weight onto my heels does nothing to loosen his grip on me, but it does allow me to put a small amount of space between us. He's definitely going to leave a bruise. It's the one thing I dislike most about my fair skin; how easily it is to bruise.

When he tries to pull me into him again, I know there's nothing else to do.

The way I see it, I have two choices.

Fight, or let him do whatever his drug-fueled desperation thinks is a good idea to keep me here. There's no way I'm going to let him hurt me more than he currently is. Pulling my free arm back, I swing forward and connect my fist with the left side of his face.

I never back down from a fight.

Will steps back, shock written all over his face.

"You hit me," he whines, his palm splayed out on his cheek. The spot I hit burns a bright red on his pale face. It might not have been my best, but he will have a nice bruise later and it had the desired effect.

"You were hurtin' me. What did you expect? I'm leavin' now, and I suggest you don't try to stop me again." Just to be on the safe side, I pull my phone out of my pocket, ready to dial 911, should he try anything funny.

Turning on my heel, snatching up my keys before I march out of the door, tugging my suitcase behind me. I'm grateful that he's at least not following me now.

I pick a direction and start walking. The city is still warm into the evening this time of year, so I don't mind walking for a while even with my aching feet. The adrenaline coursing through my veins takes some of the edge off the pain anyway. It'll at least help me calm down and figure out where I'm going tonight because the sun will start setting soon. I'd rather not be hauling a suitcase around the city too late.

As I walk, I try to come up with a plan, my mind running through everyone I know that lives in the city. My best friend, Cecila, who I've known my whole life, moved to Minnesota for work last month, so she's off the table. Sasha lives in a studio apartment and with her getting up every day at 4am to open her bakery, staying with her is also out of the question.

How have I lived in New York for as long as I have, and only managed to make acquaintances? Nobody else in my contacts is someone I could call and ask to sleep on their couch. They probably wouldn't even answer the phone.

When I get two blocks away, I've got a plan. *Call Jack, and beg to stay at his place until I can figure out how to get the rest of my stuff back.* I'm not even sure what's in this suitcase. Turning to open my duffel and grab a sweater to throw on later, I come up short.

Oh, crickets.

How could I be so silly?

A picture of the bags I dumped by the front door at Will's populates in my head, taunting me. The ones with my make up, straighteners and the majority of my personal and very necessary belongings. That's going to be another expense to cover; replacing everything that was in them.

Maybe I can get them when he's had a chance to calm down.

There's nothing I can do about it and I'm certainly

not going back there now. I pull my phone out of the back pocket of my jeans, and move over to a quieter part of the sidewalk. Not that anywhere in New York is quiet.

A sense of ease washes over me as I dial Jack's number. My brows tug together when an international dial tone rings in my ear. I don't remember him telling me he's going away. It hasn't been that long since we last went for lunch. Has it? It feels like an eternity before the call connects.

"Sav? What's wrong?" Worry only an older brother could feel laces his voice, mixed with a sleepiness, that tells me I've woken him.

"Where are you?" I ask, ignoring his question.

Jack pauses for a moment and when he speaks, he doesn't bother to hide the hesitation in his voice. "I'm in England, Sav. I moved here."

"What? Why? When did you leave New York?"

I try to do the math for when I last spoke to Jack. It's been a while, but surely he would have told me he was moving out of the country? That isn't just something you do on a whim. I'm lost in my racing thoughts when Jack's voice pulls me back into the moment.

Resignation coats his words as he says, "A few months ago. I needed to get away and I thought I'd oversee the new project. I did tell you this, Sav."

I'm such a bad sister. How could I forget that my brother told me he was leaving the country. Distractedly, I ask, "When are you coming back?"

He doesn't sound much like my larger than life big brother when he replies, "Honestly? I'm not sure."

'If he ever will' are the unspoken words that hang between us. I don't press him on why he's left, there obviously is something—or someone—but I know that he'll tell me when he's ready. I hope. It wouldn't be a surprise if he didn't though, not when I wasn't even around to say goodbye in person.

"I'm sorry, Jack." I scrub a palm over my forehead and my mind works at double speed to come up with a solution to my predicament.

There's a soft chuckle on the other end of the line before Jack asks, "What are you sorry for, little sis?"

"For being too busy to notice you left the country. For only calling you when I need something. The list is endless, Jack." I throw the arm not holding my phone up in the air as I release an exasperated sigh, earning a few curious stares from passersby.

Jack is quiet for so long that I end up pulling the phone away from my ear to make sure it's still connected.

When he does speak, I can hear the smile that I imagine is tugging at his lips. I close my eyes as tears, that I won't let fall, burn my eyes. Damn, do I miss him and the life that seems to have passed me by.

"You know you can always call on me to help you with whatever trouble you get yourself into. Even when I'm in another country." He yawns and I can hear the sheets rustle as if he's sitting up in bed. "What do you need, Sav?"

My voice is strong and sure as I say, "It's okay, I'll figure it out. I live in New York, there are a million hotels to choose from."

Well, none that I can afford that aren't infested with bed bugs. I silence the voice in my head because it isn't being very helpful right now.

"Hotel? Why do you need a hotel? What happened?"

"I don't really wanna talk about it right now," I say, not wanting to pile onto whatever Jack's dealing with. "I just need somewhere to stay for a couple of nights."

"Oh. I would offer you to stay at my place but I've hired contractors, and the place is being gutted and renovated. Let me make a few calls, I'll see if I can find you someone to stay with."

I know who that *someone* is that Jack's referring to and there's not a chance in hell am I staying there. Him calling that one person I've actively and successfully avoided for too long to stop now is off limits. I know my brother well enough to know that *he* would be the first person Jack calls without him even saying his name.

"It's okay, big brother, I'll figure this out. Believe it or not, I'm a grown up. I can look after myself." Hell, I just punched a guy. Finding somewhere to stay, at least for tonight, is going to be a piece of coconut cake in comparison.

Jack hesitates, probably because he already knows

the answer. "Do you need me to send you some money for a hotel?"

Pulling in a breath, because I know he only means well, I reply, "No. Thank you. I have money. It was more about the company side of things. I sorta miss you, big brother."

There's a reluctance lacing his words as Jack replies, "If you're sure." He pauses, deciding something. A heavy sigh travels down the line before he continues, "I don't like it but I'll accept it. Promise me, as soon as you get there and you're settled, you'll text me where you're stayin'. I mean the full address, room number, floor, everythin', okay?"

I roll my eyes, because you wouldn't have guessed I was a whole twenty-seven years old with the way he treats me sometimes.

Sucking in a breath and moving further into the corner I'm huddled into, I reply, "Fine. Go back to sleep and you'll wake up to a message with the details. What time is it over there anyway?"

"It's nearly midnight," he yawns again. "If there isn't a message, I won't hesitate to call the cops, Sav."

Geez Louise, and I thought I was supposed to be the dramatic one.

I disconnect the call and pull up the web browser on my phone. A notification pops up on the screen, telling me I've got twenty percent charge left. As if this day couldn't get any worse.

Within five minutes, I'm on the move again, to a hotel. It was the only one in my budget that didn't look like a murder hotel. I'll have to figure out somewhere else to stay longer term, but at least for tonight and tomorrow, I'll have somewhere to sleep.

TWO

Savannah

When I arrive at the hotel, I've half a mind to call Jack back and see what friends he might have in the city that I could stay with. The outside is dingy and dark, and when I tug open the heavy glass door, the inside doesn't look much better, making me pause on the threshold.

If I was certain I could make it back to the subway station without being followed, I'd try and find somewhere else to stay. As it is, and with my safety in mind, this is where I'll be resting my head tonight.

Pulling back my shoulders, I march through the door letting it swing shut behind me. My steps are sure and steady as I walk across the lobby to the check-in desk.

It's only one night. I chant, because the further I walk into this seventies throwback of a foyer, with its faded blue carpet and floral wallpaper, I'm wondering if this isn't a real life *The Shining* hotel.

The guy sitting behind the chipped and battered reception desk doesn't look up as I approach. He doesn't look like he's been out of college very long, his interest more on the video playing on his phone rather than in checking me in. Thankfully, this means he wants me out of his way, so the process is quick and efficient.

But it also means he doesn't know who's coming and going.

Great. Now I'm even more creeped out than I was before. Give me a true crime documentary or have me go toe to toe with a grown man and I'm fine, but the second I watch a horror or a thriller movie, I'm as nervous as a cat in a room full of rockers, and this hotel gives me the heebie-jeebies.

I hurry to my room, shooting a text off to Jack with the details of where I'm staying. Taking in the dirty, stained walls, the faded carpet of the hallway and the loud noises that seem to come from every other room I pass, I pick up my pace, praying that I'll at least be able to get a decent night's sleep.

A high-pitched scream echoes around the elevator as it moves between floors and I grip the handle of my suitcase a little tighter. *Well, this gon' be fun.*

When I arrive on my floor, I stick my head through the open doors, looking from left to right before darting out of the elevator. The signage on the wall in front of me ensures I head in the right direction.

It feels like a layer of grim has fallen over me by the time I let myself into my room. Even the door handle is sticky and I can only hope that this is where the stickiness ends. If I had any other choice, I wouldn't be staying here.

Flicking on the light switch, I determine that my room ain't much better than the public areas. The overhead light flickers with a low buzz sounding, before righting itself. I need to find somewhere else to stay tomorrow. My skin feels dirty just standing in this space.

The sheets on the bed look more brown than the white I'm certain they're supposed to be. The furniture looks battered and bruised and the walls look like someone might have started small fires at random places in the room.

Using my suitcase to prop open the door, I do a quick sweep of the space. When I'm certain there's nobody hiding out, I close the door pulling over the chain and locking myself in.

I don't want someone finding my dead body here in the morning. The dark stains spotted around the carpet, mixed with what looks like holes made by fists in the plaster, tell me that I wouldn't be the first person to be murdered in here.

Calm down, Savannah. It's not that scary.

I throw my suitcase on the stand next to the dresser and spin on the spot, biting my lip as I look around. I really need to go back to Will's and pack up the rest of my stuff at some point, but I don't exactly want to bring it back here. I think I'll wait a week before I do that.

Maybe once I've found somewhere a little more permanent to live. Hopefully he'll be at work when I do go, so we can avoid any more drama.

I'm lost in my thoughts when I unzip my suitcase and flip open the lid.

Oh no.

An array of lingerie and sweats surround my family photos. Smiling faces of Mama, Dad and Jack look up at me among the silk and lace of some of my more fancier sets.

Sucking in a breath, I blow it out of my mouth before I move to the bed, precariously perching on the edge as a laugh bubbles up and spills from my lips. Could this day get any worse? It feels like an *SNL* skit or something.

I need a good night's sleep and then tomorrow I can figure out a plan of action. Moving to the suitcase, I rummage through the contents in the hope that there's some actual clothing inside.

Stripping down, I walk into the bathroom, turning on the shower that's hanging over the off-yellow bathtub. It's a small miracle when the water runs clear and steam starts to coil around the bottom of the tub. The overhead light flickers, much the same as the bedroom, as I look at the bruises forming on my arm. Already, you can see the distinct marks where his fingers gripped me. I'm mesmerized by the imperfection on my usually flawless skin.

When the mirror fogs up, I turn away from my reflection and step into the shower to wash away the grime of the day. It's not quite the bath I'd wanted, but there's no way I'm lying down in this.

The water runs over me, drenching me from head to toe, my muscles slowly relaxing as I close my eyes. It's in the semi quiet of the bathroom, with the water drowning out the noise of other residents that I can finally take stock of the day.

So much has happened in such a short space of time. I've lost my main job, my boyfriend, and my home. If you can even call it that. It didn't feel like my home. *New York hasn't felt like my home*. I feel like an imposter every day. As if I'm barely existing.

A single stray tear slides down my cheek and I swipe at it angrily.

It's all I'll allow because I refuse to cry over all this.

This doesn't get to break me.

I'm not weak.

Distracting myself from wallowing in my self-pity any longer, I squirt some of the hotel shampoo into my hand, lathering it together before I massage it through my hair.

Almost immediately, I regret using the cheap stuff provided by the hotel. It smells like chemicals and has my hair forming in dry clumps as I massage it through.

As if my day couldn't get any worse.

Rinsing the shampoo out, I hold my breath as I pick up the conditioner and hope for it to at least smooth out the dryness that the shampoo seems to have caused. I finger-comb it through, twisting my hair around into a loose knot on the top of my head then scrub my body clean with the body wash provided before rinsing myself from head to toe.

Stepping from the water that's slowly getting cooler, I grab a towel that could be likened to a carpet and wipe away the water. The starchy fabric scrapes across my skin. Satisfied that I'm dry enough, I wrap the towel around my hair and walk back into the bedroom naked.

Removing a pair of gray sweats and a cropped, sleeveless hoodie, I close the case and place them on top. Tomorrow I can wear what I had on today but past that, I'm going to need my clothes. My luggage feels like the only clean thing in the room and even though I've just showered, I already feel grimy again.

Suddenly, conscious of the fact that this hotel looks sketchy as hell and I didn't check it out for hidden cameras, I dress quickly.

While I'm towel-drying my hair, standing in the middle of the room, I hear a loud knock at the door. Actually, I wouldn't classify it as a knock. It's a very aggressive banging and it's most certainly at my door.

This ain't a knock you'd hear from the hotel manager, this is more like one you'd hear from a S.W.A.T. team doing a raid. I freeze in the middle of the room, pulling the towel from my head as my eyes dart around for somewhere to hide.

Heck, it would be the cherry on the top of this already crappy day if I were murdered right about now.

The banging sounds again, this time more forceful than the last—if that's even possible. As quietly as I can, I creep toward the door, wondering how many true crime dramas have this exact scenario? Single female, creepy hotel, hiding behind the door when it's inevitably battered down, blood spattered across the carpet...

I need to stop watching true crime documentaries.

Perhaps very stupidly, I'm more curious about who it could be than the fact that they could shoot me through the peephole.

I try to control my shallow breathing and make myself as quiet as possible. Of course to me it's all in surround sound: the thumping of my heart, every breath I take and the sound of the carpet crunching under my feet as I move across the room.

Gently, I place my hands on the door, pushing myself onto my toes to look through the peephole. What I see nearly has me cursing to high heaven.

It's worse than a serial killer.

So much worse.

Now *this* is the cherry on top of the crap cake of a day.

My head knocks a little too loudly against the door as I lean forward. I suck in a breath, praying he hasn't heard me.

"I know you're in there, angel."

My eyes close as I try to compose myself.

Of all the nicknames I've picked up over my life, I hate that one—coming from him—the most, because at one point it meant the world to me.

I hate the history that comes with *him* calling me that.

THREE

Noah

T he sound of my phone vibrating across my desk pulls my attention away from the contract I'm reading through. I'm glad for the distraction when I look down and see Jack's name appear on the screen. He's been my best friend since senior year of high school, and even though he's in England, we still speak regularly given his involvement in my business, so it's not unusual for him to call.

What is unusual is the sense of foreboding building inside of me at the sight of his name. I do the math on the five hour time difference and the fact that it's got to be close to midnight over there does nothing to ease it.

Something must've happened.

Either that or whatever he's calling me about is going to end up with me doing him a favor. I lean back in my chair, twisting my pen in my hand as I contemplate my next move. I can't not answer.

Snatching up my phone, I connect the call and say, "Hey, man. How's it going? Is London treating you good?"

Almost distractedly, he replies, "Hey, No. I'm okay, thanks. How are things with you and Sutton?"

I learned long ago that Jack seems to be incapable of using full names with people he cares about. For some reason, he seems incapable of saying one extra syllable in my name. I don't bother correcting him any more because it just makes him do it more.

"We're all good over here, man. Isn't it late over there?" I ask, already knowing the answer but wanting to cut to the chase without being disrespectful.

"Yeah." There's a hesitation in his voice and I picture him tugging on the back of his neck as he paces the room. "That's why I was calling." There's a long pause as he chooses his next words. "It's Savannah."

My stomach plummets and I pray to God it's not bad news. That she's at least unharmed. We haven't seen each other in so long, but it doesn't mean I care any less about her now than I did then.

"Is sh..." My voice comes out as a croak. I clear my throat, straightening in my chair as I try again. "Is she okay?"

Jack seems oblivious to my torment, as he rushes, "I think so. She was a bit vague on the details but she said she needed somewhere to stay. That's kinda why I'm calling you. She sent me the info on her hotel and, let's just say I don't feel comfortable leaving her there. Would you mind letting her stay with you for a bit? I'd let her stay at my place, but I have contractors in and they aren't due to finish for a few weeks."

He pauses to suck in a breath and I take that as my opportunity to respond, because if Jack says it isn't safe, then it isn't safe. "Send me the details."

A relieved sigh sounds through the phone. "Thanks, No. I owe you one. I'll send you the info now."

"Anytime, Jack. I'll let you know when I've got her."

We disconnect the call and I stand from my desk, gathering up the papers I was working on so I can finish it when I get home. My phone chimes in my pocket and I expect it to be Jack with the details for Savannah's hotel, but it's not.

SUTTON

I'm meeting some of the girls for dinner tonight.

NOAH

Okay.

Sutton is my girlfriend of three years. We've been living together for the last year but not much has changed in our relationship. Sutton is understanding of the long hours I have to put in as a CEO and is more than happy to entertain herself. Some might say we live separate lives but it's what works for us.

My phone buzzes in my hand again. This time it's Jack with the hotel details. Plugging the address into the search engine on my phone, I immediately see why Jack was so concerned. It's a goddamn shithole. I know that Savannah can look out for herself, but even I wouldn't feel comfortable staying in a place this sketchy.

Opening my contacts, I dial the car service I use on the rare occasions I can't take the subway. Holding my phone to my ear, I grab my jacket and briefcase, making my way to the elevator. As I jab the call button the ringtone in my ear switches over to a male voice.

"Evershed and Whitehall Cars. How can I help you?"

I know immediately who has answered the call. "Hi Eddie, is Rupert available for a last minute trip this evening?"

"Mr. Parker, of course. He's on his way to you now. The office, right?"

Fuck. Maybe I have been working too much lately. "Yes, Eddie. Thank you."

The elevator arrives as I disconnect the call and shoot a text to Rupert with our destination before stepping inside. The ride down is quick and when I exit into the deserted lobby, my strides eat up the space between the elevator and the door.

I opt to wait on the sidewalk and take in the last of the late July evening. Anything to calm the storm raging inside of me at what I might find when I get to the hotel. When I push through the door, a cool summer breeze hits me and I regret having spent the majority of my day cooped up inside.

My wait isn't long and I've filled it by scrolling through my emails, answering a few and forwarding some to others to pick up. It's enough to keep my hands busy and my mind occupied.

The sleek town car pulls up next to me, gleaming in the last of the summer sun, and I reach for the back passenger door. Rupert knows that I think using a car service is luxury enough without him getting out to open the door.

"Good evening, Mr. Parker," Rupert greets me as I slide into the backseat.

"Evening, Rupert."

My thoughts are racing with all of the worst case scenarios of what I could stumble upon, as well as a nervousness at seeing Savannah again. Why I'm nervous, I have no idea. Yes, it's been a long time since I've seen her, but that's no reason for my mouth to be dry and my heart to be racing. My knee bounces with the restless energy coursing through me.

Rupert navigates us through Lower Manhattan and across the bridge as I pull up the hotel details again. The screen fills with images and news articles of a dilapidated and seedy looking hotel. Why she chose this place out of all the establishments in the city, is beyond me.

It isn't long before we pull up outside the hotel—if you can call it that. The pictures don't do it justice, or rather they made it look better than it actually is. Looking at the screen in my hand and then back at the building in front of me, I would have guessed the hotel had been around a lot longer. It's safe to say, nobody has been taking care of the place.

When I step out of the car, my nostrils fill with the scent of rotting garbage mixed with dog crap. Exhaling, I will my stomach to hold because I don't want to let my guard down while throwing up my lunch.

My stride is purposeful as I move toward the entrance. The lights are out on either side of the door, casting the entryway in shadow. Perfect. It's like she was just asking to be kidnapped, or even worse, murdered.

Swinging the door open with a tad too much force, I step into the lobby of the hotel. It's about as well looked after inside as it is outside. The muffled sound of my footsteps on the shag carpet—*seriously?*—have the guy sitting behind the desk looking up from whatever video he's watching.

He swallows audibly as I approach the front desk. "Can I help you?"

My voice is gruff and commanding, leaving no room for doubt, I throw a hundred dollar bill on the counter as I reply, "Room 571 is checking out."

Neil, according to his name tag, types into the computer in front of him, a frown pulling at his brow when he realizes I'm very much not the five foot something woman who checked in. "I think you might have the wrong room, sir."

Apparently Neil didn't get the memo. A muscle in my jaw twitches as I grind my back molars, because there is nothing I dislike more than having to explain myself. "*She's* checking out."

He must see something in my face because he doesn't

47

question me any further, he just taps away on his keyboard. When he's done, he hands me the invoice. Snatching it up, I stalk toward the elevator, ignoring Neil when he calls, "She'll need to give back the key."

I impatiently wait for the elevator to arrive and when it does I step inside and jab angrily at the button.

When the doors open on her floor, I head straight for her room. The walls are a combination of dirty cream and black marks. Screams can be heard coming from one of the rooms but I can't tell if it's on this floor or another. My body is on full alert. I can't believe she's put herself in this position. Holding onto the anger, I let it feed my movements, pushing down the concern that bubbles beneath.

As I reach her door, they subside, giving me a reprieve.

Standing there, my body relaxes. It's only now that I realize how tense my shoulders were and how rigid my jaw was. Raising my hand, I knock. The bang echoes around the corridor as I wait for her to answer.

There's silence on the other side and so I knock again, listening intently for the sound of movement. Anything to tell me she's inside.

That's when I hear it.

A faint knock on the other side.

Leaning in, I call through the door, "I know you're in there, angel."

Almost immediately, I curse myself for using the name I gave her so long ago. I don't get to call her that anymore. I don't want to call her that anymore. That nickname comes with a whole history that needs to be left in the past.

It feels like an eternity before the door opens and she's standing there in front of me looking like a goddamn fucking real life angel. There's a halo of light behind her and for a moment it's just us in the here and now. An overwhelming urge to pull her close and ask her to stick around this time overtakes me.

It's like the girl I knew five years ago is no more. She's bloomed into a beautiful woman that's sure of herself and doesn't hide behind the veil of her hair.

Hair that I know is soft to the touch.

Her fair skin is clear and blemish free making the four beauty marks around her mouth, chin and on her cheeks stand out. With a slightly upturned nose and full lips, she looks alluring.

It's when my focus is bouncing around her face that I catch, in my peripheral vision, the distinguished markings of a bruise forming on her arm. My gaze darts to the mark. Its dark, ugly imperfection glares at me from her otherwise perfect skin, my jaw grinds as my nostrils flare. That tenseness that left me moments ago, returns with full force.

Swallowing thickly, I point to her arm and ask, "Who hurt you?"

Her wide gaze drops to the marks on her arm as if she didn't realize they were there. Covering the bruise from my sight, as if that will wipe it from my memory, she lifts her chin, defiance clear when she says, "It's nothing. What are you doing here? Did Jack send you to check on me?"

Ignoring her questions, I tug at the cuff of my shirt. Anything to distract myself from the rage that's burning through my blood. I don't believe myself entirely when I say it's because she's like a sister to me. "It's not nothing, ang—Savannah." I correct myself before continuing, "Tell me who did it?"

I can see the cogs turning in her pretty little mind before she responds. "To be honest, it's none of your business, but if you must know. My Daddy Dom got a little too rough during our latest session. Don't worry though, he more than made up for it with the aftercare." She folds her arms over her chest as she watches me for any reaction.

Spluttering, I reply, "Wha... How do... You know what? It doesn't matter."

Savannah cocks a brow, tilting her head to the side. "You sure? It might be your thing. Maybe a madame would suit you better."

I jut my chin as I run a finger under my collar. *Why's it so hot in here?*

Looking over the top of her head and into the room, I ignore her question, refusing to engage. I'm not getting sucked into whatever game she wants to start playing.

Fuck, I forgot just how tiny she is.

Berating myself for even thinking about the past, I look around the room. It looks like a throwback to the seventies. A faded orange blanket lays on the bed and stained brown shag carpet covers the floor. I'm not entirely sure what color the carpet originally was, especially with the lighter patches around the room.

Or maybe it's from bleach.

My stomach churns at the thought of leaving her here alone.

Yeah, it's not happening.

I incline my head toward her half open suitcase, asking, "Is that your luggage?"

Narrowing her eyes, there's a curious, questioning note in her tone when she replies, "Yes."

When I take a single step forward, I come up short as she takes a hold of the doorjamb and door, blocking my way and refusing to move.

I don't have the time or patience for this right now. The sooner I get her back to my place and I can bury my head back in work, the better. "Get your luggage, Savannah. You're coming to my place."

Her mouth falls open as a bark of laughter leaves her lips. Blinking rapidly, she tries to process my statement. If it's what Jack wants, it's what Jack gets. He's my brother. Not in the literal sense, but since the day I met him, he's had my back. This is the least I can do for him.

"Excuse me?" she scoffs.

Running a hand through my hair, I breathe out an exasperated sigh. "You heard me. I promised Jack I'd look out for you and the best place to do that is at my apartment, not some..." I pause, looking around as I try to aptly describe the hovel she's staying in. "Rundown hotel in Brooklyn."

Not exactly the words I would use in other company to describe this place, with its peeling wallpaper and faint scent of urine, but it'll do.

Squaring her shoulders, Savannah lifts her chin, replying, "First of all, I don't need to be looked after. I'm a grown woman not some dependent child you need to coddle. Second of all, I wouldn't stay with you if your apartment was the last place on earth."

She's part way to shutting the door when I wedge my foot between it and the frame. She's not getting rid of me that easily. I have one job to do—keep her safe—and typically that involves not leaving her in a shithole like this.

In a last ditch effort, based on the desperation coating her words, she tries to reason with me. Her efforts are futile, but I let her have her say as I try to reign in my frustration at her and the situation she's put herself in.

"Look, I can call Jack and tell him that you came by and that where I'm staying is perfectly acceptable. You'll be off the hook, and I can finally go to bed because you're giving me a headache."

Certain that she's finished with recounting her foolish plan, I put enough weight on the door to have her step back. She moves further into the room, her arms wrapping around her small waist as I stride in with purpose.

Concentrate, Noah.

My eyes move around the room, taking in the lack of personal items that are out of the suitcase. We can be on the move in a matter of minutes, if she just gets her shit together instead of standing there staring at me. I can feel her gaze on me, burning through my skin and deep into my soul.

My voice is gruff when I say, "Get your things together, Savannah. Or I'll pack for you."

Folding her arms across her chest, she stares me down, refusing to move. "I'm not coming with you. I'm fine here."

I've had enough. She doesn't get to act like she hasn't disrupted my evening. Like she hasn't brought to the surface all of the protective instincts for *her* that I've worked so hard to bury.

In a carefully controlled tone, barely holding onto the anger that's built inside of me, I reply, "It wasn't a choice, Savannah. Pack your bags or I'll do it for you. I'm not leaving you here to get carried out in a fucking body bag tomorrow morning."

She doesn't move, so I maneuver around the room, swiping up her wallet, phone and discarded clothes, praying to God I don't come across anything intimate.

I'm not sure I could handle it.

As I stride over to her suitcase, she finally springs into action, darting across the room, blocking my path.

"Move out of the way, Savannah," I snap, my control slipping. I'm certain the vein in my neck is bulging if the way my pulse races is anything to go by. Sucking in a breath, I try to calm my frustration. "You need to understand that I'm not leaving without you, so either you come with me willingly or I drag you out of here."

"I'd scream," she murmurs distractedly.

My response is quick and without thought. "Nobody would care."

Almost immediately I regret my choice of words. *Christ. Foot meet mouth. What is wrong with me?*

Dropping eye contact with me, Savannah nods before clearing her throat and moving past me into the bathroom.

I don't bother defending my word choice. My focus needs to be on getting us out of here, not on soothing her ego.

Pinching the bridge of my nose, I shake the feelings churning inside of me away and step up to her suitcase. When I lift the lid I can't help the curse that slips from my lips. Variations of lace and silk lay before me and my first thought is 'Who the fuck is she wearing this for', before I realize that's not any of my business.

Damn you, Jack for asking me to come here.

Throwing her clothes in the suitcase, I slam it shut, zipping it up and lifting it off the stand. I wait impatiently by the door for her to finish up in the bathroom.

Savannah returns to the room and acquiesces with a heavy sigh before following behind me as I lead the way out of the room and toward the elevator.

It feels like an eternity as we wait in silence, the

sounds of the other residents filling the void. When the elevator does arrive, we step inside and I push the button for the lobby. Neither of us utters a word. I don't even know where to start with what to say. How do you act toward the one person you've always wanted but can't have? Especially when you haven't seen them in years.

I know what she's been up to because of Jack, but has she ever asked him about me?

The rational side of my brain tells me no. She would have reached out if she wanted to know anything.

The doors slide open with a ding and I step out, not checking to make sure she's following.

I can already tell that having Savannah O'Riley living in my apartment is going to be hazardous. Do I want her living there? No. Will I set her up in another more reputable hotel? Also no.

When I told Jack she could stay with me, I meant just that. Savannah will be staying with me, at least until she has somewhere more permanent to live.

Now to break the news to Sutton.

FOUR

Savannah

S urely Noah Parker, my brother's best friend—
who I haven't seen in over five years—doesn't
truly *want* me to stay with him.

Noah's only doing this as a favor to Jack, not because he wants to.

He has to be crazy to think I would ever live with him, even temporarily. Anyway, I'm fairly certain he has a girlfriend, and I have no intention of listening to the two of them bumping and grinding into the early hours of the morning.

I just know he'd have stamina.

What is wrong with me?

I can only blame the fact that I haven't seen him in so long for the way my body reacted to him. It was like that first time in the school hallway all over again. Only this time, I knew what was happening to me and that trying to stop it would be useless.

I pull in a breath as I practically run after Noah. His stride is at least twice as long as mine, but he doesn't seem to take this into consideration. Either that or he just doesn't care.

Maybe I can turn around and go back inside. Surely staying here has got to be marginally better than staying with him.

When I opened the hotel room door it was like seeing the boy I'd loved but in man form. A million emotions ran through me, and for half a second, before he spoke, it was like everything that happened between us hadn't.

There's a hardness to him now, but I'm certain it's just the black suit he's wearing and that underneath it, he's still the boy that called me angel and told me how much he loved my hair as he ran his fingers through it.

"I'm sorry, angel. You're like a sister to me."

Heavens, even now, it still hurts. A wave of embarrassment crashes over me and I shake my head, clearing the bad memory and bringing myself back to the present.

My gaze drinks him in as he stalks toward a black town car that's idling at the curb. The material of his suit stretches over his magnificent shoulders. He was always built, way more than any other boy in school, but now he's a man and he's even bigger than I could have imagined.

Of course, I've thought about him occasionally since I last saw him, but my imagination never did him justice. He didn't have a beard in any of my thoughts, but it suits him. He looks like a viking that's been dropped into Manhattan, but with short hair.

A light breeze whips around me and I curse myself again for having forgotten my duffel bags. Goosebumps form on my skin and I rub my hands up and down my bare arms. It's unseasonably cold tonight for this time of year. Perhaps it's a foreshadowing of what's to come should I get into the car.

Or perhaps it's just the weather, Savannah.

My pace picks up as I try to reach him before he gets into his car. "Noah," I call.

He stops mid stride and I realize that's the first time —in a very long time—that I've said his name out loud. Noah doesn't turn around, instead he keeps his back to me, his shoulders rigid as he waits for me to speak.

"I know you're just doing this as a favor to Jack. But to be honest, I'd rather not stay with you and your girl-friend. I'd only cramp your style and I'm a grown up, in case you hadn't noticed. It was nice of you to come fetch me, but I really am okay with staying here." I look back at the hotel. The lights that are out in the signage and the peeling paint on the brickwork, all signs that I should quit my jabbering and get in his car.

When I look back at him again, he's turned around and his hazel eyes are studying me. He scrubs a hand over his beard as he chooses his words. A muscle ticks in his jaw and I know he's close to the limits of his patience. "You're right. I am just doing this as a favor to Jack. That's why you're coming to stay with Sutton and me.

This isn't up for debate, Savannah, so quit trying and get in the goddamn car."

I can't see a way out of this. If I don't get in the car, I know that he'll put me in it; that his promise to Jack means that much to him. Defeated, I mutter, "I need to at least check out."

"It's already done."

There's a finality in his tone, and if my mind wasn't so preoccupied with trying to get out of staying with him, I might have paid more attention to it.

I march over to the car, flinging the front passenger door open before I climb inside. The driver, who barely looks old enough to have a license, stares at me in surprise, before righting himself and looking straight ahead.

"Hello, I'm Savannah. It's nice to meet you."

He tips his hat toward me. "Rupert, ma'am."

For the first time all night, a genuine smile pulls at my mouth, and my light laugh echoes around the car. "I'm not old enough to be called ma'am. Please, call me Savannah."

The back door opens and Noah climbs in behind Rupert, his spicy cinnamon scent enveloping me in a hug. I can't help the dig as I say to Rupert, "Or, you can call me angel."

"If you value your job and your life, Rupert, you won't call her that."

I roll my eyes as Rupert straightens in his seat, replying, "Yes, sir."

And just like that, all of the fun has been sucked out of the car.

Resting my hand on the back of his shoulder, I lean over and whisper in Rupert's ear, "Don't worry, you can call me angel when we're alone. I won't tell."

Rupert swallows audibly and I brush an invisible speck of lint from his shoulder, my eyes darting to the man occupying the back seat. Noah's gaze is burning a hole into Rupert's shoulder, where my hand still rests. His jaw grinds while his knuckles go white as he tightens his hand around the phone clenched in his palm.

This could be fun.

As Rupert pulls out, I relax back into my seat before a thought occurs to me. It might just be the way to get out of this and if it doesn't work, I can always keep messing with him by flirting with Rupert. I'm sure he'd hate that. He was never good at hiding his dislike for any boys I brought around. Noah was ten times worse than Jack for that.

What if he fires Rupert?

No, he wouldn't do that. Although, I don't know Noah. Not anymore.

I won't bring Rupert into my games.

"Does Sutton know I'm coming to stay?" I ask, my curiosity getting the better of me.

My question hangs in the air. When I turn in my seat, his hazel eyes connect with mine. His head is tipped back against the headrest, angled toward me as he stares, and a tense silence fills the void between us. He looks stressed; like the weight of the world rests on his shoulders.

His tone is filled with exhaustion when he replies, "She knows."

I can tell there's so much more to what he's said. Yet he isn't offering it up. *Did they argue about me? Does she know everything?* So many unanswered questions run through my mind.

No. I'm not gonna go there.

Turning back to face the front, I think over a plan that doesn't get Rupert fired nor cause Noah anymore stress. He didn't ask to have Jack as a best friend. Neither did he ask for Jack to call him up and demand he look after his little sister.

Pulling my phone from my pocket, I send out several texts to see if I can pick up some more shifts at any of my jobs. It's my last ditch attempt at making the best out of a bad situation—be too busy to even see my new roommate.

I spend the remainder of the drive planning out my schedule, packing it full. Whenever I'm not in a show, I tend to fill my days with odd jobs, like teaching theatre classes to kids or helping out in Sasha's bakery or even working in a dive bar.

When the car pulls up to an apartment building in the Financial District, I check the clock on the dashboard. It's ten past ten. That means I can grab a good six hours of sleep before I have to get up to make it to Sasha's bakery. It's going to be a long few weeks if everything goes to plan.

Noah steps from the car, and I race after him with a hurried goodbye to Rupert. He's already at the bank of elevators when I finally catch up.

"You know, some of us weren't blessed with long legs," I snip, annoyed that he keeps walking off without waiting for me.

I can practically feel the frustration roll off of him. It's very possible that I may have poked the bear one too many times this evening. He can't say I didn't give him an out.

He's only got himself to blame for this weird sense of obligation that he has toward my brother. I've never been able to understand it, but it's there and has been for years.

Noah ignores me. This is going to get real old, real quick.

As we step into the elevator, I turn to give him a piece of my mind but he speaks first, halting any outburst I might have. "Savannah, it's been a long fucking day and I don't need you to lecture me about whatever the hell it is you've got an issue with. If you want to stay somewhere else, feel free, but it's going to need to be somewhere better than that rat-infested hovel I've just picked you up from. Otherwise, just be grateful and stop trying to look into things that aren't there. I'm your friend, doing you a favor in your time of need."

My friend? That's laughable. Since when did I become his friend?

Don't friends usually hang out? All the times I was shut out or told I was too young to hang out with him and Jack come at me full force.

To me, that doesn't scream friendship. Friends don't tell you to go away, or laugh at you before shutting the door in your face.

No, Noah Parker is not my friend. I've never seen him as a friend and I'm not about to start now. I'm going to keep to myself and get that deposit saved as quickly as possible so things can go back to how they used to be. Even if it means cutting back on some of the very few luxuries I afford myself like my dance lessons or that weekly Starbucks I've become accustomed to.

I don't bother replying to him. What would be the point? We spend the rest of the ride to the thirtieth floor with the gentle murmur of the elevator as the only sound.

When we arrive on his floor, the doors open to a dark corridor, lit only by mood lighting next to each apartment door. The walls are a muted gray and the dark beige carpet much more luxurious than the one at the hotel.

A strange sense of anticipation fills my body as I follow Noah to the door at the end of the corridor. There are only five doors on this floor, with none of them near his. I assume that means he has the biggest apartment on the floor.

I guess I'll find out soon enough.

I've never met Sutton before, mainly because, for the last seven years I haven't been as close to Noah as I once was. Not that we were ever that close, but I would at least see him for the holidays.

My curiosity is piqued and a burning desire to know what she's like and what it is about her that he loves fills me.

Noah unlocks the door and steps over the threshold, depositing my luggage next to the table to his right before he removes his suit jacket, throwing it over his arm.

When he steps aside, a woman with long brown hair that falls in waves over her shoulders comes into view. She's standing next to the TV that's hanging between the floor to ceiling windows, as she looks out over the city.

My attention moves around the room taking in the furniture and low lighting. I can't quite make out the color of the couch but I do know it's dark and looks like a cloud. Accent cushions cover it and I immediately know that it's not something Noah would have done. Maybe it's a Sutton touch.

There isn't much in the open plan space in terms of personal effects. On the right side of the room I spy a mahogany sideboard with candles and picture frames adorning it. I can't make out who is in them, but I'd like to imagine it's at least Noah and Sutton.

A large dark round dining room table takes up the rest of that end of the room. I can't quite picture Noah—

from the guy I knew—being the type to hold dinner parties.

The kitchen is visible through an archway. It looks brand new. From the front door I can just about make out the cabinets lining the walls, the gleaming refrigerator and kitchen island.

Why is everything so dark in here?

My gaze shifts back to the woman in front of me, watching her every move. There's an air of sadness about her, but when she turns around it's like she hides it away, forcing a welcoming smile onto her lips.

Sutton is stunning and the complete opposite of me. Mama would whop me upside the head if she heard me comparing myself to another woman, even in my own mind. She's always told me that comparing myself to another person is like trying to compare two snowflakes; we're naturally different. Sutton is tall and elegant, and when she walks toward me a warmth radiates from her. She holds out a delicate hand, her equally delicate features coated in a mask of sympathy mixed with friendliness.

"It's so nice to meet you, Savannah. Jack..." At the mention of my brother's name, a rosy glow fills her cheeks. That's interesting. "Well, Jack's told me so much about you. I feel like we're already best friends. We missed you at his going away party. I just wish we were meeting for the first time under better circumstances."

Taking her hand in mine, I give it a brief shake as I reply, "You and me both, Sutton." An awkwardness surrounds the three of us, and I'm certain it's to do with my presence. Picking up my suitcase, I turn to Sutton and say, "I am pooped and have to be up early. Would you mind pointing me in the direction of my room?"

"Of course, come. I've put some fresh sheets on the bed. We've got you a key, so you can come and go as you please. And help yourself to anything in the morning. We have some granola and yogurt in the fridge."

She's as pretty as a peach and nice to boot.

Sutton shows me to my room as Noah stalks off in the opposite direction. I wish I could say that's the last I'll see of him, but living in the same apartment is going to make that impossible.

"Don't worry about him. He's stressed about some big acquisition at work. I don't bother with the details because it goes over my head. Hopefully, when it's all over, you'll get to see the nicer side of him."

"Oh, I won't be staying that long."

Nope, I'm going to leave tomorrow. It was a mistake to come here at all.

"You can stay as long as you need to." Sutton opens the door to the guest room. "This is you."

It's plain and very white. A bed with white linens takes center stage in the middle of the back wall. Both sides have glass bedside tables with intricate steel lamps on them. The flooring is white washed hardwood with one—what I hope is faux—gray fur rug on either side. The rest of the furniture is white, and if I was staying, I'd definitely add some pops of color. As it is, it has the necessities and will at least allow me to have a good night's sleep tonight.

"The bathroom is just across the hall. I left you some toiletries in there so help yourself and, please, shout if you need anything."

With a murmured 'thank you', I lock myself in the room, burrowing under the covers praying for sleep to take me over.

But my mind is plagued by memories I've tried so hard to keep buried.

FIVE

Savannah

T ears stream down my cheeks as I race through the backdoor and into the kitchen. Thankfully my parents aren't home, and although Jack was here when I left, I know he'll be in his room, building something or other.

Closing the backdoor behind me, I lean back against the cool wood. My chest heaves and I hold a hand over my mouth to muffle the sob that spills free. The faint sound of a lawn mower fills the quiet, mingling with my crying.

Boys suck.

And Johnny Lake sucks the most.

Getting the lead in the school play had me on cloud nine. But I crashed back to earth when I heard him laughing with his friends. About how someone as boring and ugly as me could land the lead and that he'd need a gallon of mouthwash waiting in the wings after having to kiss me. I'm not sure how I'm going to be able to do the show alongside him. Not when I know that's how he really feels.

Why does it hurt so bad?

I'm gasping for breath, unable to pull in enough oxygen. It feels like I might suffocate. My throat feels tight and burns with the pain of trying to breathe.

Is this how I die? Crying about a boy being mean?

Stop, Savannah.

It doesn't work. Nothing is working.

The tears keep coming. A headache is forming behind my eyes.

A noise somewhere in the house finally has my sobs easing as I freeze, listening for where it came from. A hiccup leaves my lips just as I lift my gaze, and connect with a set of worried greenish-brown eyes. Noah's standing at the end of the hallway by the front door assessing me. He doesn't move.

Hurriedly, I swipe at my wet cheeks, praying he hasn't seen me. The thought is laughable, because of course he has. He's looking right at me.

Dipping my head, I skulk down the hallway, determined to escape to my room and cry in peace. A weight crushes my chest with each step. Even now, the tears still come. I'm mad at myself for being hurt over a boy's stupid words. But they did hurt.

I grab the bannister with one hand, and swing myself

around onto the first step. My progress is halted by Noah's arm blocking my retreat. His hand rests in front of me, forcing me to stop.

I look up at him, confusion furrowing my brow. He's much closer than I expected and his proximity has my whole body tingling. When my lips part as I suck in a much needed breath, his gaze dips to them before he swipes his tongue out over his own. Heat engulfs me at the movement.

Noah lifts his hand, wiping away a stray teardrop that rolls down my cheek as I blink up at him. It would be so easy to turn into him. To take the comfort I see hovering in his gaze. But that would just lead to rejection, and I'm not so sure I can handle anymore hurt today.

Concern laces his words as he asks, "What happened?"

My voice is hoarse when I reply, "Nothing. I'm fine."

Noah reaches out his hand, freezing mid air as if he's realized his mistake. He drops his arm and a flame of frustration sparks behind his eyes, before he blinks and it's gone. "Don't lie to me, Savannah."

Who does he think he is?

I shove his arm as my anger flares, forcing him to take a step back. "Leave me alone, Noah. I..." The weight of the day and his sympathy—which I don't want or need—has me choking on a sob. Hurtful words spill from my lips like poison. "I don't need you. You don't need to pretend that you care about me. Despite what Jack might have said, you aren't my brother."

Racing up the stairs, I barrel through the door of my bedroom, slamming it shut behind me. I throw myself on the bed as sobs wrack my body and I let go. My cries are muffled by the comforter, but to my ears, they're loud and gut wrenching.

"Go away," I shout into the mattress at the sound of my door opening.

Whoever it is ignores me.

Can't I cry alone?

The bed dips under their weight and when he touches me, I know it's Noah. His hand rubs soothing circles on my back as he asks softly, "What's wrong?"

Shrugging him away, I sit up, rubbing my face. Scooting to the head of the bed, I hug my knees to my chest as we stare at each other.

He's waiting expectantly for my answer, and I want to tell him so bad, to get it off my chest. But I can't. He probably agrees with what Johnny said and I don't think I could handle that.

When I can't take the silence any longer, I ask, "What do you want?"

Noah smooths his hand over the comforter, a calmness filling him as his shoulders relax. "Despite what you might think, Savannah, I do care about you. I just want to make sure you're okay."

I need space.

Moving to the edge of the bed, I stand, pushing down the fabric of my dress. Noah tugs on my hand, and I freeze as a spark of electricity spreads through my skin where he's touching me.

His thumb rubs small circles across my knuckles and we both watch, fascinated by the movement.

My voice is a husky warning when I say, "Noah."

He looks up at me with wide eyes as if he's just realized where he is and what he's doing. He blinks once, twice, three times, before he seems to come to his senses and drops my hand.

I take two steps back when he stands quickly, towering over me. "If you won't tell me what's wrong, then I'll tell Jack and see if you'll open up to him."

He wouldn't.

But he would.

My mind is trying to think of a way out of it but I'm coming up empty.

When I come to the realization that I have no choice, I cross my arms over my waist, hugging my torso as I drag in a deep breath. Exhaling slowly, I reply, "You don't need to tell Jack. I overheard someone I'm in a play with at school talking about me and, well, he wasn't very nice. And what makes it worse is we both got the leads and have a lot of scenes together."

Noah pulls me into a hug, his masculine spicy and vanilla-like scent enveloping me. I pull in deep breath after deep breath, luxuriating in the comfort he's offering.

There's a calmness to his voice as he asks, "Who was it, and what did they say?"

I pull away, my gaze searching his face. There's no hesitation when I reply, "I'm not telling you."

His hands move to rest on the top of my arms and he squeezes them softly. "I can't help if you don't tell me."

"How would you knowing help?"

Noah looks away, rubbing his hand over his jaw before he returns his gaze to me and says, "I will help him to understand what he can and can't say about you."

Rubbing my arms, I move back to my bed, flopping onto the mattress as I laugh. "Right. And then I'll be a pariah in school. No, thank you. I'll handle this myself. He'll regret his words more than you can even begin to imagine."

Noah doesn't respond for the longest time. His gaze assesses me before he nods, as if accepting that I can deal with Johnny Lake on my own.

Tipping his head to the side, his brows tugging together, he says, "I didn't know you were doing a play. And you got the lead? That's amazing, Savannah. You should be so proud of yourself. This is just the beginning for you, and if that boy can't see it, then he's a fool."

A giddy feeling takes me over and I can't help the grin that spreads across my face. "I know, right. The freaking lead."

Noah chuckles, the sound deep yet light. My breath catches in my throat. Suddenly I'm nervous and nauseous. "You should get back to Jack."

With a knowing look, Noah squeezes my shoulder before he walks out of my room. The door clicks softly behind him and I'm left with the words of Johnny and the feelings Noah ignited in me fighting for supremacy.

As is always the case, I replay the interaction with Noah over and over again.

SIX

Noah

F rustration rolls off of me as I walk into my home office. I can't even say that Jack will owe me for taking Savannah in, because it's the least I can do. He also has no control over the feelings that she ignites inside of me. Only I do.

Forcefully, I hang my suit jacket on the hook by the door, surprised I don't rip a hole in the fabric.

It feels like a weight is resting on my chest that I can't seem to move. My breaths are coming in labored pants and I run my fingers through my hair, tugging on the strands. Tipping my head back, I try to focus.

Never in a million years did I think seeing Savannah again would have me losing my fucking mind.

Today was the first time I've seen her in years, and yet she still has the same hold over me. Even when she was trying to get a rise out of me with Rupert, it was like I fell into the same old routine. An almost animalistic need to make it known that she is untouchable overtook me, and I fucking threatened his life. *And I meant it.*

Dropping my arms, I walk to the glass topped desk that sits in the middle of the room. It's best if I see as little of Savannah as possible. Out of respect for my relationship with Sutton, I can't have the feelings Savannah brings to life stirring inside of me.

How did she end up in a place like that?

Christ, if she's in trouble she should know that she can go to Jack. She could even reach out to me. *Not that she would.*

I take a seat at my desk, loosening my tie with one hand as I pull the papers I was working on before Jack called out of my briefcase. Right now, I have work to do and that doesn't involve reminiscing about the five foot one temptress down the hallway.

I blink to focus on the words in the profile sheet of our latest prospective acquisition.

It's no use.

My conversation with Savannah and the reason she gave for the bruises forming on her arm push through for my attention.

What the fuck is a Daddy Dom?

None of my fucking business is what it is.

Whatever Savannah gets up to in her free time is none of my concern. I've done what Jack has asked me to do and I don't need to get involved in her life or whatever it is she's into. But I'm really fucking curious.

My fingers tap away on the laptop in front of me.

Pressing 'enter' has my screen filling with websites and images about BDSM. My eyes widen and my jaw drops as I click around the sites.

Dumbfounded, I close the web browser.

To each their own, I guess.

But Savannah?

She really has grown up.

I look down at the papers strewn over my desk. It's getting late, but I need to get these valuations finalized for the meeting with Dew and Olsen tomorrow afternoon.

The words blur as I read over the same line for the fifth time.

Jesus, I could kill Teddy for fucking this up. Who goes and falls in love with the granddaughter of the CEO of the company we're trying to takeover?

There's a gentle knock at the door interrupting me from my distracting thoughts. When it opens, Sutton's voice fills the room as she asks, "Are you coming to bed?"

I don't look up, instead I continue reading over the document and making a note to check with finance on the accuracy of the figures provided by Dew and Olsen. "Not yet."

Sutton pauses, and I know she wants to ask more about Savannah. Getting a text message when we were pulling away from the hotel and then me ignoring her calls has given her plenty of time to think over possible scenarios, I'm sure.

"I need to get this done." For the first time since she

knocked, I look up from the papers in front of me. "I know you must have a million questions, and I will explain but, please, let me finish this."

She steps into the room, closing the door behind her. Dropping my pen on the table, an exasperated sigh leaves my lips as I lean back in my chair and wait for her to speak.

"I know you have work to do, but you at least owe me an explanation, Noah. Why did you ignore my calls and texts?"

My mind whirls, searching for an answer to her question. It's a simple enough question, but at the same time, it's not.

Do I know why I ignored her? No.

Do I want to hurt her more than I obviously have already? Of course not.

I know that I should have responded, but I just didn't want to get into an argument about something that was going to happen. This is something that should be spoken about in person. Just not right now.

"I'm sorry, I should have answered you. It was wrong of me to not respond."

She folds her arms across her chest as she leans back against the door. "I have no issue with her staying here, but why is she?"

"Jack called me. He was worried about her, and I said I would help."

"And you didn't think to call me? To check if I was okay with her staying in *our* home?"

'No', is my immediate response. My heart pounds as my stomach drops at the silent admission. I'm not that much of an asshole, am I?

Holding my hands up, I reply, "I'm sorry. I should have asked you first, but I owed him and couldn't say no."

Her brow furrows, and I immediately regret my word choice. "So what Jack wants is more important than whether or not I feel comfortable living with a woman you have a history with?"

"I don't have a history with her, Sutton. Other than her being my best friend's kid sister, Savannah means nothing to me." *Liar*.

She studies me for a moment before she shakes her head and pushes away from the door. "I guess it's only for one night."

Scrubbing a hand across my forehead, I sigh heavily. "I think it will be longer than that."

The corner of her mouth lifts. "She doesn't seem to think so."

Smoothing down my beard, I reply, "If having her in the apartment makes you feel uncomfortable, I can put her up in a hotel. But I can't let her go back to the place she was staying. It wasn't safe."

Sutton thinks about it for a moment, and I know her well enough to know that she won't let Savannah live in a hotel when we have a perfectly good guest room.

"She can stay for now, but don't take that to mean I'm happy for her to stay forever."

Nodding, I pick up my pen again. "Thank you. And for what it's worth, I am sorry. The second she outstays her welcome I'll move her into a hotel."

"Okay. I'm going to bed."

I can feel her gaze linger on me, but I don't lift my head to meet her eyes. She walks out of the room, softly closing the door behind her.

It was a mistake to bring Savannah back into my life. If I don't handle this carefully—by keeping Savannah safe but at a distance—it could all blow up in my face and ruin the longest relationship I've ever had.

Allowing myself a moment of reflection, I replay the moment I saw her again after so many years. She still packs a punch with her dark gingerbread hair, striking dark blue eyes, petite features and curves that drag you in.

She's dangerous.

Even if I wasn't in a relationship, I'm not about to ruin my most important friendship for her. Jack's seen what I've come from, and instead of walking away, he's stood by my side. He's stood up for me and helped me make something of myself.

I lose track of time as I fall into a tunnel of focus. A noise coming from the kitchen disrupts me. I look around my office, the only sign that it's not yet morning is the fact that it's still dark outside. I've been so caught up in the valuations for this meeting. A quick look at my watch, has my brows lifting in surprise that it's half past three in the morning.

I need to get some sleep.

Organizing the papers, I place them in my briefcase before standing from my seat and stretching my aching body. I should have taken a break sooner. Thankfully, my meeting isn't until one, so I can get some sleep.

Pressing send on an email to Jerry in finance, I close the lid of my laptop, placing it on top of the papers. Another sound from the kitchen pulls me from my distracted thoughts.

Certain that it's going to be Savannah because Sutton sleeps like a rock and wouldn't be up this early, I don't rush to get out there. My steps are slow and steady. It feels like I'm wading through water, the sudden onslaught of fatigue catching me off guard.

As I enter the kitchen, I come up short when I find Savannah crouched on the floor, muttering to herself as she sweeps up what looks to be granola with her bare hands. Blinking, my eyes roam over her and I slowly come to the realization that she's fully dressed, shoes and all. My brow tugs into a frown as I wonder what the hell she's up to.

"What are you doing?" I ask.

She lets out a husky yelp as she spins to face me, a fist —no doubt holding granola—pressed to her chest as she collapses against the kitchen cabinet. "Oh good gracious, you gave me a fright. You shouldn't be sneakin' up on people like that."

Her southern drawl has my heartbeat quickening as my throat grows thick. I fucking adore her accent.

Not appropriate, Noah.

Clearing my throat, I look away and out of the window at the end of the kitchen. "I wouldn't say I was sneaking. What are you doing?" As if drawn to her, my gaze darts back to drink in her every movement.

Savannah returns to sweeping up the spilled granola before she answers me, her focus on the task in front of her. "I was making some breakfast but knocked over my bowl. I'm just going to clean this up and then I've got to run."

I smooth my hand over my beard, pulling at the hair on my chin. "Why are you having breakfast at three in the morning?" I ask as I move to the cupboard under the sink for the dustpan and brush.

When I turn with it in my hand, Savannah moves to the trash can, throwing out the granola she'd picked up. "Why're you still dressed?" Savannah asks, her brows tugging together in confusion as she ignores my question.

Bending to sweep up the remaining mess, I don't respond to her as I concentrate on making sure nothing gets missed. With it all swept up, I turn to face Savannah, my question on the tip of my tongue.

She's closer than I expected her to be. I suck in a breath, lavender assaulting my nostrils as I get a look at the depths of her dark blue eyes and the rings of gold around her irises. My hand itches to reach up and smooth away the strand of hair resting on her cheek.

Savannah closes her eyes before inhaling deeply and clearing her throat. When she opens them, she ducks her head and moves away from me to the other end of the kitchen, grabbing up a bag I hadn't noticed. "I have to go."

I stand in the moonlight as it streams through the open window, the gentle click of the front door telling me she's gone.

Pinching the bridge of my nose, I walk back to my office, snatching up my phone from my desk.

NOAH

> Where would Savannah be going at 3:30 in the morning?

JACK

What do you mean? Why are you even awake at 3:30?

NOAH

> We have a takeover. She was—

My phone vibrates in my hand as Jack's name flashes across the screen.

"Hey man, you okay?" I say as I connect the call.

There's a hum of background noise on the other end of the phone as Jack speaks, "Hey, yeah, all good here. Thank you for picking Savannah up by the way." I imagine him walking to work, with the sound of London coming alive around him.

"Anytime."

There's a hint of worry in his tone when he asks, "So, what do you mean where would she be going?"

"I was heading to bed and found her in the kitchen fully clothed, shoes and all, making breakfast." I chuckle as an image of her on the floor surrounded by granola pops into my head. "Well, she was making a mess, but that's nothing new. Then, well, then she left."

"I'll give her a call and see what's going on. Thanks, man. I gotta go. Catch ya later."

The call disconnects and I place my phone back on the desk and head to bed.

SEVEN

Savannah

At midday, I walk through the door of Noah and Sutton's apartment. My body aches from being on my feet since before the sun rose. I've been kneading all varieties of dough and mixing cake batters at Sasha's before walking two dogs for a job I picked up through my job app.

I want to rest my head on my pillow and sleep for the rest of the day. It feels like an eternity since I last packed out my schedule this much, but I don't have much choice.

I'll get in a power nap, and then make a plan to get some more clothes because I can't keep re-wearing the same stuff over and over. Especially if every day is going to be as active as this one.

Instinctively, I throw my key in the bowl filled with mail on the table by the door. If this was my own apartment, I'd kick my shoes off and strip out of my clothes as

I zombie-walk to bed. As it is, I'll have to make do with just kicking off my shoes.

I don't want to outstay my welcome but I'm also very aware that I need to add to my meager savings to be able to afford a deposit for my own place.

Eyes on the prize.

In all my adult years, I've never lived by myself. I've always lived in a shared house or with my parents. I don't even know if I'd like living on my own.

That sounds like a problem for future Savannah to figure out.

I'm in a world of my own when Sutton exclaims, "Great, you're back."

Oh, my stars!

Screaming, my hand flies to my chest, resting over my racing heart. I spin on my heel and seek her out. I was so intent on getting to my room and then having that nap I've been promising myself since I started lagging this morning, I didn't even realize anyone was home.

I'm going to die of shock if Noah and Sutton keep jumping out on me like this. *Does nobody know how to delicately announce their presence?*

Sutton moves around the couch, her palms up as she approaches me cautiously. "I'm so sorry. I thought you knew I was here."

My hand falls to my side as I pull back my shoulders and reply, "It's okay. It's already been a long day and I was just gonna steal a nap and then head out to get some clothes. I was in a bit of hurry when I..."

I trail off as it dawns on me that I'm rambling and Sutton doesn't need to know about the disaster that is my love life. Scratching the side of my head, I take a step back in the direction of my room. As I lift my hand and open my mouth to speak, Sutton cuts me off. "I could come shopping with you? I know some good places around here."

My eyes dart down to the designer clothes that she's wearing. Definitely not in my budget.

When I meet her clear and friendly gaze, I give her a tentative smile and say, "That's very kind of you, but I was thinkin' about goin' to some thrift stores or even a discount store. I'm kinda on a budget if I'm going to get out of your hair any time soon." With one final smile, I turn down the hallway to my room.

Sutton's voice is soft and there's a hint of vulnerability there when she calls, "I don't mind going to a thrift store or a discount store. I think it would be good for us to get to know each other."

Pausing in my tracks, I face her again, my mouth moving before I can think of any reason to turn her down. "Okay. I'm still gonna need that nap though. Maybe we can go in a hour or two?"

It wouldn't be very gracious of me to say no. Especially given how she has welcomed me into her home with what I'm assuming was no notice.

Clapping her hands together in excitement, Sutton replies, "Fantastic, I can't wait."

At least one of us can't. I'd rather walk across a

piping hot floor furnace than spend the afternoon shopping with Noah's girlfriend. Not because she isn't lovely
—she's very welcoming—but, well, avoiding Noah
seems to go hand in hand with avoiding Sutton.

With a whole lot less enthusiasm, I murmur, "Great.
Me neither."

EIGHT

Savannah

R efreshed after my nap, I threw on a black t-shirt I found in the bottom of my suitcase and the same pair of jeans I've worn for the past week.

If I'd been asked, on a scale of one to ten, how much I would enjoy a shopping trip with my brother's best friend's girlfriend, I would have said negative ten, not at all.

I'd have been very wrong about that.

Although I should be upset because my efforts to distance myself from her have failed—miserably—today has been surprisingly fun.

We've laughed and gossiped about anything and everything. When Sutton told me about her love for nineties chick flicks and music, I just about proposed to her. We listed our top five Meg Ryan films, giggling uncontrollably as we reenacted the orgasm scene from *When Harry Met Sally*. This afternoon has been a blast.

It certainly helps that between each store, we stop at a bar for a drink. Now I'm slightly tipsy and definitely spending more money than I planned, but you only live once. At least that's what Sutton keeps telling me as she guides me to the cashier with each purchase.

Sutton throws her arm around my shoulder, practically bending in half to rest her chin on my shoulder as she dangles a scrap of material in front of me.

"You have to try this dress on."

It's beautiful, but there ain't a whole lot being left to the imagination. I might as well be naked.

"I don't think that will cover everything it should," I giggle.

Sutton hiccups and we stare at each other before bursting into a fit of giggles, attracting glares from the uppity sales associates. We're in one of the fancier department stores in the city and I'm very aware that in my non-designer clothes, I stick out like a sore thumb.

Stepping back, Sutton thrusts the dress into my chest, simultaneously turning me in the direction of the fitting rooms and taking my bags from me. "I won't take no for an answer on this one," she slurs.

Maybe we've had enough to drink.

Obeying her demand, I weave my way through the store, clutching onto the dress like I might lose it. The woman manning the fitting rooms eyes me from head to toe. Just to spite her for making assumptions about me that are most likely true, I'm tempted to drop the dress on her folding table and leave.

She hands me a card and dismisses me as she goes back to folding the cashmere sweater in front of her. It seems like not having manners is a necessity in this store. Heck, it's a necessity for this city.

I find an empty stall and step inside, closing the door behind me. Dim lighting overhead gives the room a soothing ambience, with the mirrors on three of the walls lit from behind, adding to the soft glow.

Hanging the dress on the back of the door, I cross my arms over my stomach and pull my t-shirt over my head. There's no point in hanging around. I could just stand in here and pretend to try the dress on, but a tightness in the pit of my stomach tells me to follow the signs.

Signs of what, I have no idea.

Next to go are my sneakers, socks and then my jeans. Standing in my underwear, I contemplate whether I can get away with leaving my bra on, but the built-in cups make that decision for me. I'm definitely wearing the wrong panties for this dress. For half a second, I contemplate removing them too before discarding the idea. A red G-string might not be ideal, but it will do.

Carefully, I remove the dress from the hanger, holding it up against my body. Three stripes of black material, that get progressively thicker the further they go, are broken up by sheer mesh. The three bands of fabric go in a diagonal direction from my waist to my hip, then from my hip to my thigh and finally from my thigh to my knee, repeating on the back.

The bust is black and very exposed, with the mesh material underneath covering the space between the cups of the dress and the first black stripe. Spaghetti straps hold everything up.

Okay, here goes nothing.

On a sigh, I face the door and pull the dress away from my body. Carefully, I unzip the fragile fabric before stepping in. I can just picture how silly I'm going to look in this dress. Images of it drowning me in fabric with areas exposed that shouldn't be flit through my mind. I'm certain it wasn't made with someone as short as me in mind.

Tugging up the zip, I smooth my hands over my hips, glad that I'm the only one about to witness my embarrassment.

Pulling in a breath for courage, I blow it out slowly as I turn to face the ambush of mirrors. My jaw drops. It's stunning. Never in my wildest dreams did I think it would look as good as it does.

I think I'm in love.

The cut outs of sheer material hint at the treasures hidden beneath, yet the black material is positioned perfectly to keep my modesty. You can't even see my underwear, although if I was to wear it, I'd go commando.

This is a dress that was made with seduction in

mind. Maybe, when I'm ready to get back out there, I could wear this dress.

With the right pair of heels, everything will look tight and toned. Twisting and turning, I admire my body unashamedly. The material is stretchy and clings to my body like a second skin without being so restrictive that I couldn't dance or let loose.

I *need* this dress.

I'm just not sure I can afford it.

Releasing a heavy sigh, I pull my phone out of my bag and snap a few pictures. I'm not about to let a potentially good profile picture go to waste.

A knock sounds on the door and Sutton's soft voice calls, "Open up. I want to see."

My body tenses, and for a moment I wonder if I can ignore her. After an afternoon of shopping, I know that Sutton will convince me to buy this one. Not that it'll take much.

Swinging open the door, I brace myself for her reaction.

Sutton's eyes widen, and she rests a hand on her collarbone. "Oh, my God. Savannah, it looks perfect. You have to get it."

I face the mirror, twisting and turning to see all angles of the dress again. "I don't know. It's a bit too much... well, maybe it's better to say there isn't a whole lot of coverage."

"No. It highlights your curves to perfection. This is the perfect dress to seduce a man. You're getting it."

Sutton hiccups before covering her mouth. "I'll wait for you by the jackets."

My brows lift and my eyes widen as she sways on the spot, "You okay?"

She nods, and when she takes a step back, I watch as she slowly moves out of the fitting rooms.

Closing the door behind me, I allow myself one final look, then tug on the zip and push the dress down over my hips. The material smooths over my skin, and even without looking at the price tag, I can tell it's going to be way out of my budget.

I could just buy it now and stay with Sutton and Noah for another week.

Yeah, not happening.

The sooner I can get myself together and find my own place, the better.

Placing the it back on the hanger, I dress quickly. When I pull open the door, Sutton is standing on the other side. Her cheeks are flushed, eyes wide with a goofy grin on her lips as she waits for me with our shopping bags.

She pouts, "Oh, I'm just waiting for you."

With a chuckle, I reply, "I thought you were waiting by the jackets."

"Nope, I thought I'd stay here to make sure you actually brought it."

She's definitely had too much this afternoon. I think it's best if we get home. Linking my arm with hers, I steer her toward the exit of the changing rooms.

Pulling me to a stop, with a serious look on her face, Sutton asks, "You are going to get it, right?"

Pasting on a smile, I reply, "It's beautiful, but way out of my budget."

Not that I looked at the price.

Sutton's face drops and she looks down at her fingers, playing with the strap of her handbag. "Oh. I mean, it's part of the sale, with fifty percent off. I just thought it was meant to be but I guess not."

My ears prick up at her statement. I've always been a sucker for a sale. Hurriedly, I search for the price tag. When my fingers land on the small card-like label, I briefly close my eyes before I glance down. A bright orange label beams up at me.

Eighty five dollars.

Instinctively, I clutch the dress tighter to me. I'm taking it home and ain't nobody gon' stop me.

"Sutton," I murmur conspiratorially. "We need to buy this dress and then immediately go home. Otherwise, I'll be living with you forever."

Giggling, Sutton whispers, "I've had so much fun today. Can't we keep going?"

Tapping my finger on my chin, I pretend to consider her request before I nod. My face splits into a grin that matches Suttons, high off of having found a deal and the alcohol still coursing through my veins.

Pointing her finger in the air, Sutton declares, "To the checkout and then the bar," before bursting into a fit of giggles.

I can't help but join her as we move toward the cash register. Dragging Sutton away from every other rack of clothes, I pay for the dress, breathing a sigh of relief when it goes through at the sale price.

As we strut our way through the store, Sutton whispers to me, "Have you ever wanted to have a *Pretty Woman* moment? Not the prostitute part, but the 'you made a big mistake' part."

Laughing, I reply, "Hasn't everyone?"

We stare at each other, silently agreeing, before we reach the exit and give out a chorus of the scene with Vivian and the snobby saleswoman.

Bursting onto the sidewalk in a fit of laughter, we merge into the crowds at a leisurely pace I know will be frustrating to the other pedestrians.

Every so often, we stop to peek in the store windows. It's while we're gazing through at the shoe display of one store that Sutton asks, "Are you going to tell me why you left your ex's place with no clothes? Did he burn them all? Or stuff them into the trash compactor?"

I'm admiring a pair of neon purple platform heels when I chuckle. "You say that like I've refused to tell you all day. It's really nothing so... extravagant, although that would make for a better story."

Sutton pouts before chuckling, "Fine, call me out like that, why don't you. I didn't want to be nosey, and you didn't exactly bring it up."

Touché. "Well, if you must know, I walked in on him having sex with my old roommate when I came home early from a work trip. And in the rush to leave because he got physical, I forgot to pick up the bags I'd left by the door."

The admission sobers us, and Sutton reassuringly squeezes my arm as we fall quiet, the city passing us by.

I don't need to look in her direction to know that her face is filled with sympathy as she says, "I'm so sorry, Savannah."

I allow myself a moment to let the reality of what happened a week ago at Will's sink in. Yes, I was able to get myself out of his place, for the most part unscathed, but I admit, for a moment, a flare of panic consumed me. I've always tried to be so tough. And I certainly haven't talked to anyone about it.

Throwing a smile on my face, I turn to Sutton, shutting down the thoughts. "It's fine. I knew he wasn't for me anyway. I punched him in the face, so I don't think he'll try it again."

Sutton's eyes widen and I see a flare of admiration before she nods and links her arm with mine, turning us to walk further down the sidewalk.

"You're brave, Savannah. I don't think I'd have had the courage to do that."

With a small smile gracing my lips, I reply, "That's what growin' up with an older brother and his friends did for me."

Sutton chuckles and we fall into a comfortable silence as we walk. At least until my curiosity gets the better of me. "How do you know my brother? I mean, I know he's Noah's best friend, but that doesn't explain why he'd talk to you about me. No offense."

Sutton looks away, a blush rising in her cheeks. I think I've stumbled on something with my question.

Clearing her throat, Sutton steps up to the window of a bookstore. "None taken. He was how I met Noah. We were really good friends in college but drifted apart. You know how it is. When I moved to the city, I reached out to him, hoping…well, it doesn't matter, but he invited me out with a bunch of his friends. You, more than anyone, knows what Jack's like when it comes to connecting people. Noah and I spent most of the night talking about Jack. He surprised me when, at the end of the night, he asked me on a date. And the rest is history, as they say."

Was Sutton hoping that Jack would be the one to ask her out?

My mind gets stuck on what she's not saying. It certainly seems like her interest was more in Jack than Noah, but… surely she wouldn't have gone on a date with Noah if that was the case?

I'm lost in my thoughts when Sutton speaks again, changing the subject. "I have an idea. Why doesn't Noah go with you tomorrow to get your things from your ex's? He'll make sure the scumbag doesn't lay another finger on you."

"Oh, that's not necessary, honestly."

Pouting, Sutton loops her arm through mine as we continue down the sidewalk. "It would make me feel better. Especially as you don't know what you'd be walking into. What if he wants revenge for you hitting him? Even though it was self defense, I'm sure he doesn't see it like that." She pauses before almost reluctantly continuing, "And I know it would make Jack feel better."

I doubt Noah would even want to go with me. And even though I can handle myself, I still find myself replying, "Okay."

Maybe she'll have forgotten by the time we get home.

I'm not certain I'm ready to go back to Will's just yet, even if it is to get my things. I know I have to because who knows what he might do with it all, but barely a week after everything, it's still a bit too soon.

NINE

I'm reclined on the large navy L-shaped couch watching *ESPN* when the front door swings open just after seven. It's been a long day and my meeting with Dew and Olsen didn't go so well. It's never a good thing when you have a combative CEO, and the antics of my business partner—who didn't even fucking show up—didn't help. Apparently Teddy and Mr. Olsen's granddaughter haven't been in touch.

Even if Teddy had been in contact, I don't think I'd have anything more to say to him than 'fuck you, Teddy'.

Savannah and Sutton stumble through the door. It bangs on the wall, bouncing off and closing behind them. Seemingly unaware of the damage they're causing, they giggle to themselves, a low hum of chatter emanating from them.

With the sportscaster talking excitedly about a punt return from a game the other night, I can't make out what exactly Savannah and Sutton are saying. It at least looks like they've had fun and done some bonding. Part of me is happy they're getting along because it means there won't be any drama. But another part is worried about how much of our past Savannah might share.

Sutton's face lights up when she sees me, her speech slightly slurred when she says, "Noah, great, you're here." She grabs hold of Savannah's hand, dragging her across the open space until they're standing at the back of the couch.

Now that they're closer to me, I see the matching flushes covering their cheeks and the glassy eyes staring back at me. At least from Sutton. Savannah hasn't so much as looked at me, her focus on the TV, although I doubt she's actually watching it.

Sutton speaks, pulling mine and Savannah's attention to her. "You'll do it, won't you? I said you would so you can't not. I mean, that would kind of be a dick move. Especially for your best friend's little sister in her time of need."

My eyebrows rise in question, silently asking what exactly it is that she's signed me up for. I ignore the frustration bubbling away inside of me at the fact that Savannah has yet to look in my direction. It irks me but it shouldn't.

Savannah turns to Sutton, her back to me as she rests a hand on Sutton's arm, muttering something to her that I can't hear.

Completely unfazed by Savannah's hushed tones,

Sutton replies to her in a louder voice, "No, because he might try and hurt you again."

My stomach clenches and a heat flashes through my body. *Who hurt Savannah?*

I'll fucking kill them.

It's what Jack would want. He'd do the same. He would feel like this. Conflicting thoughts barrage me as I try and fail to process what Sutton could mean. Berating thoughts for feeling this way about someone that isn't Sutton and justifying ones, because it's Savannah.

They continue their conversation, cutting me out. Leaving me to fantasize about all the ways to end a man. At least until I catch myself. I'm not normally a violent person, but there's just something about Savannah, a need ingrained so deep inside of me to protect her.

I move toward the edge of the couch, desperately trying to listen in and understand who hurt Van. A tightness pulls in my chest as I try to figure out what has happened.

Why am I feeling like this?

In an attempt to silence the noise inside my head, I ask, "Is someone going to clue me in?"

Silence falls over them before Sutton turns to face me. "Well, I was mistaken." Her eyes dart to Savannah before returning to me. I don't believe her for a second. "But, would you mind going with Savannah tomorrow to collect her things from her ex's?"

I don't even consider it, replying, "Sure."

It's what Jack would want and goes hand in hand

with his request for me to look out for his little sister. That's all this is. These feelings of anger at Savannah being mistreated are just because she's like a sister to me. Nothing more.

I breathe out, my shoulders relaxing as I lean back into the couch. That's all it is.

Sutton claps her hands together. "Great. I'm going to put my things away and then we can figure out dinner." With that, she leaves the room.

I'm staring at the TV, not really seeing what's playing out. My mind is a whirlwind of confused thoughts that I don't have the capacity to process right now.

I feel a headache starting. Rubbing at my temples, I tip my head back against the sofa, releasing a heavy sigh. Is it too much to ask for a break? It just seems to be one thing after the other recently.

Breaking me from my thoughts, Savannah says, "Thank you for offering, but you really don't need to come with me tomorrow. I only went along with it because Sutton's had a few too many and it's not worth gettin' in a tussle over."

"I said I would."

Under her breath, but loud enough for me to hear, she utters, "Right, 'cause you mean everything you say."

Her nose is wrinkled in an infuriatingly adorable way as she shakes her head. It's on the tip of my tongue to call her out on her shit, to tell her that for as long as she lives under my roof, she can't keep bringing up the past. But she picks up her bags and heads in the direction of her room.

What I wouldn't give to go back and undo the mistakes of my past. The thought is unwelcome. The past has happened and you can't hide from it. The only thing you can do is embrace it and keep moving forward.

Right now, my moving forward looks a lot like dropping Savannah off at the nearest hotel.

TEN

Savannah

The evening after my shopping trip with Sutton, I walk in the door at six. Immediately, my eyes connect with Noah from his position perched on one of the uncomfortable stools at the kitchen island. Neither of us breathe a word.

My skin prickles as I feel his gaze track me, as I dump my keys in the bowl on the table by the door and kick off my shoes. I'm tired, and don't have the patience to argue with him about whether or not he's coming to Will's with me.

Earlier today, I decided I was going to go and collect my things tomorrow rather than today. Every movement is an effort and I can barely keep my eyes open and I don't know what's waiting for me when I get there. I'd rather not be half asleep in case I run into him.

I'm the first to break the tension building in the room with each second that passes. "Hello."

"Hi." He pauses briefly, before standing and asking, "Are you ready?"

I take a step forward and reply, "You really don't need to come with me."

He straightens his red tie with one hand, smoothing down the fabric with the other. My eyes track the movement before I catch myself and look away.

"I know, but I'm going to. I told Sutton I would."

Right. I huff out a laugh at his statement. Better than anyone, I know that whatever Noah Parker says, he means. Even if it's that you're nothing but a sister to him.

"I'd rather you didn't."

Noah shoves his hands deep into his pockets as he rocks back and forth on his heels. Nodding, he replies, "That might be so, but I'm going to."

We stand, silently staring at each other, until I roll my eyes and turn toward my room without a word.

Looks like we're getting this over and done with today.

In my room, I strip down and throw on a pair of denim shorts and a white t-shirt. Grabbing my phone and a scrunchie from the dresser, I walk back into the open living room. The hairs on my arms stand on end as I feel Noah watching me.

Keeping my eyes down, I tie my hair up into a messy bun, only looking up at him when it's done. He clears his throat and looks away. I take that as my cue to move to the front door and put on my sneakers.

Snatching up my keys, I wait for Noah by the door expectantly. As he strides across the space, an awareness

I shouldn't be feeling ripples through me and my breath hitches as he gets closer.

I spin on my heel, throwing open the door and all but running to the elevator, jabbing at the button as if he's an axe murderer, and this is my only escape. It's hard to not miss the deep chuckle that rumbles in his chest as he comes to stand next to me.

"I'm not going to hurt you, Van. You don't need to run from me like I'm a murderer."

How did he do that?

I eye him skeptically from the corner of my eye. He doesn't know me well enough to be able to read my mind like that. Not any more.

Choosing to keep quiet, I aimlessly scroll through my phone until the elevator arrives. We ride down without a word being spoken.

It's only as we're walking across the lobby that Noah speaks again. "The car should be at the curb."

I hum a reply, intent on making this as painless as possible. Any time I'm in his vicinity, I'm reminded of everything we've shared and how heartbroken he left me.

Neither of us attempts to make conversation with the other as we ride to Will's place. I chat to Rupert, and Noah busies himself with his phone.

When we pull up outside the house, I suck in a breath, preparing myself for whatever might be beyond the door. Climbing out onto the pavement, I take in the almost eerie emptiness of the block. You wouldn't think you were in New York if the skyscrapers weren't peeking above the skyline. I walk up to the front door, using my key to let us into the brownstone.

As we step inside, the lingering smell of cigarette smoke and rotting food hits me. My eyes water and my stomach turns.

I've been gone for a week. What happened?

Further up the hallway, between the kitchen and bathroom, I spot fistholes in the walls. I hope Noah doesn't notice.

My eyes go to the spot where I'd dumped my bags, finding it empty. "I left 'em by the door, but I'm guessin' he moved 'em. I'll just—"

My words are cut short when Will steps into the hallway from the kitchen at the back of the house. If at all possible, he looks like he's lost weight in the few days since I left. I know I shouldn't, but I can't help but compare him to the man standing behind me. Where Noah looks like he could crush you with a hug, Will looks like you could push him over with one finger.

Will's movements are skittish and his gaze wild as he moves toward us. Noah's hand lands on my hip, and I ignore the jolt of electricity only partially dulled by the layers of my clothes. Noah moves me to stand behind him, my view now filled with the broad expanse of his dark navy suit covered back.

Peering around him, I watch as Will scratches at his arm. He looks between me and Noah before he asks, "Who are you?"

It takes a moment for me to process what Noah's just done by moving me behind him. *Who does he think he is?*

I push past him, eyeing him. When I'm standing between them, I answer Will, my voice soft and cajoling, "We've just come to get my things, Will."

This isn't the guy I knew.

Did I even know him?

My eyes don't leave him, certain that he's high on something or other.

"Who are you?" Will asks again, taking a step forward, his unfocused stare on Noah.

Noah and I talk at the same time.

"This is Noah, he's my—"

"I'm her new boyfriend."

A warmth pools in my stomach at his declaration before I catch myself.

Excuse me?

He did *not* just say what I think he said.

Will's hands ball into fists at his side and I watch as a red mist takes him over. Dragging in deep breaths through his nose, he exhales them noisily, trying to get a hold of his anger. All the while, staring daggers at an unphased Noah. That's literally the worst thing Noah could have possibly said right now.

Spinning to face Noah, I smack him on his very solid chest before turning to face Will again, ignoring the throb in my hand at the contact.

Will splutters, "He's your new boyfriend? How could you do that to me, Savannah?"

My mind doesn't quite catch up with my mouth when I respond, "Are you serious? You were screwing my old roommate in our bed. So what if I've moved on? We were through the second you touched her."

Will rushes toward me, his movements surprisingly coordinated. I brace myself for whatever he might try. But before he can reach me, Noah moves around me in the small space, stopping Will in his tracks. With his hands fisted, Noah stalks toward Will. For each step he takes, Will takes one back.

I can feel the anger radiating off of Noah. And, even though I don't know all the details of his childhood, I know that he doesn't tolerate men putting their hands on women.

"Noah," I call softly.

He doesn't acknowledge me, instead, he continues his approach toward Will.

Worried that he might do something he'll regret, I plead with him. "Don't do anything stupid, Noah. He's not worth it."

Pulling in a breath through his nose, Noah growls, his eyes still on Will, "Go and find your bags, Van."

I don't move. I can't. I'm frozen to the spot, replying, "Promise me you won't hurt him."

Will smirks, and Noah lunges for him, grabbing onto the front of his dirty white tee. The smile that was forming drops from his face when Noah responds, "I can't do that, angel."

That stupid nickname.

My eyes burn with unshed tears as I contemplate my next move. Seconds pass before I spring into action, certain that the quicker I am, the less likely Noah is to do any real damage. "Where are my bags, Will?"

Will squeaks out, "In the bedroom closet."

My legs burn as I race up the stairs, taking them two at a time. On the landing, I stumble on my undone shoelace, righting myself as I move through the house.

Pushing into the bedroom, my focus is on the partially closed closet door. When I pull it open, I send up a silent prayer that my bags don't appear to have been opened. A quick look inside each confirms everything is still in them.

Throwing one bag onto my shoulder and the other onto my forearm, I run through the room, down the hallway, and then the stairs. My sneakers squeak on the hardwood floor as I step off of the last step.

Moving toward the front door, I call, "Noah, I've got them. Let's go."

Releasing Will, Noah steps back, adjusting the cuffs of his shirt. From my position by the now open front door, I can't hear what Noah says to Will before he follows me to the door. But I don't miss the way his shoulders relax as he steps over the threshold and into the warm July air.

The sun beats down on us and as Noah falls into step next to me. He takes one of the bags from me, throwing it over his shoulder as we walk to the town car parked just down the street.

I can practically hear his mind whirling as he processes what's just happened.

Unable to listen to him tell me, yet again, what a poor choice I have in men, I speak up before he can. "I don't want to hear it, Noah. And don't you dare tell Jack what happened. Something is wrong with Will, because whoever that was back there." I point in the direction of the house. "That wasn't the guy I was dating."

Holding his hands up, he replies, "I won't tell him. I promise."

I stop next to the car, throwing my hands on my hips and staring him down. "And what the heck was that? Telling him you're my boyfriend? I don't need you to fight my battles for me."

Noah opens the door, indicating for me to get in before he replies, "I know you don't."

On the drive back to his apartment, as we sit in comfortable silence, I shut down the voice that's questioning why he called himself my boyfriend and why I felt the way I did when he said it.

Regardless of the reason, it should never have happened.

ELEVEN

Savannah

This past week has flown by. I've barely had time to breathe, let alone sleep. I'm definitely running on empty, operating in a haze of what's become a habit.

I'm walking back to Noah's from my fifth shift at O'Malley's Bar this week. If every week for the next twelve carries on like this—I'll likely be dead—but, I should have enough for a deposit and first month's rent for my own place.

Not that my current living situation sucks exactly.

I don't pay rent. That's the plus. But I'm also living with the guy I had the biggest crush on in high school and who I'm not sure I'm over. And let's not forget his amazing girlfriend. I haven't seen Sutton much since our shopping trip, but when I have, she's been nothing but kind to me.

In fact, on the rare occasions that I've had some

downtime and been in the apartment, I haven't seen or heard much of Sutton or Noah. It's kind of peculiar. The whole apartment almost feels... abandoned. If it wasn't for the housekeeper coming in once a week, I'd have thought nobody lives there.

"Mornin', Billy," I call to the concierge as I smother a yawn.

"Good morning, Miss O'Riley. I hope you get some sleep at some point this week," he calls back.

"You 'n' me both, Billy. You 'n' me both."

I jab the button for the elevator, willing my eyes to stay open just a few more minutes. When the doors swish open, I step inside and just as I push the button for my floor and lean against the back wall, a voice calls out.

"Hold the elevator, please."

Lunging forward, my finger hovers over the door close button as my sleep addled brain processes the arrow direction. Seconds before the doors close fully, I jab the door open button and they spring open. A stunning woman dressed all in black steps in, struggling with a box that she places on the floor.

Her caramel highlighted hair is tied into a messy bun on top of her head and a light sheen of perspiration covers her brow.

As she straightens and turns toward me, her dark brown eyes are filled with hesitation. "Do you mind holding the elevator? I'm just moving in, and it's been a pain going up and down with just one box at a time."

"Oh, let me help. Where're your boxes at?"

She places a hand on her chest as she looks over her shoulder before returning her gaze to me. "You don't need to do that. In fact." She bends, and picks up the box she'd just put down, continuing, "You take this one and I'll wait for another one."

Taking the box that she's holding, I place it back on the floor to keep the doors open. Turning to her expectantly, I reply, "My mama'd kill me if she knew I took this elevator and left you to move in on your own. Many hands make the load lighter and all that."

When she doesn't move or say anything, I hold my hand out, a grin on my face as I say, "I'm Savannah. It's nice to meet you."

She looks a little taken aback by my willingness to help. Maybe even a little scared.

"As you can probably tell, I'm not from New York. But where I'm from, it's totally normal to offer some help. You don't need to be afraid."

My statement elicits a reaction out of her and she laughs, taking my hand and shaking it with a firm grip. "I'm Alex. It's nice to meet you too, Savannah. I've actually only got a couple of boxes as the movers brought most of the stuff in. This is just the last few bits."

We walk across the lobby to the front desk. Neatly stacked next to the desk is a pile of six boxes that I'd missed when I walked in. My sleep deprived brain too focused on getting to my bed.

"You know, Billy could help you with these, right?"

Alex shrugs a shoulder before replying, "I know, but

115

this is my first building with a concierge and doorman and it just didn't feel right having them carry my stuff like I don't have arms."

I offer up an understanding smile. "That makes sense. It takes some time gettin' used to, that's for sure."

It doesn't take us long to get the boxes loaded into the elevator, and when I press the button for the thirtieth floor, I turn to ask Alex for her floor number. She lets out a huff of a laugh, her eyes on the panel of floor numbers.

In need of something to laugh about, I ask, "What's funny?"

A smirk pulls at her mouth as she says, "It's... well, you won't believe this, but it looks like we live on the same floor."

I turn to the control panel as if needing to check before replying. "No way. Well, that's it, we're meant to be friends."

"You know what, Savannah? I couldn't agree with you more." We share a laugh, before Alex asks, "What are you doing now?"

Sleeping. "I was going to take a shower and head to bed," I chuckle.

Alex pouts. "Just one drink? A 'thank you' drink?"

I don't take much convincing because it might actually help me to have a sleep that isn't plagued with memories of a girl I used to be. If the drink's strong enough, I might even be lucky enough to pass out completely. "Sure, that actually sounds good."

When the elevator arrives on our floor, Alex carries a

box to her front door as I start moving them out of the car. It doesn't take us long to carry the boxes from the elevator and into her apartment.

As we carry in the last two boxes, Alex turns to me. "Which apartment do you live in?"

"I live at the end of the hall. But only temporarily."

"Oh, are you..." Alex waves her hand in the air as if trying to think of the right word. "Housesitting?"

If only.

"I'm actually stayin' with my brother's best friend and his girlfriend. It's convenient since I don't pay rent, so most of what I earn can go toward a deposit and first month's rent for my own apartment."

"That's smart. And, if you ever need to not be around them when they're having all that hot sex all over the place, then you can come over here. I, for one, am having zero hot sex."

At Alex's mention of hot sex, my brow pulls together. I haven't heard any signs of sex going on in the apartment, which is unusual for a couple. Right? In fact, most nights when I come home, Noah either isn't there, or he's working in his office with the door shut.

I shake my head to clear the thoughts.

Just because I haven't walked in on them having sex doesn't mean that they aren't having it. They could just be super quiet, or maybe he's boring in bed. The thought has a smirk creeping onto my lips.

Imagine that.

Actually, no. Think of puppies. Anything but that.

Alex is rummaging through boxes when she turns to me with a glass bottle full of clear liquid. She holds it up triumphantly with a giant grin on her face. "We have tequila. I hope you don't mind, but it's kind of my drink."

"Tequila sounds amazing." My mouth pulls into a smile that matches Alex's as I move toward the pink couch in the middle of the room.

Now that I'm not lost in my own thoughts, I take a moment to look around her apartment. It's much smaller than Noah's place, and even though she's just moved in, I can already tell it won't be as clinical. Bright pops of color fill the space, peeping out of the boxes that surround us.

Looking a little lost, Alex returns to rummaging through more boxes. "We just need some glasses," she utters, distracted.

She walks into another room. I assume the kitchen because although her apartment is smaller than Noah's and not so open plan, the layout looks very similar.

Returning with two coffee mugs, Alex declares, "These will have to do. I'm not that picky about what holds my drink, just what that drink is."

"Same, girl, same."

Throwing herself on the couch next to me, Alex hands me one of the white ceramic mugs, gripping her own between her thighs as she unscrews the tequila bottle. When we both have a drink, she places the bottle on the floor between us before leaning back on the couch, completely at ease.

"Moving sucks, and I really hope this place will be it for me for a while." There's a comfortable pause as we both sip on our drinks.

Alex asks, "Tell me about yourself, Savannah. Where are you from?"

I relax back into the couch, weirdly comfortable around this woman I've only just met. "I was born and raised in Montgomery, Alabama. I've been in New York for nearly five years now. Have you always lived in New York?"

"Oh, wow, Montgomery is a really historic city for civil rights. I was born in New York but moved to Sacramento when I was five. How come you moved to the city?"

"I went to college and I've been sluggin' away tryin' to make it big on Broadway. It's goin' real well, as you can tell by my complete lack of stardom." I turn to face Alex, kicking off my shoes and tucking a leg under myself. "When did you move back to New York?"

There's definitely something about her energy that just puts me at ease.

Alex takes a sip of her tequila, her brows tugging together as she thinks over her answer. "Well, it's got to be close to eight years now. I went to college in Chicago and then moved to New York right after. Do you love the city or wish you were back in Montgomery?"

I look down at the clear liquid in my mug, swirling it around as I think over her question. Alex doesn't press me for an answer.

Finally, I reply, "It's unbelievable how lonely this city can make you feel. I'm not entirely sure I haven't gone a bit mad because I've started a little game with myself."

Alex smiles, asking, "Yeah?"

"Don't judge me, but when I wanna entertain myself a little, I like to test out some of my many accents. Sometimes I nail them, other times I don't. Pretendin' to be someone else is all part o' bein' a performer. You take on the persona of your character and I like to practice that even when I'm not on stage. Although, y'all do really love my true southern accent."

Chuckling, Alex replies, "People in New York, for the most part, love different. I can just imagine what sort of reactions you must get if you lay your own accent on thick. It's so cool that you can almost turn it on and off though."

With a chuckle, I reply, "It's taken a lot of practice, believe me."

We chat for an hour or so, making our way through half the bottle of tequila before I glance at my watch and realize it's two a.m. Thank goodness it's Thursday tomorrow and I can at least sleep in until six. I'll be half drunk and as dead on my feet as I normally am when I walk Miss. Dixie in the morning.

The lights are all off when I stumble my way through the apartment, using the wall for support. I drop my bag on my bedroom floor before I start slipping out of my clothes, throwing them around haphazardly. It's only when I'm standing in my navy blue lace bra and matching G-string that I remember I need to brush my teeth.

Standing in the middle of my room, I hesitate for a moment. Do I put something on or take a risk and run to the bathroom as I am? Whatever I put on, I'll only end up taking it off when I get into bed. I really doubt anyone is going to be up at this time of the morning. And Noah and Sutton have an ensuite anyway.

A quick look in the corridor tells me nobody is around and I decide to take the risk and dart across the hallway to the bathroom. Safely inside, I breathe a sigh of relief before I pee and then brush my teeth.

Maybe I can blame it on my alcohol and sleep-addled brain, but it doesn't even cross my mind to check the hallway again before I head back to my room. If I had thought to, I wouldn't have found myself face to face with a very broad and very bare chest in the moonlight at the end of the corridor.

Neither of us says a word.

We stare at each other like we've been caught in a compromising position. I guess in some ways we have. My head swims from the alcohol and the fire that's sparking to life in my gut.

I can feel his gaze on me even as I try to shrink back into the shadows, which is hard to do with the bathroom light still on. My labored breathing is the only sound I can hear. My eyes are glued to his defined abs and the two lines on his hips leading to the intimate parts of him hidden by his low hanging black sweats. I take him in almost greedily, a hunger clawing inside me. Every part of him is big and even as far away as we are he makes me feel delicate.

Not appropriate, Savannah.

This is your FRIEND's boyfriend.

Look away.

A longing, I have no right to feel, settles in the pit of my stomach.

He'll always have my heart.

The heck he will.

This living situation is one of convenience and my stupid emotions are not fifteen years old anymore. Flicking off the bathroom light, I rush into my room, shutting the door behind me as I sink against the cool wood.

That was stupid of me. To have gone out there without covering up. He's probably going to think I was trying to seduce him and kick me out. No, he wouldn't do that. Jack would be pissed.

I just need to be more careful.

I need to put more distance between us.

Climbing into bed, I pull the covers over my head, closing my eyes as I will sleep to come.

As with every night since I've been here, my mind is plagued with fantastical dreams of a boy who's now turned into a man.

Only unlike reality, in my dream, this one wants *me*.

TWELVE
Noah

I pause in the light of the refrigerator, my brow furrows as my ears strain to hear the sound again. It was like something had dropped, which considering it's two thirty in the morning, is odd.

Maybe Sutton or Savannah has knocked something over. *Maybe I'm just hearing things.* Despite standing completely still for a good five minutes, there isn't any more noise.

Of course, it's possible that it's just Sutton going to the bathroom, but when I went and changed out of my suit, she was fast asleep and she never wakes in the night.

Grabbing a bottle of water from the refrigerator, I close the door and make my way through the kitchen and out into the hallway. The moonlight lights my path.

All of these late nights have me hallucinating. That's got to be what it is. This merger is draining me. Several times over the past few weeks, I've considered walking away. It's not worth the stress it's causing me. *Teddy isn't worth the fucking stress.*

I'm walking out of the living room when a light at the end of the hallway near Savannah's room catches my eye. Instinctively, I look over, certain it's another trick.

My gaze connects with Savannah's wide eyes. I can't help the way I take her in as she stands frozen at the end of the corridor.

Neither of us says a word or makes a move.

An awareness ripples through me, settling into the pit of my stomach where it tumbles and tightens. She's only wearing lingerie and it barely covers parts of her body I have no right to see. The light from the bathroom creates a spotlight behind her, simultaneously hiding her from me but hinting at her curves.

My tongue feels heavy in my mouth, and I swallow thickly trying and failing to get my feet to move. This is wrong on so many levels.

Savannah seems to come out of her fugue state first and turns off the light, shrouding the corridor in darkness before racing into her room.

When the soft click of her door closing echos down the hallway, I blink, taking an involuntary step forward. I catch myself before I go any further.

Fuck, what the hell was that?

I've known Savannah since she was fourteen, seeing her in her underwear can't be the reason for the currents of electricity coursing through me.

She's like a sister to me.

She can't be more than that to me.

Scrubbing my hand over the back of my neck, I move through the dimly lit apartment until I reach the closed door of my bedroom. A sharp intake of breath is all I allow myself to gather my racing thoughts before I turn the doorknob, push the door open, and step into the room.

Sutton is my girlfriend and I'm in love with her.

Aren't I?

The question pops into my mind but I push it away. I don't have the answer. If my body is reacting the way it is to seeing another woman half dressed, can I really say that my feelings for Sutton are as strong as they once were?

A small gap in the drawn curtains affords me enough light to make it to the bed. I can see Sutton laying on her side, facing me.

As quietly as I can, I move toward the bed, pulling the covers back before shucking off my bottoms. The sheets are cool against my heated skin as I lay down.

Reaching out a hand, I rest it on Sutton's hip on top of the cover, almost desperate for a connection. Anything to remind me of my commitments.

Even if we're more like friends than lovers.

Sutton shifts, rolling away from me and out of reach, murmuring, "I've got to be up early."

It's been like this for months. The intimacy that ran rampant between us when we first started dating has diminished to the point we're more like roommates than partners. We're both to blame for it, but I can't help but feel that I should have tried harder. That she's pushed me away because I haven't made the effort to keep our connection alive.

I don't even remember the last time I hugged Sutton or tried to initiate sex.

Maybe that's why my body is reacting the way it is to having seen Savannah in next to nothing. My balls are practically blue and I'm certain it's my dick's way of telling me that it's fed up with my right hand.

That's all it is.

With one last look at Sutton's back, I close my eyes, praying for a dreamless sleep. When an image of Savannah, moments ago, dances behind my closed eyes, I open them, staring up at the white ceiling above me.

This, what happened tonight, can't happen again. Not when I'm in a relationship, no matter how unhappy it is.

A commitment is a commitment, and a promise is a promise. Neither should be taken for granted or treated like they mean nothing.

Tomorrow I'll find Savannah somewhere else to stay.

A memory of the conversation I had with Jack when we were seventeen, and I'd just moved to Montgomery, flashes into my mind. Before he'd introduced me to Savannah that day at high school, he'd told me about his nerdy kid sister.

When she'd walked towards me, it was like she was

fucking floating and I was done for. Her pillowy lips had called to me as her wide eyes drank me in. It took all of my restraint to not ask her to be mine.

It must have been obvious for Jack to see, because that night, when I left his family's home, in the driveway next to his Cutlass Supreme, he told me that Savannah was off limits. I made a promise to him that I wouldn't touch her. That I would treat her like my own kid sister.

At the time, his friendship meant more to me than any girl ever could. But with each passing year, as I got to know Savannah, I questioned whether making that promise was a mistake. I still value his friendship—he means the world to me—but so does she.

If only I'd known that in telling *her* no, I'd lose her anyway.

With a huff, I roll onto my side, disappointed with myself for dismissing my friendship with Jack. Shit, he's been there for me through thick and thin.

He's the only person that's been a constant in my life since I was a teenager. It's like the second I met him, he knew what was happening at home and pulled me into his inner circle. Jack became so much more than a friend.

He's my brother.

It was solidified the night he helped me save my mom. Nothing I can do will ever repay that debt to him.

I'm going to put everything that's happened tonight and the thoughts that have filled my mind down to having had a stressful week. All I need is a good night's sleep and then everything can go back to normal.

THIRTEEN

Savannah

I t's been six weeks of awkwardness since Noah and
I ran into each other in the hallway, both half
naked and me a little past tipsy. Almost out of a
sense of guilt, and definitely embarrassment, I've been
trying to avoid both him and Sutton.

Of course my plan has been in vain because of Alex.
On a handful of occasions the four of us—Sutton, Noah,
Alex and I—have been out to the clubs around the city.
Alex has invited them every time.

What makes all of this worse is that I really like
Sutton. She's been so welcoming and easy to talk to. But
a seed of guilt has been blossoming inside of me over
that night. And no matter what I do, it won't go away.

I shrug into my gray zip up hoodie as I walk through
the apartment from my bedroom. Tonight, I'm going to
relax with my friends and forget about everything that's
been making me feel anything but fantastic lately.

The front door opens and I consider for a second darting back to my room. It can only be one of two people and I'd rather not see either of them right now.

This is no way to live, avoiding the people I share an apartment with.

Sutton walks in, closing the door behind her, oblivious to my presence. She places her bag in the closet next to the door, and shrugs out of her jacket, hanging it on one of the hooks. When she turns, a soft smile spreads across her face as her gaze lands on me. "Hey. I feel like I haven't seen you in ages. How are you?"

I move to the table on the opposite side of the door and swipe up my keys before turning toward her. "I'm great, just working a lot. How are you?"

The smile drops from her face and she looks away. I watch, fascinated, as she seems to shrug off the cloud that coated her and straighten her spine.

Ignoring my question, Sutton tilts her head taking in my burgundy oversized sweats and white t-shirt. "Are you going out?"

"Oh." I look down at my outfit before continuing, "Yeah, just to Alex's. Meghan and Ben are coming over too and we're gonna put on a movie."

Sutton looks away, a wistful smile on her face as she closes her eyes, before returning her gaze to me and replying, "That sounds like a nice evening. Have fun."

She goes to walk away but gets no further than a couple of steps when I say, "Did you, maybe, want to come? We're gonna order takeout and do some face masks."

I'm gonna regret this.

But I can't not invite her. It feels like I owe her, not just for accepting me into her home without any anger— because she had every right to be mad about that—but also because of what happened six weeks ago.

Briefly, I wonder if Noah told her about what I've been referring to as 'the incident', but I almost immediately dismiss the thought. He probably thought it was so insignificant that it didn't warrant telling Sutton. And anyway, I'm fairly certain that he couldn't see anything. Not really.

A genuinely big smile takes over Sutton's face. "I would love to. Just let me get changed."

Sutton walks away toward her bedroom, the sound of her shoes on the floor growing quieter with each step she takes. I listen intently until the only noise filling the space is the sound of the air leaving my lungs.

How can I spend the evening with Sutton when I haven't been honest with her?

Honest about what exactly?

About how in love with her boyfriend I still am? That the feelings he stirred in me when I was seventeen are the same, if not amplified now?

This is why it's better that I don't spend time with either of them.

It's so much easier to forget everything when you aren't being mocked by the constant reminder. Whether that be the amazing woman he's chosen to make his or the way he looks at me like I'm nothing more than a friend.

My phone vibrates in my hand, pulling me out of my spiraling thoughts. I flip the screen over, reading the message from Alex.

> **ALEX**
>
> Hurry up, Savannah!
>
> We're going to order the food. Still up for pizza?

> **SAVANNAH**
>
> I'm coming. And I'm bringing Sutton.
>
> Pizza sounds great.

> **ALEX**
>
> Okay, what pizza does she want?

Alex's question stumps me. Is that something I should know? I've lived here for two months and yet we've only shared a handful of meals together. I'm ashamed to say that when we have eaten together, I haven't paid much attention to what Sutton picks. Does that make me a bad friend?

Regardless of my internal struggle, I do consider Sutton a friend.

Tucking my phone into the pocket of my sweats, I call out to Sutton. "Do you eat pizza?"

Sutton chuckles as she walks around the corner. "Who doesn't eat pizza?"

I've never seen her wear something so casual. She's

in a pair of black leggings and an oversized forest green sweater with fluffy slippers adorning her feet. Despite her relaxed outfit, she still looks like a million bucks.

Especially in comparison to me.

Mentally brushing away the comment, I return her smile and say, "Good point. Alex wanted to know what type of pizza you eat, but we can just let her know when we get there."

Turning toward the door, I pull it open and walk through, waiting in the hallway for Sutton to lock up. Noah isn't home, but if I had to guess where he is, I'd say at the office. Out of the two, he's been the easiest to avoid because he's either working in his home office or out in his main office.

It takes us all of ten seconds to walk the few steps to Alex's door. Alex and I aren't quite at the point that I can just let myself into her apartment, so I knock and wait for her to answer.

Moments later, she swings the door open, holding her arms wide as she does. Behind her, I can see Meghan and Ben chatting animatedly on the couch.

"Oh my God, what took you so long? I'm starving. Is pizza still okay?" Alex's eyes are a little crazed as she looks between Sutton and I.

Chuckling, I walk into the apartment, pulling Alex into a hug before I step back and reply, "It's so good to see you too, Alex. Pizza is great. I'll have a couple a slices of anything."

I walk over to Meghan and Ben, greeting Meghan

first with a hug. Her long blonde hair is tied back in a high ponytail and her face is free of make up, allowing her petite features to shine. She's stunning and I kinda hate her for it. She looks like a grecian goddess with a white flowing dress covering her baby bump.

Ben pulls me into his arms, barely giving me time to release Megahn. To say I was disappointed when Ben told me he doesn't date women, is an understatement. He's one of the most good-looking guys I've ever seen. He has a straight nose, eyelashes any girl would be envious of and high cheekbones that should have him gracing the cover of a magazine. Tonight he's wearing a white fitted t-shirt that shows off his tattoo sleeves and navy sweats.

Alex introduced me to Meghan and Ben not that long ago and even though I've only known them a few weeks, they've pulled me into the fold and it's like we're old friends.

My gaze meets Sutton's over my shoulder, finding her closer than expected.

With a smile I'm certain doesn't reach my eyes, I say, "Sutton, this is Meghan. Let me try not to butcher this. Meghan is married to Cooper, who is Alex's boss. Alex and Meghan grew up together and Alex got Meghan the interview for the job she had workin' with Cooper. Right?" I turn to Alex and Meghan and they nod in unison, matching smirks on their faces. "And this is Ben. Meghan and Ben live next to each other just outside the city. Ben recently broke up with his boyfriend so any time we go out, we're always on a mission to find him the 'one'. Everyone, this is Sutton, Noah's girlfriend and my current roommate."

Ben stands, pulling Sutton into a hug. "It's so nice to meet you, Sutton."

Sutton steps out of Ben's embrace and straight into Meghan's.

"It's nice to meet you, too. Come on, let's get comfy and then we can start grilling you," Meghan laughs.

I watch as Sutton relaxes, allowing Meghan to guide her over to the couch.

"Can I get you ladies a drink?" Alex asks, standing in the kitchen entryway.

Turning to Sutton, I raise a brow in question.

"I'll have whatever you're having."

"Two beers it is then. I'll give you a hand, Alex." I indicate to Sutton, before walking over to Alex in the kitchen.

"You know I could carry two beers, right?"

I laugh, although it doesn't sound genuine to my own ears. "Sorry, I thought you might be gettin' one for yourself."

Alex bumps my shoulder, a smirk on her lips. "You get the beers and I'll order the pizza, because if I have to listen to them argue anymore about pizza toppings without actually having a pizza in front of me, I'll go mad."

This time my laugh is genuine. I busy myself with grabbing the beers from the refrigerator before following

Alex back into the living room. Meghan and Ben are still arguing over what pizza topping is the most superior.

"No, you have to have a barbecue base with all the meats. It's the new thing."

Meghan holds a hand over her mouth and dry heaves. "Gross. That's a crime against pizza. It's got to be a tomato base."

Ben turns to face me, and I make the mistake of making eye contact with him. "Come on, Van. You have to agree with me."

My brows lift as my eyes widen. I head to the chair opposite the couch, taking a swig of my beer to buy myself some time. "No way am I arguin' with a pregnant woman. And anyway, Meghan is right. It has to be a tomato base on pizza."

"I can't ever win around here." Ben pouts and we erupt into a fit of giggles.

This is just what I needed. To be surrounded by my friends, drinking beer and eating good food.

My stomach is full and a little bloated from all the pizza I've eaten tonight. Add in the four beers I've had and I look and feel like a beached whale.

The conversation has been flowing nicely all evening and we're currently wearing the sheet masks that Ben brought. Alex put some 'spa music' on and the calming sound of the rainforest fills the room.

Meghan shuffles herself further into the couch, one hand resting on her belly and the other holding her mug of tea. "So, Sutton, tell us, how long have you and Noah been together?"

Momentarily, I close my eyes, before I open them again, looking around the room. Alex's knowing gaze assesses me and I fight against the urge to look away. I told Alex about the bathroom incident, but she doesn't know anything beyond that. Nobody in this room knows anything about my past with Noah.

Sutton takes a long sip of her beer before she replies, "Just over three years."

"Do you think you'll marry him?"

Ben's question catches me off guard, and I choke on the sip of my beer I've taken.

A twisted part of me wants to know the answer. As if it will solidify their love and I can then switch off my feelings for him. But I'm not sure my heart could take the finality in the truth.

Coughing, I mutter something about my drink having gone down the wrong way and excuse myself to the bathroom. The sounds of chatter I can't quite make out follow me down the corridor. Like a ghost haunting and mocking me with each step. I lock myself in the bathroom as my eyes sting with unshed tears.

What is happening to me?

Almost in a daze, I stand in front of the mirror, my eyes roaming over my reflection. I look composed and as normal as a person can with a sheet mask on. But the swirling and churning inside of me tells a different story.

I operate on autopilot, removing the mask and massaging the residue into my face. It does nothing to quiet the rushing noise deafening me. With perhaps too much force, I turn on the faucet, splashing the cool water on my face, as I pray for the tightening in my gut to ease.

A soft knock sounds on the door followed by Meghan asking, "Savannah? Is everything okay?"

Grabbing a towel off the bar, I pat my face dry before pasting a smile on my face and opening the door. "Sorry, do you need to use the bathroom?"

Meghan looks at me quizzically before her eyes narrow into slits and she replies, "I do, but that's not why I came down here."

Taking a step to the side, I make room for her. She remains in the doorway, her hand rubbing over her bump absentmindedly. Her focus is on my face and it's almost as bad as when Alex assessed me.

I need to put on a show.

I'm supposed to be an actress for goodness sake. It's my job to play pretend.

So why is it so hard to do now?

On the edge of breaking, I send up a silent thank you as Meghan steps into the bathroom, allowing me the room to escape.

"Oh, by the way," she pauses, waiting for me to turn to her. "She said no. She doesn't think she'll marry him."

With a nod and Meghan's words echoing around my mind, I walk back to the living room.

Why wouldn't Sutton marry Noah if he asked?

Does she not love him?

I have so many questions. But I know I won't get any answers because it's not my place to ask them.

Taking a seat, I'm pulled back into the conversation when I hear Alex ask Sutton, "So, it's basically over if he doesn't come through for this event?"

Leaning forward slightly, I tilt my head, feigning nonchalance as I listen intently, waiting for an answer.

Sutton looks at me, a look I can't quite decipher taking over her face. "Pretty much. Our relationship has been slowly dying for months. I'm very aware though that neither of us has been making any effort. In my mind, this is the revival. He knows how important it is for me so I know he'll be there. But if we can't get that intimacy back... what are we even doing together?"

Ben reaches out and holds onto Sutton's hand, comforting her. As her friend I should be doing that, but I just can't get past my own feelings, and I feel like the worst person for it.

For the rest of the evening, I'm stuck in my own head. Questions swirling, demanding answers. The most prominent being, how could I have not seen that they were *that* distant?

Now more than ever, I need to get the money together to move out. Because if Noah and Sutton break up, I can't stay living with him. Not with it being just the two of us.

FOURTEEN

Noah

I t's been a long fucking day of unexpected meetings and endless paperwork. Sometimes I question why I decided to make mergers and acquisitions my career. But then I remember all I've achieved and what I was able to do for my mom. All of the long hours and crushing weight of responsibility has been worth it.

Has it?

The question hovers at the forefront of my mind giving me pause. What have I had to give up in order to become a billionaire before I turned thirty?

A wave of what could have been envelopes me, desperately trying to drag me into its pit of despair. Shaking my head, I clear the thoughts from my mind. There's no point in thinking about shoulda, woulda, coulda, events.

I'm grateful for everything I do have. Like a mom

that's safe, a home to call my own, a thriving business and Sutton.

But I'm not happy with her.

Christ, I haven't been happy in this relationship for so long.

I know Sutton can give me everything I've ever wanted in a relationship. But something's holding me back. It's stopping me from being all in. I'm just not entirely sure what *it* is. So I've buried myself in work. Taking on tasks that can be delegated to my more than competent team, until I'm working sixteen hour days nearly seven days a week.

Pulling off my tie, an object flies past my head, hitting the wall opposite the bed with a dull thud. My eyes narrow as I try to make out what it is. I turn in the direction that it came from just as Sutton storms into the room, slamming the door behind her. A fire burns bright in her eyes as she looks at me with a mask of fury.

With a calm tone that somehow seems to say nothing is wrong at the same time that it conveys her anger, she asks, "How could you? I never expected you, of all people, to do this to me."

I blink, trying to process what she could mean. How could I do what? My mind races through the events of the last few months and anything I could have possibly done wrong. The only thing that sticks out is that night over a month ago. I should have told her. She had a right to know. Guilt consumes me. Ready to plead for forgiveness, I reply, "I'm sorry."

With a defeated tone that tells me just how done she is, Sutton replies, "I just don't understand why you didn't turn up, Noah?" Her wide, hurt gaze lifts to mine as she continues, "You knew how much this meant to me. I looked like a fool, standing there waiting for my boyfriend, like some high schooler waiting for a date that never shows."

My body relaxes before I catch myself.

What the fuck am I doing?

Apologizing for seeing Savannah half dressed flies out of my head as I let Sutton's words sink in. Why do I feel relieved that my girlfriend is pissed at me not showing up for her?

Shit.

Sutton's partner dinner was tonight. I fucking forgot. My mind has been so preoccupied with cleaning up Teddy's mess that it wasn't a priority.

And just what does that say about how much I value my girlfriend?

My throat feels thick as a heaviness settles onto my chest. The guilt threatens to eat me from the inside out.

I watch, at a loss for words, as Sutton kicks off her patent black heels. Her hands move to the side of her black dress, pulling down the zip. As she uncovers her body, I feel nothing. No stirrings, no immediate lust for her. Nothing.

Sutton looks deflated, her shoulders stooped and her usual light dimmed. She looks broken and at that realization, my chest tightens. I'm to blame for this. Sutton moves to the bathroom pulling her hair out of its ponytail.

Before she can shut the door, I close the distance between us, resting my palm on the smooth surface. Stopping her from shutting me out. "Tell me how I can make it up to you."

Looking up at me with glassy eyes, Sutton replies, "I don't think you can, Noah. This was a really big deal for me."

An almost desperate need to make it up to her makes my next words spill from my mouth. "Please, there has to be something."

For reasons I can't quite identify, I need to make this right, because the look on her face tells me she's close to walking away. And if she does that then it'll just be me and... fuck, I can't even think of that. She has to stay.

Maybe if I wasn't in a tunnel of desperation, I'd analyze my motives for wanting her to stay. But blinders have me focused on this one objective; nothing else matters.

Sutton's eyes roam over my face. It feels like an eternity passes before she tentatively replies, "I guess, you could come out with me tomorrow night. It feels like we've lost that spark, Noah. And something needs to change because I can't keep feeling like this. Ignored and unimportant."

Without an ounce of hesitation, I reply, "Consider me there."

A smile lights up her face, her relief at my agreement

palpable. I've really been a terrible boyfriend. Whatever is missing between us, it needs to change. I know it does. But you can't force feelings.

"Thank you, Noah. For this to work, we both need to make an effort and I'm very aware that neither of us has for a while. I'll shower and then let Savannah know you'll be coming with us."

My face remains neutral as I nod in agreement with her while inside a heaviness settles in my core. The thought of working on our relationship doesn't fill me with excitement. Instead, I feel a sense of dread. I move to the bed as Sutton closes the bathroom door. Collapsing back onto the mattress, my arms cover my face, leaving me in darkness.

A million things run through my mind, from work, to guilt over having missed Sutton's dinner, to why I'm holding onto a relationship that seems to have died long ago.

It's not fair on either of us.

FIFTEEN

Savannah

I wince at the burn as another shot slides down my throat. Right now, I need all the liquid courage I can stomach. When we invited Sutton out, I never expected her to have Noah tag along.

Especially not after everything she said at Alex's.

Alex tops up my shot glass, eyeing me cautiously as I throw it back and tip my head to the glass for more.

"Are you okay?" she asks tentatively.

I nod before replying, "Just keep 'em coming."

Popping the top back on the bottle, Alex moves it out of my reach before resting her hands on my shoulders. "I don't know what is going on with you right now, but you look hot and we don't want to get into hot mess territory so I'm cutting you off. Let's get going."

I consider her statement for a moment before deciding that she's probably right. Nobody wants to hook up with a sloppy drunk.

Tonight, I've done my eye shadow in a smokey effect with my lips nude—because it's one or the other, never both. Smokey eyes suit my dark blue irises and fair skin tone better anyway. My dress is a backless, long sleeved, bright blue mini dress and I've got a pair of white platform heels on my feet. I'm determined to have fun.

We grab our coats and make our way down to the street as Alex calls a cab through a service app. It doesn't take long for us to be pulling up to Siren.

As Alex steps out, I hand over a twenty dollar bill to the driver, telling him to keep the change before I follow suit. Even though it's still early September, we've had to throw on some warm coats to ward off the unseasonably cool evening air.

Alex stands in front of me as I swing my legs out and onto the sidewalk. She's amazing, making sure I don't show my goods to the partygoers.

Tonight, Alex has on a fitted white cut out dress that showcases both her curves and skin tone to perfection. She's styled it with a pair of five-inch strappy gold heels that wrap around her calves and a gold clutch. Her caramel highlighted, chestnut brown hair falls down to her chest, each strand perfectly straight.

Linking arms, we sway our way to the front of the queue in a fit of giggles. We've agreed to meet Noah, Sutton, and Ben inside at the table we've reserved. I think they'll have a lot of catching up to do with us after all the shots we had at Alex's. Although I'm not sure Alex is as drunk as I am.

She's a bit of a feeder—if that's even the right word —when it comes to drinks.

The bouncer lets us in without question and we walk through the dark corridors brushing past couples making out and people having conversations in a quieter area of the club.

After dumping our coats at the cloakroom, we push through a door at the end of the corridor and the main part of the club is spread out in front of us. The music that was just a dull thud amplifies, enveloping us.

Alex throws an arm around my shoulders as she talks into my hair. Even in my heels, I barely reach her chin. "Let's go get a drink, find the others and then hit the dance floor."

I do a little excited wiggle, drawing the attention of a tall, mysterious and handsome guy dressed in black jeans and a white shirt, leaning on the bar. Our eyes connect and he raises his glass toward me.

I might not be ready to go home with a guy but I'm up for flirting.

Swaying my hips as the opening notes to *I'm Real* by Jennifer Lopez and Ja Rule blasts through the speakers, I grab Alex's hand and move toward the bar. My gaze doesn't leave the hot guy.

I can already tell it's going to be a good night.

Not only is it old-school R'n'B jams night—my favorite—but I've got good company in Alex and a hot guy to flirt and dance with.

Alex stands behind me as I lean over the bar to grab

the attention of the bartender. When she reaches me, I order two glasses of champagne and whatever the hot guy I'm standing next to is having.

I can feel his gaze boring into my bare back and when I turn my head to face him, there's heat in his eyes. Stepping back from the bar, I hold my hand out for him to shake. Almost immediately he slips his own into mine. It's warm and slightly calloused, but based on the rich smell of his cologne and the tailored cut of his clothing, it's more likely from the gym than any hard labor.

There's no spark.

Internally, I roll my eyes. Whatever happened when Noah touched my hip was a fluke. A static electric shock. Not some spark between us in the romantic way. That stuff only happens in romance books, not real life.

Holding my hand for what some might consider a beat too long with no action, he bends, his lips brushing over the shell of my ear as he murmurs, "Jamison Monroe."

Wow. The deep timbre of his voice travels through my body, leaving goosebumps in its wake. I mean, I'm not getting flutters down there like I used to with a certain someone but I can appreciate a delicious man as much as the next woman.

But I didn't get that with Will either.

And look how well that turned out.

"Savannah." I'm not stupid enough to give a stranger my full name.

As the bartender drops our drinks off, Alex reaches

through us, forcing him to drop my hand. Picking up a glass of champagne, she drops some bills on the counter. "As nice as it is to watch you two eye fuck each other, I don't really go for voyeurism. It's nice seeing you again Jamison, take care of my girl. Have fun kids and be safe." With that she walks off, no doubt to find the others.

Jamison and I both chuckle before I turn back to the bar and pick up my drink, throwing it back in one gulp.

Putting the glass back on the bar, my curiosity gets the better of me. I lean into him—he smells woodsy. I like it. My voice is raised to be heard over the music as I ask, "How do you know Alex?"

Jamison leans in close, as he replies, "She's best friends with my friend, Cooper's, wife."

I process the information, a question dancing through my mind that I need to know the answer to before I go any further with him. "Have you two..." My question trails off, but I know he understands what I'm asking.

"God no. She's been hooking up—although not so secretly—with one of my other friends, Sebastian. He'd kill me if I went near her. I think they do a lot of hate fucking."

With a nod, I put a pin in that, making a note to ask Alex about Sebastian another day. I wonder if he's the guy Alex has hinted at but refused to give me any details on. I know Meghan knows, but they've both been tightlipped about him.

"Wanna dance?" I hold my hand out to him as he

downs the amber liquid before discarding the glass and taking my hand. He leads the way to the dance floor as the track changes to *Drop It Like It's Hot* by Snoop Dogg and Pharrell Williams.

My hips swing to the beat as we move, until we're in the center of the crowd. Jamison twirls me and tucks me into his body so my back is to his front. We move as one to the rhythm, grinding against each other, losing ourselves to the music.

In the back of my mind, I'm vaguely aware of the fact that I haven't so much as said hello to the others. Tonight is for me though and screw my manners.

Mama would whoop me so hard if she knew.

Sorry, Mama.

Jamison and I alternate between dancing, drinking and talking for a few hours until the guilt gets the best of me. As much as I try and act like I can just forget my manners, they're so deeply ingrained that I haven't been paying attention to Jamison for the last thirty minutes— which is also rude.

I leave him at the bar with the promise that I'll return and if I'm not back in an hour, he can hunt me down. I'm a sweaty mess from all the dancing, and at least one drink over from my limit, but I find the table easily enough. When I arrive, it's just Sutton and Noah occupying it.

There's a heavy tension filling the air and if I had better use of my faculties, I might notice how they aren't sitting that close, or even talking to each other.

Confusion must show on my face as I approach because Sutton gives me a welcoming smile before she says, "Alex and Ben are over there dancing." She points just over my right shoulder and my gaze follows.

"Oh well, I just wanted to come say hi."

Sutton gives me a soft, sad, smile. "Hi. I love your dress."

I look down and smooth my hands over my hips. "Thank you, I love yours too."

Sutton leans back, showing me more of her black sequined mini dress. It's short and sparkly with spaghetti straps giving it a delicate look. "Thank you. Have you been having fun?"

"The best time."

It's awkward.

Like super awkward and I want to leave.

Noah is staring at me with a look of, what I can only decipher as, brotherly disappointment. While Sutton looks like she's seconds away from dragging me to sit next to her and act as a buffer.

Taking a step back, I bump into a solid body behind me as a set of powerful masculine hands land on my waist. "Oh, I'm sorry," I shout over the music, turning to see who I've stepped into. An easy smile fills my face as I smile up at Jamison.

He leans down, his hands wrapping around my waist as he says, "I got tired of waiting."

He's eager, I'll give him that.

With a chuckle, I turn to Noah and Sutton, "This is Jamison Monroe. We're going back to dancing."

I don't wait for them to reply, instead, with a distracted wave, I turn with Jamison leading me back to the dance floor. We only stop to get refreshments the whole time and when we leave Siren, he comes with us to Passion, a club I've wanted to go to for a while.

It's impossible to miss the gap that seems to have formed between Noah and Sutton as the night wore on. Or the way that Noah can't seem to control the ticking muscle in his jaw as I laugh and chat with Jamison.

SIXTEEN

Savannah

I've had an amazing night with Jamison, but he still hasn't tried to kiss me. It's on the tip of my tongue to ask him why, when I feel a familiar presence standing behind me. Ignoring Noah, I continue grinding into Jamison. I'm practically straddling his leg, his hand low on my back as my hips roll to the tempo of the music.

"Looks like my time is up, cupcake."

A frown forms on my brow as I look up at Jamison, his words momentarily confusing me. I thought we were having fun. At my unspoken question, he juts his chin indicating behind me. When I glance over my shoulder, I come face to face with a rather pissed off looking Noah.

No, that's got to just be the lighting. It is dark in here.

I shout over the music, my voice thick with lust. "It's okay, Noah. I can find my own way home. Y'all can leave without me."

He doesn't move. *Did he not hear me?* I mean, it is loud. Stepping away from Jamison, I rest a hand on Noah's shoulder and stand on my tip toes.

I didn't think this through.

His spicy scent assails my nostrils and my hand tingles as I touch him. Even with the fabric of his white t-shirt acting as a barrier there still seems to be a current passing between us. I want to step away but I can't seem to move.

Noah rests his hand on my hip as he dips his head to hear me, seemingly unfazed by our close proximity and the effect he has on me.

An elbow in the back from some random dancer has me falling into him. With my chest now pressed to his, my whole body feels on fire. My breath hitches as I struggle to breath.

What is going on?

I can only blame this on too many drinks, too much of a height difference and too many people crowding around. There is nothing between us. It's all in my drunken imagination.

Some of my bravado is gone when I say, "Y'all can leave, I'm stayin' out."

His fingers flex on my hips as he inhales through his nose. I wait for him to tell me how he's got to keep me safe and blah, blah, blah.

Taking a step back, I give him a smile that I hope conveys how much I need this, and that I can look after myself. And none of the confusion I feel at my body's reaction to him.

Why can't it be like that with anyone else but him?

Sutton appears at Noah's side. A blush spreads over her cheeks as she gushes, "Hey, Savannah. I feel like I haven't seen you all night." Her eyes flit behind me to where I'm sure Jamison is still waiting. "We're heading home. You coming?"

I swallow thickly, as if I've just been caught doing something I shouldn't. I guess I have, because I shouldn't be touching Noah at all.

Jamison wraps an arm around my shoulder, whispering in my ear, "This is quite a situation you're in, cupcake." He straightens as he holds his hand out to Noah, "We didn't get to meet properly earlier, Jamison Monroe."

Right, 'cause Noah was too busy sulking about whatever.

Noah doesn't take Jamison's hand. A weird tension rolls off of him. Sutton and I watch as Noah and Jamison seem to be having some unspoken conversation.

"Okay, well this is gettin' weird. I'm gonna get a drink. I'll see y'all at home and you..." I stroke a hand down Jamison's arm before continuing, "At the bar."

When I step between them to head in the direction of the bar, Noah goes to grab a hold of me, stopping inches away. I can feel the heat of his palm on my skin and even though there is no physical contact, he might as well be dragging me under water. My breath stalls in my throat as I look up at him with wide eyes.

I don't know how long we stand like that, but it's as if everything but that near touch is muted. The lights dim and the music is only a dull hum somewhere in my subconscious.

He drops his hand, taking a half step away for good measure. "We're all going home. You've had enough for tonight."

I twist my face as I look up at him, because surely I just heard him wrong. "Look, *big brother*, you don't get ta tell me when I've had enough. You don't have no say ov—"

My words are cut off as Noah swoops down and throws me over his shoulder.

This guy has gotta be off his rocker.

His strong arm bands over the back of my bare legs and I'm very aware of the fact that my ass is probably on display for the whole club to see as he marches out. If it wasn't for the fact that heat is pooling in the pit of my stomach at the feel of his bare skin on mine, I'd be hitting and kicking at him.

As it is, I'm paralyzed; my whole body focused on the fact that he's *touching* me.

Maybe later, when I'm alone in my room, I will berate myself for feeling like this. *Maybe.*

Sutton trails behind, shouting over the music. "Noah, what the hell are you doing?"

Good question.

Even when we get outside, he doesn't put me down. Instead he strides over to the town car, bundling me into the back seat and slamming the door shut. I'm surprised the glass doesn't shatter.

Blinking as I stare down at my lap, my mind works a mile a minute as I try and fail to process what the hell just happened. How does he think what he just did was appropriate?

Your thoughts and feelings weren't exactly appropriate.

That's not the point.

He shouldn't have done that. If he didn't, then I wouldn't have had those inappropriate thoughts. Or felt like I was about to combust just because his hand was holding my thigh.

Noah and Sutton arguing on the sidewalk pulls me out of my whirling thoughts. I have no intention of being in the middle of that. Being in the middle of a couple mid fight is a total buzz kill and I'm here to party.

An idea forms. I'm going back inside. Even if it's to only get Jamison's number. And maybe a kiss.

I need to time my exit just right. Lifting my gaze, I look around the car until my eyes connect with Ruperts. Bingo. "Hey Rupert, how are you?"

"Good, thank you, Miss O'Riley. Did you have a good evening?"

"It's Savannah, Rupert. And yes, I did have a good night. Right up until your boss decided the fun should end."

The door opens and Sutton climbs in the back with a huff, just as Noah opens the front passenger door and gets one leg inside. With a wink to Rupert, I open my door and dart out, rounding the trunk and racing—as quickly as my short legs and heels will let me—back to the club.

There's an element of confusion in his voice when Noah shouts after me, "Savannah, what are you doing?"

I don't bother answering him.

Throwing him a cheeky grin, the bouncer opens the rope divider, and I dart through calling back 'thank you'.

I'm a woman on a mission and nothing is going to stop me. My first stop is the bar. I hurry down the length of it until I find him. Jamison looks up, a lopsided grin on his face when he spots me.

"You're lucky, I was about to leave."

With my best sultry smile, I smooth my hand down his arm as I purr, "Now, you wouldn't've left without my number, sugar."

He throws his head back, a throaty laugh erupting from him. "No, I wouldn't, cupcake." Jamison composes himself as his gaze moves over my left shoulder. "I better be quick, your dad's back."

I turn away from Jamison, my eyes connecting with a furious Noah as he pushes his way through the crowd toward us. I can't contain the eye roll that sends my eyes to the back of my head. Or the smirk that falls on my lips at having pissed him off.

Serves him right.

Facing Jamison, I pick up his phone from the bar, entering my number into a new message thread. I send a text to my phone, waiting until it buzzes in my purse before handing it back to him.

My next move is completely impulsive but also comes from a need to know if there is any chemistry between us.

My fingers cup Jamison's face, pulling him down to me as I push up onto my toes. Our lips connect briefly, before his arm wraps around my waist tugging me closer. When he kisses me the second time, it's the perfect blend of power and softness. His tongue demands entry into my mouth and when I grant it, he dips inside.

Pulling away, I take a step back, a smirk on my lips. "Catch ya later, sugar."

"Oh you will, cupcake."

I sashay toward the exit, a grin on my face the size of Manhattan. Noah is standing a few steps away, a look on his face I don't care to analyze. Waving my phone at him triumphantly as I pass, I think over the kiss with Jamison.

It was nice enough, but there just wasn't any spark there. Maybe I'm asking for too much, after all, life isn't like the movies.

Not every kiss will be like my first kiss.

They won't all set me on fire and have my lips tingling for hours afterward. I think I might need to lower my expectations or at least come to the realization that maybe that kiss wasn't as grand as I'm making it out to be.

It happens all the time. People remember things being truly amazing but when they experience it again, it lets them down. This is just like that. Except I won't be experiencing it ever again.

Picking up my coat from the cloakroom on my way out, I step out onto the sidewalk and walk to the car with Noah not far behind. Climbing into the front passenger seat next to Rupert, I buckle myself in. When Noah is settled, we pull away from the curb, the car shrouded in silence.

There's nothing I hate more than silence.

"Rupert, do you like R'n'B music? It's my favorite." I don't wait for him to answer as I switch on the radio and fiddle with the buttons until I find a station with late night jams. Resting my head on the cool glass of the window, I sporadically sing along to a popular song by *En Vogue*.

"You have a beautiful voice, Savannah," Rupert compliments.

"Thanks, Roops. Years of singing lessons sure have helped."

The motion of the car, the alcohol flowing through my body and the exhaustion that has shrouded over me recently has my eyes fluttering closed. I hope that Noah and Sutton figure out whatever has caused this divide between them.

Maybe it's me.

No, I've hardly been there.

It feels like it could have been five minutes or five

hours when the car comes to a stop outside our building. I hang back as Sutton and Noah exit the car and walk toward the doors, an obvious tension following behind them.

"Thanks for the ride, Rupert. Wish me luck." I throw him a wink and a cheeky smile, before reaching for the door handle.

Rupert gives me a warm smile before I step out onto the sidewalk.

I think I'm going to need more than luck to be honest.

SEVENTEEN

Noah

Both Savannah and Sutton are having an issue with me at the moment, if the slamming of doors on either end of the apartment are anything to go by.

The start of a headache throbs at the base of my skull. Tonight has been the least entertaining night out I've had in my thirty-one years of life. It went downhill the moment Sutton came home with a cloud hanging over her. And it got progressively worse when I saw Savannah looking like she'd just had sex on the dance floor.

Jack would have been disappointed too, I'm sure of it.

At least that's how I've rationalized away the clawing feeling that settled in my gut at the sight of her. I hope, for his sake, I never meet Jamison Monroe again. What sort of name is that anyway?

Fuck.

A heavy sigh leaves me as I walk down the hallway to the bedroom I share with Sutton. When I enter the room, the ensuite door is open and I can hear the sound of water running. She must be getting ready for bed. She's barely said a word to me all night.

Except to tell me what an ass I was for carrying Savannah out of the club. I don't know what came over me but I wasn't leaving Savannah alone with that guy.

The tension between Sutton and I has been building for the last few months. I can't put it all on tonight, but I know that I need to do something about it. It's not fair on either of us for this disconnect to continue.

Sitting on the edge of the bed, I remove my shoes and pull my t-shirt over my head. My body feels tired, a level of exhaustion I haven't experienced since college settling on my chest. With my head hanging, I barely notice when Sutton walks into the bedroom, switching off the bathroom light, shrouding the room in darkness.

With an effort, I drag myself to stand next to the bed. Walking to the laundry basket, I throw in my t-shirt and socks. When I face the bed, I can just make out the shape of Sutton, her back to me.

"I'm sorry," I murmur.

She doesn't respond for the longest time and I wonder if she's heard me. I take a step toward the bathroom but Sutton turns to face me.

Resignation coats her words as she says, "It doesn't make it better, Noah. I can't even begin to imagine how Savannah must have felt."

There she goes, thinking about the feelings of other people over herself. It's one of the qualities I loved about her.

Loved?

Ignoring my own question, I reply, "I know. It was wrong of me, but more importantly it was disrespectful to you. I don't know what I was thinking."

"You weren't, that's the problem. Get ready for bed, Noah. We can talk more in the morning."

Sutton rolls onto her side, dismissing me. I stare at her back, my eyes having adjusted to the darkness before I walk into the bathroom.

When I climb under the covers moments later, I relax back staring up at the ceiling. Many thoughts race through my mind, keeping me awake. It's as I lie in the quiet of the night, the soft sounds of Sutton sleeping beside me, that I come to a decision. One that's been in the making for months.

Tomorrow, I'll find the time and do what I should have done a long time ago. Instead of burying myself in work, I should have stepped up and done what needed to be done.

There's been an almost natural separation from both of us and at this point we're just existing in the same space. Deep down I've known, just as I'm sure Sutton has, that this is over.

EIGHTEEN

Noah

Daylight spills through the curtains the next morning, the brightness burning red through my closed eyes. I stretch my arm out almost instinctively, looking for any signs that I'm not alone.

It's futile.

Sutton will have been up for hours already. She's always been an early riser, even after a late night.

Throwing my arm over my eyes, I slowly blink them open, adjusting to the brightness. Despite asking her, on many occasions, to not draw back the curtains when she gets up, Sutton likes to have them open as she dresses for the day.

When I can see without feeling like a torch is burning my retinas, I drop my arm onto the mattress with a thud. I didn't drink much last night, but the headache that started when we got back is still there. A dull ache at the base of my skull.

Swinging my legs over the side of the bed, I scrub my hands through my hair, tugging on the strands hoping to redirect the pain. I need a painkiller and a glass of water.

As I sit on the edge of the bed, the events of last night replay in high definition. My fingers flex where they're rested on my knee as an image of Savannah dancing with that guy taunts me. When she called me her 'big brother', a feeling I don't want to even try to understand overwhelmed me. I should be relieved that she thinks of me that way.

So why does it cause a lead weight to sit in my stomach?

The ensuite door opens and Sutton walks into the room dressed for the day.

She's fastening an earring when she says, "We should go for dinner tonight. I think it would be good if we talked." There's resignation in her tone, and I know she's on the same page as me. Last night—my actions—was the tipping point.

Clearing my throat, I reply, "Yeah, I think that would be good."

"Okay, I'll book a table at Rust for seven. We can meet there. I think my meeting with Julien will probably run over."

I don't reply, instead I nod in agreement. Sutton's eyes linger on me for a moment, then she turns and walks from the room.

My body goes lax as all of the tension leaves it. I'd buried myself under my work so deep that I hadn't even noticed the physical impact the strain of this relationship was having on me.

Laying back on the bed, I listen to the sounds of the apartment. It's quiet and I wonder if Savannah is still asleep or if she's left for the day. She's working herself into the ground, for what reason I'm not entirely sure. I'm surprised she's still fucking standing. She's welcome to stay here as long as she needs. I'm hardly ever here, so if she's avoiding me, she doesn't need to.

One conversation at a time.

Standing from the bed, I stretch my arms above my head. I need coffee, food and painkillers. My body is craving pancakes. Maybe I can grab some after I've hit the gym. Walking to the kitchen, I run through my plans for the day.

It's Saturday, and although I don't technically have to work, I know I'll be putting in a few hours. Sacrifices have to be made when you own the company and your business partner has gone AWOL.

In the kitchen, I run my hand along the black granite countertop as I move around the island to the coffee machine. Pulling a mug out of the cabinet above the coffee maker, I place it under the nozzle. Grabbing a pod, I insert it into the machine and press start. I lean against the counter, my ankles crossed as I wait for it to brew.

My focus is out the window, at least until Savannah walks into the room. She's wearing a pair of black leggings that hug her every curve and a simple black t-shirt. Her hair is mussed, like she hasn't quite got around to running a brush through it.

"I'll have a cup if you're makin' it."

A nervousness washes over me, one that only comes when she's near or we're alone. It sits heavy on my chest as butterflies flutter in my stomach. Even with her having been here for nearly two months, it hasn't gotten easier seeing her like this. It's a little too intimate for my comfort.

I turn back to the coffee maker, pulling out the mug I'd made myself. Placing it on the counter, I incline my head toward it, indicating for her to take it.

As she moves about the kitchen, she says, "You know, you had no right last night to drag me outta that club like I'm some toddler pitchin' a fit in the Piggly Wiggly. I wouldn't be surprised if Sutton is ill at you for your behavior. I know I would be."

With my back to her, I pull in a breath, busying myself with making another coffee. She's right. Of course she is. I had no right to do what I did. I'm just not entirely sure *why* I did what I did.

Keeping it simple, I reply, "Sutton isn't mad about it, but, like you said, she has every right to be. I'm sorry."

Please don't ask me why I did it.

As much as I might say I don't know why, I do recognise my own reaction when I'm jealous. And feeling possessive. But these are all things I have no right to feel. Feelings that are so wrong for me to have.

"I'm glad you're man enough to admit when you're wrong. And that y'all are good."

"Yeah. We are." *No, we're not.*

"Great." She practically bounces across the kitchen, away from me. When she reaches the threshold she pauses and says, "I might just go and call Jamison. See if he wants to take me out for dinner tonight."

Of all the things she could have fucking said. My jaw grinds as I try to keep my reaction under wraps. Part of me wants to lock her in a room and tell her she's not going anywhere. Another part of me understands that, regardless of our history, that isn't something I should even be thinking about. Let alone acting on.

"Sutton and I are going out for dinner tonight, so enjoy yourself," I blurt, more as a reminder to myself than anything.

"Oh. Well, maybe I'll invite Jamison over here. I can cook him a homemade meal and *really* take care of him." Savannah winks, her gaze trained on me.

Deep down, I know she's just messing with me—to see if I meant my apology—but I'll be damned if that man steps foot in my apartment. I make a mental note to give his description to the doorman and concierge before I leave for the day.

Savannah floats out of the room, a soft chuckle filtering back to me. I lean back against the counter again, my head now pounding as I look out over the city.

It's going to be a long *fucking* day.

NINETEEN

Noah

The screendoor slams shut behind me. The sound of it banging against the frame echoing around the cul-de-sac. Nausea bubbles up inside of me as I double over and pull in lungfuls of cold December air. A rush of anxiety crashes into me over and over again. It crushes me under its weight.

He's gone.

It's okay.

He's gone.

It's okay.

She's safe.

I know that he'll be gone for the night. Every time it happens the same way. He gets angry about something she's done—or not done, who fucking knows—and hits her. This is why I didn't want to go to college. She tried to tell me she'd be fine but the bruises don't lie.

This past week, everything seemed to be okay, but he just couldn't stop himself this morning. *On Christmas of all days.* The flare of surprise before the angry mist took over told me that he didn't expect me to get between them, again.

As if on instinct, my feet carry me across the street and down the sidewalk. Even though I'm focused on getting to my destination, I can't silence the screams in my ears. A tightness grabs a hold of my chest, squeezing and twisting at the muscles. Clenching my fists, I push down the anger bubbling under the surface.

I hope he doesn't come back.

My feet come to a stop outside of Jack's house. The living room window faces out onto the street, a large green fir tree fills the bay window. From my position on the sidewalk, its twinkling lights mocks me as it blocks out the view into what I know would be a happy Christmas morning.

Briefly, I look back over at my house. In comparison to Jack's, with its fresh looking shutters and pristine front porch, mine looks rundown and unkept. A gray cloud hangs heavy over it, a true representation of the misery contained inside. There are no Christmas lights, no tree with presents underneath and certainly no happy family.

"Are you gonna stay out here catching a cold or come in?" Jack calls, humor lacing his voice.

I don't look over at him right away, because if I do,

his humor will turn to sympathy and I don't want to bring him down. Not today. No, for one day, I'd like to play pretend and not drag my best friend into my pit of despair. Jack's already seen it all. But after that one time, when he helped me more than I could have imagined, I vowed he'd never see it again.

Pasting a smile onto my face, I turn to Jack, walking up the driveway. The stones crunch under my sneaker clad feet and I shiver as a gust of wind blows past me.

Jack claps me on the back as I step over the threshold into the house. He wraps his arm around my shoulder, the closest thing to a hug we give each other. "You can borrow one of my jackets when you go home later. Come on, we just started opening presents, then it's about time we stuffed our faces."

The smell of turkey and stuffing fills the house and my stomach gurgles. I haven't eaten since Jack and I went to the mall yesterday afternoon. There's never really any food in the house. My mom finds it hard to get to the store when my dad's always gone with the car. Of course, he can bring beer home, but not anything of sustenance.

I pull back out of Jack's embrace, not wanting to intrude. Christmas is supposed to be about family, right? Surely that means I shouldn't leave my mom alone.

What if he comes back?

Resting both hands on my shoulders, Jack turns me, his face serious. His voice is soothing in a way I hate to hear and sounds far older than his twenty-one years of age. "She'll be fine, you can take a plate home for her later. We want you to join us, No. You're our family."

Sometimes I hate that he knows so much about me and what's going on in my house. That I've had to make him keep a secret, even when it's caused him pain and worry that something could happen. I hate that he's seen my worst, and that he felt he had to help me fight against a grown man. *My father*. If he hadn't, I'd have probably died.

Nodding my head and pushing away the dark thoughts, I follow him into the living room.

As has been the case too often lately, instinctively, my eyes seek out Savannah. She's sitting in reindeer pajamas on the couch, her legs tucked under her and her hair piled into a messy bun on the top of her head. When her soft gaze lifts to mine, I feel my body relax as the tension leaves me. A small smile graces her lips before she looks away shyly.

I could look at her all day.

Her skin is clear and she almost looks ethereal in the daylight spilling in the window.

Fuck, if she isn't an angel.

Sadie speaks, pulling my attention to her. My stomach drops, like I've just been caught doing something I shouldn't. "Hey Noah, we're so glad you're here, sweetheart. You want some hot chocolate?"

Scrubbing my hand over the back of my neck, I reply, "That would be great."

I don't want hot chocolate, I want to keep looking at Savannah.

Jack elbows me in the ribs forcing my gaze away from her. His brow arches as he says, "Come on, man. Eyes off my sister."

My face flames at having been caught and I avert my gaze looking down at my lap.

She soothes me by just being present, she doesn't have to say or do anything. She's my life raft in a sea of uncertainty. Always there to ground me and bring me to shore safely.

I'm losing my mind.

With a smile, and completely oblivious to my inner turmoil, Sadie walks from the room, but not before saying, "You've come just in time for presents, Noah."

Presents? Shit.

I've known Jack for three years and this is the first year I've crashed a holiday. Sure we've hung out during the holidays, but it's usually *after* family time.

This family has welcomed me into their home without question. It's too much. There's no way I can repay them. I didn't get them any gifts. Not that I could afford any, I don't get the trust fund my grandparents left me until I graduate college.

The trust fund is the only reason I've gone to college. I'd have never left my mom if getting that money wasn't a possibility. It's our way out and away from *him*.

Plopping down onto the couch between Jack and Savannah, the faint hint of lavender engulfs me.

Savannah rests her hand on my knee, using it to push herself up from the couch before she darts from the room. Just that small touch sends a spark of energy surging through my body from head to toe. I wonder if she feels it too.

Christ, Noah, it doesn't fucking matter if she does.

It's probably just a figment of my imagination anyway.

Sadie returns carrying a mug overflowing with whipped cream and mini marshmallows just as Savannah bounds into the room.

"Be careful, it's pipin' hot," Sadie warns, handing over the mug.

I place the mug between my feet, careful not to spill any of the hot liquid as Savannah hands me a gift. I turn it over in my hands. It's less than a centimeter thick and half the size of a piece of paper. It's been wrapped neatly in snowman wrapping paper. She eyes me for a moment before she sits back on the couch. The warmth of her leg pressed against mine a constant reminder of her presence. *Why does she feel so much closer than moments ago? I shouldn't have sat here.*

"Lennie, baby, do you wanna give everyone a present to open?" Sadie asks.

Savannah and Jack both exclaim excitedly as they rip at the paper on their gifts. Tuning them out, I slide my thumb under the first tab, gently pushing at the wrapping paper, urging the tape to come free.

With as much care and precision as I can, I unwrap

the gift until it's uncovered and laying in the middle of the creased paper. Lifting the piece of cardboard laying on top reveals a copy of the latest *DC Superman* comic book. My breath catches in my throat and I swallow around the lump forming.

A dainty hand lands on my arm and I lift my attention to the dark blue gaze looking back at me, that same soft smile on her lips. Her voice is a hushed whisper as she says, "I hope you don't already have that one, but I wanted to get you something I knew you'd love."

Savannah's eyes dip to where her hand rests on my arm before she lifts it and tucks a strand of hair behind her ear. I feel the loss of her skin on mine, the faint touch forever burned into my memory.

"If you do have it, I can take it back. Maybe get you a gift card. It's not a problem."

My voice cracks, overwhelmed with her generosity and proximity. "It's amazing, Van. I..." Swallowing thickly, I look back at the comic book in my lap before continuing, "Thank you."

She shrugs, like it's no big deal, but it's the best gift I've ever received.

Because it came from her.

Jack nudges my shoulder, drawing my attention away from Savannah. "What did Sav get you?"

"A comic book," I reply, flicking through the pages.

"Nice one. Sav got you a better gift than she did me." Looking around me at Savannah, Jack jokingly says, "I expect more from you next year, Sav."

"Maybe if you stopped calling me by that stupid nickname, you'd get a better gift."

Savannah's response has a smirk forming on my lips. It brightens my mood, and for the rest of the day, I refuse to allow myself to feel guilty. Instead, I luxuriate in the company of the family that has taken me in and shown me what love truly looks like.

TWENTY

Noah

Sutton sits across from me surveying the menu, a tension of what is to come hovering above us. We were seated twenty minutes ago. We've barely said a word to each other—aside from the usual courteous greetings—the entire time.

When the waiter passes by for the third time, I give a small shake of my head indicating we still aren't ready. It wouldn't surprise me if he approached and told us we needed to leave. It's a busy Saturday night. The sound of cutlery scraping across plates, mingled with mood music and the loud chatter of people all add to the ambience.

I don't know about Sutton, but I won't be able to relax and eat until we've had this conversation. It's been a long time coming after all.

Sutton puts down her menu and looks over at me, a sad smile on her face. "I'd like to start, if that's okay?"

I follow suit, placing my menu on the table. Inclining

my head, I pick up my glass, taking a sip of the icy water. "Go ahead."

"I'd like to think that this conversation isn't coming as a surprise to you. Especially as I feel that you and I have grown so distant over these past six months. You've been working so much and I've been filling my time with jobs here and there and vacationing without you. I hardly ever see you, and even when I do, it's not like we do anything that couples should be doing. For you, there was always an acquisition in play or a merger that needed to be executed, but in truth, I wasn't putting in the effort either.

"I could have forced you to come away with me, or take me out for dinner, but I was quite content to just live my life. In a way, I had the protection of a boyfriend, but without any of the affection I so desperately need. It's not fair on either of us, to be dating ghosts of who we used to be. For the last couple of months, I've really been reflecting on what I want and who can give that to me. And I'm going to caveat what I'm about to say with, I love Savannah and I am so glad I got to meet her."

When I go to interrupt, she holds up her hand and says, "Let me finish. I think I was using her staying with us as an excuse to not have this conversation. In a way, she was a buffer, at least to a certain point. But when she started working just as much as you, it amplified my loneliness. For both of our sakes, I think it's better if we walk away before we resent each other for not giving us what we need."

Blowing out a breath, my body sags with relief. Christ, she's right. This conversation has been long overdue. I should have stepped up long ago and ended things between us because I've known that it's been over for a long time.

"I agree. I'm sorry I haven't been there. You know I'll always be honest with you and maybe I shouldn't tell you this but I need to get it off my chest. It was never anything you did, just know that. Us ending, isn't on you. It's on me. Instead of being a man about it, I threw myself into my work and neglected you because the things I felt when we first started seeing each other had diminished. I don't know why or when but I'm sorry I couldn't give you what you needed."

She reaches across the table and takes ahold of my hand. "Neither of us are to blame, Noah. These things happen in relationships, not everyone is destined to be with someone for forever. It's a nice idea, but in most cases, things like that only happen in the movies. I'd like to hope we can still be friends, because you still mean something to me. Just not in a romantic way."

Leaning back in my chair, I smooth my hand over my beard, pulling at the hair on my chin. "I'd like that." I pause, my gaze wandering around the restaurant as I release a breath. The weight of the evening lifts off my chest. Turning back to Sutton, I say, "I'm not really sure what else there is to say."

The corner of her mouth lifts as she shrugs a shoulder. "There isn't much to say. You wanna eat or just go home?"

"I don't mind, it's up to you."

Folding her napkin, she places it on the table. "I think I'm gonna leave. I'll stay at Monica's tonight but I'll be back to pick up some of my stuff tomorrow before we schedule in some time for me to get everything."

Nodding my head distractedly, I remain seated. Shock, at the fact that we've actually broken up, has me blinking as I stare straight ahead. I knew this conversation was going to happen, and deep down, I knew that Sutton was feeling the same way but I expected... hell, I don't know what I expected.

Maybe some drama? No, that's not Sutton's style at all.

I barely register Sutton stopping next to me as she presses a kiss to my forehead and squeezes my shoulder. "I'll text you." She hesitates, as if she's not quite sure whether to voice what she's about to say. "When you're ready, just know it's okay for you to give in to her. You and Savannah are much better suited for each other than you and I ever were. Plus, it helps that you can cut the sexual tension between the two of you with a knife."

With that, Sutton walks away, my eyes following her as she strides through the restaurant. My brow furrows as I try to wrap my head around her comments. *What the hell was that about?*

Oblivious to my inner turmoil, the waiter approaches, clearly done with me occupying a table. "Are you ready to order sir?" Pointedly he looks in the direction of the door that Sutton just walked through.

Fucking hell. "No, I'll just take the bill."

"Of course, I'll go and get it for you now."

I'm still trying to process what Sutton said about Savannah when the waiter returns. I go through the motions of paying the bill and dropping down a sizeable tip for occupying the table.

On autopilot, I stand from the table and wind my way through the restaurant to the exit. Rupert's waiting for me as I push through the doors. We aren't too far from the apartment, and the cool September evening air might help focus my confused thoughts. "I think I'm going to walk. Thanks for waiting though. Enjoy your evening, Rupert."

He doesn't question why my dinner's finished early; he's too good at his job. "Of course, sir. Have a good evening and enjoy your walk."

There's little chance of that. Not with a new weight settling on my chest. Despite what Sutton said about Savannah and I, nothing will ever happen between us.

TWENTY-ONE
Savannah

Music blares from the surround sound speakers as I shimmy my hips to the beat. I might be a bit too tipsy for cooking but I haven't injured myself yet and my craving for homemade ramen got the better of me. I'm ashamed to admit that I don't know how to cook many dishes, but this one is my specialty.

On the way back to the apartment from back to back dance and acting classes, I stopped at the store. It's definitely a day of treats. I've missed going to classes and it's really been showing in my techniques. I'm rustier than I've ever been before. Something needs to change because I can't make Broadway my career if I'm only able to afford two of each of my classes a month.

Maybe I can ask Jack for a loan.

I dismiss the thought almost immediately. In all of my twenty-seven years of life, I have never had to borrow money to get by and I don't plan on starting now. I'll figure something out, I always do.

Sipping on my red wine, I twirl with my wooden spoon acting as a microphone while I sing along to an Aaliyah song.

It's not the finest singing, and I'm certain that if my vocal coach could hear me now, she'd have a conniption. The thought has me bursting into a fit of giggles as I twirl around the kitchen, sipping on my wine and singing along to my favorite playlist.

Tonight is just what I needed. Comfort food, wine and being able to let my hair down. It's been a long few weeks.

Sutton is away on a girls trip and Noah has a business dinner. Usually, that means he won't be back until way past midnight. If we were both free when Noah worked late, Sutton and I would usually order in and do a pamper session.

Now that I think about it, I haven't seen her in a while.

I'm sure she's just busy with work.

It should only be a few more weeks before I can move out. I'm so close to having a deposit and first month's rent for my own place, I can practically feel the freedom that will come with it. Maybe I can even start dating again. The thought has a nervous shiver running down my spine.

I am not ready for that just yet.

My timer goes off and I walk back to the stove to

remove the eggs from the boiling water. Gently, I plop them into the bowl of ice cold water sitting on the counter next to the stove.

My hips move to the beat of the song playing through the surround sound speakers as I stir and taste my ramen. It's ready. Grabbing a bowl, I pour it in and then place it on the kitchen island. Unable to resist, I scoop out a spoonful of the liquid, the taste of the salty broth on my tongue making me moan.

"Do you always dance around half naked when nobody is home?"

Spinning on my heel, my hand rests on my chest as I come face to face with Noah. *What's he doing back so soon?*

Cheese and crackers. I knew I should have dressed properly. This really is a facepalm moment. And I had time while the ramen was cooking. Stepping forward, I make sure that my near naked bottom half is fully covered by the island. "Goodness. You scared me. You gotta quit sneakin' up on me."

I wait for him to say something, resisting the urge to fidget under his assessing gaze. He doesn't speak, and if he wasn't blinking I'd think he was frozen. No, this is just Noah. He's a man of few words, which works fine for me.

"What are you doing?" he asks, stuffing his hands into the pockets of his black slacks.

I look at the bowl of ramen noodles in front of me that are slowly going cold. My stomach gurgles loudly in the quiet. Why is he here? "I was making dinner."

With an air of boredom to his tone, Noah replies, "Naked?"

Rolling my eyes—because I'm not even naked—I heave out a heavy sigh, his questioning irritating me. *I just want to eat my food. Is that too much to ask?*

Reminding myself that this isn't my house so I should be polite, I paste a smile on my face, as if this man isn't getting between me and my food. "I wouldn't say I was naked. I have clothes on." *Just not a whole lot of clothes.*

"Ri—ght," he draws out the word, a look in his eye I can't quite decipher.

The tone tells me he thinks I'm lying, and based on the fact that all I have on my lower half is a v-shaped high leg thong, I'd have to say, he's right.

In the intimate confines of his apartment, where it's just us, I feel incredibly naked.

As soon as he leaves, I'll go and put some leggings on. Anything to not feel so exposed. I think the embarrassment of being caught in next to nothing would at least be lessened if Sutton was here. Maybe we could even laugh it all off. There definitely wouldn't be a weird tension swirling in the air as he stands there with heavy eyes, daring me to move.

"Would you be a peach and just leave?"

His chin jerks up, as if surprised by my request. It might be his apartment, but the least he could do is be a gentleman and give me enough privacy to get back to my room.

Oh no. What if he tells Sutton about this and she thinks I'm trying to seduce him? We've become closer in the weeks I've been staying here. I'd hate to ruin our friendship. I might still have some feelings for Noah, but I'd never try and take another woman's man. It's just not who I am. But, of course, she doesn't know that.

Noah pulls me from my spiraling thoughts. There's a lightness to his voice as he leans against the walled arch that separates the kitchen and living room and asks, "If you're not naked, why do I need to leave?"

There's a challenge in his voice. One I haven't heard since I was a kid. He's going to make me walk out from behind this counter with him standing right there. *Why's he doing this?*

I mean, it shouldn't be a big deal. I wear less than what I have on now on the beach. But it's Noah. It's different.

That night in the hallway I was in less than I am now.

Right, but that was in the dark. He could hardly see any of my lower half. I should have set the mood with the smaller lights while I was cooking. The overhead lights show every inch of my exposed skin.

Every. Single. Inch.

My gaze drops to the black granite counter as I pull in a breath through my nose, blowing it out through my lips. I steel myself for whatever might happen when I step out from around this counter.

Okay, here goes nothing.

When I look back up Noah is gone.

What the hell was that?

I can only hope he knew what I was going to do and thought he'd save us both the embarrassment of me having to go through with it. Or he got some sense and realized how inappropriate he was being. Either way, I'm grateful he left the room.

Listening intently, I slowly move, peeking around the corner into the living room. While the coast is clear, I race back to my room, only relaxing when I step inside and close the door behind me.

A pair of oversized gray sweatpants lay across my unmade bed. They'll do. My movements are rushed as I try to tug them on, my balance wavering. I stop, concentrating on the action of dressing. The last thing I need is to fall and get knocked out with my pants around my ankles. That would be worse than what nearly happened in the kitchen. A million times worse.

With both legs securely in the holes of the pants, I pull them up to my waist. When I let them go, they slide down on my hips. Shoot. These were on my bed to be adjusted. I'm short and these sweats are long.

My stomach chooses that moment to make itself known. It gurgles as a sharp hunger pang contracts my muscles. These really will need to do. Rolling down the waistband helps somewhat but it's still not perfect.

Ducking my head through the door, I look left then right before deeming it safe to exit my room. The apartment is quiet as I walk back to the kitchen. He must be cooped up in his office. It's usually what he does when he's here. Noah doesn't seem to have much of a life outside of working.

In the kitchen, I swipe up my bowl, slurping down some of the noodles over the edge. Grabbing a spoon, I turn off the music that's still playing over the speakers then fill up my wine.

With my bowl and wine glass in hand, I head into the living room. An episode of the *Bachelorette* is calling my name. I need to see who gets chosen tonight. The choices so far have been very questionable.

I'm lost in the episode as Jessica, the bachelorette, picks Dustin over Austin. For a moment, I forget that I'm not home alone and shout, "Honestly, Jessica, if that boy had a idea, it would die of loneliness. Get. It. Together. Girl."

"I forget just how Southern you can be with those sayings." Amusement laces Noah's voice.

Whipping around on the sofa, my gaze lands on him. He's wearing a pair of black sweats and black t-shirt with bare feet. It's the most casual I've seen him in the nearly three months I've been living here.

Admonishing him, I reply, "I thought we talked about you sneaking up on me?"

Noah moves toward the couch, my eyes following his approach. He sits down, making himself comfortable with a sigh that tells me he's had a long week. Dropping his head back against the sofa, exposing the thick column of his throat, he mutters, "I don't remember that conversation."

I'm distracted, openly watching the cords of his neck move as he swallows. "You need to get your hearing checked then, because it happened nearly an hour ago, over there." I point over to the kitchen, as if that will refresh his memory.

A blush steals over my cheeks when he pops an eye open, turning his head to look at me. "No, you made a comment, there was no discussion."

Turning back to the TV, I can't help the chuckle that slips through my lips. "Tomayto, tomaato."

Out of the corner of my eye, I see his lips twitch. Did Noah Parker just consider smiling about something I said? I feel like that hasn't happened in such a long time. We fall into a comfortable silence, watching the rest of the episode.

When it's finished, I flick through the channels looking for something we might both enjoy.

"You want to put a movie on and order some food?"

I don't say anything, instead turning to face Noah, I lift the back of my hand to his forehead. "Are you sick?"

That gets a laugh out of him and the sound of his rich, deep timbre echoing around the room, sends a bolt of electricity through my body. I squirm in my seat. My first thought is he should laugh more because it's delectable. My second is that it was highly inappropriate and I should leave.

Standing from my seat, I run my palms down my thighs, which of course because this night couldn't end with me making a dignified exit, has my sweats shifting lower on my hips. "I should leave you to it. I just ate anyway and I'm sure you'll want to call Sutton before she goes to bed. Or whatever it is that you two do." I don't even know where she's gone. I'm just rambling at this point.

The easy going look on his face morphs into one of confusion mixed with concern before he wipes it away and says with an air of nonchalance, "Sutton and I broke up three weeks ago."

TWENTY-TWO

Noah

"Sutton and I broke up three weeks ago."

Savannah's eyes flare in surprise as her jaw goes lax. It only lasts a matter of seconds before she masks it. I can see her mind working as she tries to process the information. Her dark blue eyes showing a storm of uncertainty that she can't hide.

After a few minutes, I continue, "I've been working a lot recently and haven't eaten all day so thought I'd come home and recharge. I'd really like some company, if you're up for it."

White teeth pull at the corner of her mouth and she chews on the sensitive flesh. I want to tug her lip free and kiss it better. And tell her to stop because she might hurt herself.

Woah. Where did all of that come from?

I genuinely just want to be her friend and hang out. Forcing my eyes back to the TV, I berate myself for having such inappropriate thoughts about her. I've been single for three weeks. It's hardly appropriate to be thinking about moving on, let alone doing things with Savannah.

It's been a while since I last sat down and just relaxed and although I have work I'll probably end up doing if Savannah says no, I want to actually take the time to reset tonight. Although, if I can't control my roaming thoughts, maybe I should go and work instead.

Savannah clears her throat, bringing my attention back to her as she straightens her shoulders and says, "First of all, I'm sorry to hear about you and Sutton. From hangin' out with her, she seemed like a great person and much too good for the likes of you."

There's a twinkle in her eye and the corner of her mouth lifts as she teases me. I can't hold back the huff of a laugh that breaks free.

Savannah sits back down, curling her legs underneath herself, asking, "What movie do you want to put on?"

With that simple question, I feel a weight lifting off my chest. Her just sitting next to me, and the light lavender scent that's uniquely her, has a calming effect on me. It's like I can finally breathe again.

The thought has my brows tugging together in confusion.

I'm only feeling this way because I'm comfortable around her. She's been in my life as long as Jack; it's normal for her to feel like a safety net. That's all this is.

The lightness is from knowing that I can take a break from the crushing pressure of my work and relax in good company.

"I'm easy. Do you want something light to eat? I'm gonna order from the sandwich shop on the corner."

A smirk tugs at her full lips, drawing my attention there again. I have to remind myself to not focus on them. I'm not sure this was a good idea after all. Shifting my gaze back to the television, I pick up the remote and navigate to one of the many subscription apps I pay for and never use.

"It's been a while since we last hung out, huh? I'm guessin' you forgot about my bottomless pit of a stomach? Do you really want a sandwich?"

I laugh at her reminder, because she's right, it has been a while and I did forget. She's so tiny, in comparison to my bulk, that it's hard to imagine her eating two meals back to back.

Unfazed by my non answer, Savannah continues, "Maybe we could order some Thai food? I could devour a Pad Thai right now."

My brows shoot for my hairline at her having remembered my favorite cuisine. *Maybe she's just guessed*. "Yes, Thai food sounds good," I mumble.

Savannah scrolls through her phone, pulling up a food delivery app. She searches through it as I find us a movie to watch. I don't really know what she likes now, so I pick a couple, add them to the watchlist and wait for her to finish ordering.

"I'm orderin' for you, is that okay?"

I turn to face her, taking in how comfortable and right she looks sitting on my couch. "Sure, I eat anything. Just let me know how much it all comes to and I'll transfer you the money."

Her brows shoot toward her hair line as she looks at me. Moments later, she wipes the look from her face, twisting her lips as she looks back at her phone.

"What was that look for?" I demand.

She refuses to meet my gaze, but her cheeks have gone a rosy hue. Briefly, I wonder if the coloring appears only when she's embarrassed or if she blushes during more intimate times.

Christ, what is wrong with me?

Clearing my throat, I say, "Savannah? I'm not going to put a movie on until you tell me, so unless you're content to sit in silence as we eat, spill."

I can see her mind whirling as she tries to think of something to say. An excuse.

"I can pay for dinner, Noah."

Pinching the bridge of my nose, I drop my chin to my chest. "I didn't mean it like that. It's just I'm forcing you to eat again and based on that, I should foot the bill."

Savannah folds her arms over her chest, at the same time snuggling into the couch. "Well, it's not a date, so you don't need to pay."

Right. It's definitely not a date. We're just two friends sharing a meal. Alone in my apartment.

Clearing my throat, and refusing to acknowledge

how right she is, I turn to face the TV, flicking to the watchlist screen. "I found three movies. An action, a horror and a comedy. You pick which one to watch."

"Can you play the trailers?"

"Sure," I reply, bringing up the first trailer and pressing play.

We end up choosing the comedy and, when the food arrives, we stuff our faces until our eyes are heavy-lidded and our stomachs are full.

Some of the tension of the last few months eases as the night goes on. Listening to the sound of her laughing has my chest feeling light and an easy smile forming on my lips.

I don't remember the last time I felt this relaxed.

Nights in with Sutton were few and far between. One or both of us was always busy with something or other. It had been a long time since we made an effort for each other.

When I go to bed that night, my body is loose and languid. I hadn't realized that the tension I'd been carrying for the last few months was from overworking myself. My relationship with Sutton and how far it was fractured, was another excuse I subconsciously used to work late into the night.

As my head hits the cool pillow, I fall, almost instantly, into a deep, dreamless sleep, at least until I'm woken by the front door slamming shut at four. I still need to figure out where Savannah goes this early in the morning, but that's a problem for later.

With my eyes still closed, I roll over, reaching out for Sutton. My hand hits the cool sheets, reminding me of my singledom. It's been a crazy couple of weeks with work. We finalized the takeover of Dew and Olsen, which was eventful to say the least.

Today is the first time I've had to actually come to terms with the fact that I'm single. It's going to take time to adjust to the thought but I'm not as heartbroken as I thought I would be.

I guess that's what happens when you've been mentally breaking up with someone for a long time. Berating myself for getting too in my own head, I turn back over, closing my eyes and forcing myself to go back to sleep.

TWENTY-THREE

Noah

I t feels like a matter of minutes since I drifted back to sleep but the sound of my phone vibrating across the bedside table pulls me to the surface. My movements are slow as I fight my way through the grogginess, reaching for my phone. With half closed eyes, I connect the call, bringing it to my ear.

"Hello."

"Noah? Hey." The relief in Savannah's voice is palpable and I picture her shoulders relaxing as she continues, "I'm so sorry to bother you but I've had a little incident and I kinda..." Savannah pauses and a loud bang sounds on the other end of the phone, followed by an eerie silence.

Suddenly alert, I bolt up in bed, rubbing the palm not holding the phone over my thigh. There's an urgency to my tone that I don't bother hiding. "Savannah? What's going on?"

The line remains quiet before Savannah's voice murmurs distractedly, "Ya know what, it's just a dog. I've got this."

Hell no. She called me looking for help, I'll be damned if she deals with whatever is happening on her own. Before she can disconnect the call I reply, injecting as much authority into my voice as I can, "Savannah. Tell me where you are."

Throwing the covers off, I climb from the bed, moving around my room as I gather my clothes, waiting for her to respond. Sporadically I check my phone to make sure the call's still connected.

Suddenly the speakers blare with the noise of a dog growling before Savannah breathlessly replies, "Honestly, Noah, it's fine. Miss. Dixie got into... somethin' and is..." She pauses as if she doesn't want to say the words. "Well, she's runnin' around the house with..." Savannah pauses again.

I hope for Savannah's sake that there is a good reason for all the dramatics.

"Jeez, how do I say this? My mama would clutch her pearls if she could see what I'm dealin' with. I swear, you better not tell anyone about this, Noah."

"I don't know what I'm not telling anyone about?" My curiosity is well and truly piqued. "Christ, Savannah, just spit it out."

My hand is on the door knob ready to push it down and walk into the hallway.

"The Great Dane has a giant pink dildo hanging out

of its mouth, Noah. I'm not a prude, but she's nearly as big as me and every time I get near her she practically knocks me over."

The dam breaks and I can't help the laugh that breaks free. A fucking dildo. The image she's painted has tears of laughter gathering in my eyes.

"I knew I shouldn't've told you. This ain't helpful, Noah," Savannah admonishes with humor lacing her words. Her voice turns throaty when she says, "You should laugh more often. It sounds good."

A warmth spreads through me, sobering me up at the same time as it acts like a cold shower. Straightening, I pass through the door and down the hallway. "Savannah, where are you?"

She heaves a sigh, and I can just picture her rubbing her thumb and forefinger across her forehead as she thinks of a plan. "Look, I don't really know why I called you. What are *you* goin' to do that I can't? I'll figure this out. I'm sorry I called and woke you up. Enjoy your Saturday."

She disconnects the call before I can say anything further. For two seconds I try and talk myself out of calling her back but the thought of her possibly getting hurt has me moving on autopilot.

Clicking on her name, I put the phone to my ear as it rings. When she doesn't pick up, I hang up and dial again. Every time it goes through to voicemail, I hang up and dial her again.

When the call finally connects, her voice is breathless

with a hint of annoyance as she says, "Noah? I'm kinda busy here."

I seize up as my cock twitches to life in my jeans. The sensation leaves my mouth dry and unable to utter a word.

There's confusion in her voice when she calls my name again. "Noah. Are you there?"

The question pulls me out of my stupor. My voice is more gravelly than I'd like it to be when I reply, "Yes, sorry. Text me the address, I'm on my way over."

I should have just left her to deal with this herself. But if something happens to her, Jack would never forgive me.

Jack.

I need to remember why she's back in my life and who brought her into it.

"Promise me, you'll look out for Sav. If you want to be my friend, she can't be hurt."

"I promise, man. You don't have to worry about that with me."

TWENTY-FOUR

Savannah

I t was a terrible idea to call Noah. What was I thinking? That it wouldn't be super awkward having the guy who only sees me as his family helping me wrestle a monster of a dildo from a dog nearly as big as me?

How does a dildo this big even fit in any holes? It would easily take me at least two hands to hold it.

You know what, I'm not even going to think about that.

Sucking in a breath, I focus on the task at hand: Getting the toy from the dog.

We're standing in the kitchen of the Eaton's home. I dog walk for them through a task assigning app, usually on Mondays, Wednesdays and Saturdays. Miss. Dixie—who I affectionately call Miss. D—is a fifteenth month old 'puppy'. I use that word loosely because this dog is too big and too powerful to be a baby. She puts fully grown dogs to shame with her strength.

She's adorable, but right now I'd trade her in for a tea cup puppy. In fact, any type of dog that couldn't have had the wherewithal to go rummaging for a toy in the back of the closet.

I'm more embarrassed about having to explain to Mr. and Mrs. Eaton how their bedroom toy became the dog's latest chew. A huge string of saliva falls from the corner of Miss. D's mouth. Her tail wags playfully as she waits for our next move.

"Okay, we need a plan of attack," Noah conspires, his eyes narrowing as he eyes up Miss. D.

Initially, when he arrived, Noah laughed at me, thinking his big muscles would be the solution. But we're both breathing heavily after having spent a good thirty minutes chasing after the bundle of energy.

She thinks it's a game, and every time I've gone to walk away, she starts chewing that darn thing before swinging it around, bashing it on the walls and cabinets.

"Maybe you can go around through the back gate, come in through the sliding doors and I'll herd her towards you."

Noah considers my idea for a moment. "I think it would be better if you went around the back. You can control the space of the door better and stop her from just running past you."

He makes a good point.

Checking my watch, I do a quick calculation on whether I'll have time to stop for lunch before my next job. I didn't have time to grab anything at the bakery as I finished late—stupid temperamental ovens—and I'm starving. It's eleven now, so I have three hours. Okay, that's plenty of time. So long as it doesn't take much longer to get her out the door. Every time I've tried to cajole her with a walk or a treat, Miss. D has been more interested in the dildo.

I can't believe my morning has turned into this.

"Okay, I'll head around now." I walk past Miss. D, not taking my eyes off her as I move to the front door.

You're going down doggo.

As I trudge around the side of the house and through the back gate, I pray that this plan works. I refuse to be taken down by a Great Dane with a giant pink dildo. It's just not happening.

When I get to the back, my eyes connect with Noah through the glass window. I give him a nod and crouch like a quarterback getting ready to catch the ball.

He starts to shepherd Miss. D toward the door. Her bum is in the air, wagging her whipping tale as she anticipates his next move. When she's close, I slide the door open, praying it doesn't squeak or scrape loudly as I do.

Miss. D wiggles her behind toward me and when I think it might be the perfect time, I dive in, grabbing a hold of her neck, hoping to all that is heavenly that she doesn't take off with me attached.

Of course she growls but then Noah, my knight in shining armor, puts a hand over her snout and pries her mouth open until she drops the plastic penis. He kicks it away, out of her reach.

"You got her for a second?"

My pulse is racing, and I swallow thickly as I look up at him, nodding. We're close and for a moment, neither of us moves. The air between us seems to spark and crackle. My breath catches in my chest and I can't help but look down at his mouth.

Please look away.

Noah clears his throat and straightens before walking over to the dildo. He picks it up and throws it in the kitchen sink. There is no way, I'm touching that. I sit up, turning Miss. D's focus to me as I cuddle her and scratch behind her ears.

Now in place of the sparks, there's an awkwardness in the air. And I can't help but feel like my open ogling of Noah's mouth caused it. *Who am I kidding? Of course it did.*

With a heavy sigh and the offending toy out of sight, I stand and walk to the front door. Picking up the collar and lead hanging on the hook, I call to Miss. D. Of course, she comes bounding down the hallway with bundles of energy that only a puppy could still have after hours of being chased around the house.

Noah follows behind at a much slower pace. I keep my eyes on the dog, afraid of what I might see in his gaze. Pity would no doubt be lingering there. At still harboring a crush on the guy who made it clear he had no interest years ago.

When Miss. D is leashed up, I've found my strength. I'm a twenty-seven year old woman now. I don't need to be ashamed of having fallen prey to an intimate moment. And I certainly won't be hiding from my feelings—I just need to have better control over them.

Turning to Noah, I paste a smile on my face, determined to brush off the insignificant moment as I ask, "Want to come on the walk with us?" When he doesn't say anything, I add, "Unless you've got things to do. I'm sure you didn't plan on spending your Saturday morning like this."

He springs into action and I stand mesmerized as he stalks toward me. This great, hulking man. I watch as his broad shoulders and flexing biceps stretch the fabric of his navy sweater when he throws on his faded, brown leather jacket.

Saliva floods my mouth and I look away, berating myself for doing what I literally just said I wouldn't. *Unbelievable*. It's like I've got the memory of a fish.

Oblivious to my inner turmoil, Noah says, "Okay, let's go, but I'm treating us to breakfast."

Well, that seems like a stupid idea. Why exactly did I invite him on the walk?

Oh right, because I spoke without thinking. As per usual. I guess it's one way to build up that tolerance to spending time in his company without making it awkward.

And I'm starving.

Turning to open the door, I reply, "That's good with me. I know the perfect spot."

With a shimmy of shoulders, I bound down the steps

with Miss. D before she tugs me down the sidewalk toward her favorite park.

The temperature has dropped significantly as we get closer to Halloween. Fall has always been my favorite time of the year, especially Halloween with all the trick 'r treaters. I imagine Noah won't get any in his building, especially as since I moved in, I haven't seen a single child.

"What are you thinking?" Noah asks, slowing his step down to match mine.

I strain my neck to look up at him as I answer, "Oh, just about Halloween and how I don't think I'll see any trick 'r treaters this year. Silly stuff, really."

He's looking straight ahead as we walk down the sidewalk, but even from my position nearly a foot below him, I can see his furrowed brow.

"Do you still dress up for Halloween?"

Chuckling, I reply, "Not how I used to."

He doesn't need to know that for Halloween nowa-days when I'm not working, my costumes usually involve being dressed up as a sexy somethin' or other. Long gone are the days of dressing up as a witch or cat because it's cute. I don't think I'll be going to any parties this year though. There are just too many things going on with work and classes for me to even consider it.

"What exactly does that mean?" Noah asks, confusion lacing his words.

Blowing out a breath, I try to telepathically ask Miss. Dixie to pull me into oncoming traffic but she ignores my request, instead taking the opportunity to walk like the well behaved puppy I know she isn't.

"I think I went as a fairy one Halloween when I was four and another year I was a scary witch. Just think of it like the complete opposite of those things and you'll maybe be halfway there."

"So you mean like *Catwoman* or *Wonder Woman*?"

My cheeks heat, because if he only knew how right he was. Last year I went to a party dressed as the *Halle Berry* version of Catwoman. Latex and all. Memories I'd rather forget of the guy I hooked up with flash through my mind. It was all going great until he asked me to crawl around his room and meow like a cat as he petted me. I don't think I've ever left somewhere so quick and all while he called out to me about what a tease I was.

A smirk of triumph slips across my lips as I remember how he soon shut down when I turned on my heel and strode toward him with murder in my eye.

"Somethin' like that," I reply to Noah, refusing to go into the details.

We fall into a comfortable silence as we walk to the park. That's until Miss. Dixie spots what I want to call a squirrel, but looks more like a hybrid rat and chases after it. I'm seconds away from being dragged face first onto the concrete.

Noah's arm bands around my waist. He lifts me off the ground like I weigh nothing as his free hand grabs onto the lead. The heat and muscles straining behind me, a stark reminder of how virile he must be.

His voice is tense and husky as he fights to pull Miss. D back. "I've got to say, angel, this feels a little too dangerous. Do they not have a smaller dog you can walk?"

The sound of that nickname again makes my pulse kick up a beat and I fight the urge to rub my thighs together as heat pools between my legs. Now isn't the time.

In fact, never is the right time.

I'm pretty sure I was just saying that. Literally five minutes ago.

Goodness gracious. It's like ever since I found out he's single, I can't keep a lid on these inappropriate thoughts. *Not that I was great at that before.*

Pushing against his solid arm, I attempt to make Noah release me but all it does is force him to tighten his grip.

"Stay fucking still, Van. I can't work on controlling you both."

Only my friends call me Van. I guess that's what he is now. *It's all he's ever tried to be*. I'm the only one that's ever wanted more, and I need to let that go and take what he's willing to give me.

Even if, once upon a time, I thought he would be so much more.

TWENTY-FIVE

Noah

Don't be stupid.

The mantra has repeated in my mind all morning. That moment with Savannah on the kitchen floor with the dog between us was nearly my undoing. I heard the way her breath hitched and I saw the way her eyes widened ever so slightly.

If it wasn't for the almost pleading look in her eyes, I might have acted on the arousal coursing through my body. She was practically begging me to be the one to break the spell.

After helping Savannah walk the beast of a dog that is Miss. Dixie—what a name—we parted ways, her to go to another job, and I came home to get some work done. My mind has been too distracted though.

I've gone over every possible outcome for if I was to act on whatever it is that is happening between us. There would be no happy ever after, because either way I would lose.

With Savannah, it could only be about sex. But just sex isn't fair to her and Jack would hate me for breaking my promise to him. I wouldn't be able to give her my time and attention. Damn, look what happened with Sutton. I was never there, and it resulted in the break-down of our relationship.

The dull throb of a headache behind my eyes has me resting my head on the back of the couch. Even just *thinking* about doing anything with Savannah has me stressed out more than any takeover ever has.

My eyes go to the clock hanging on the wall at the other end of the room. It's past midnight, and she's still not home. Worry gnaws at the pit of my stomach before I dismiss it. Savannah's an adult. She doesn't need me to baby her.

I'm sure she's just over at Alex's or something. Standing, I pace up and down the length of the living room. I stop in my tracks and turn toward the front door, my mind made up.

As I'm walking through the open space, the front door opens and Savannah steps in. She hasn't seen me yet, if the way she's creeping in is anything to go by. She drops her bag by the front door, kicking off her shoes and then shrugging out of her jacket. There's a cloud hanging over her, the exhaustion rolling off her in waves.

"Where have you been?"

A yelp of surprise leaves her lips, and she places a

hand over her heart as her gaze seeks me out. "You know what? I'm gonna get you a bell. Why on God's green earth are you standin' in the dark?"

"I'd hardly call a room with two lamps on the dark. Where were you?" I demand.

"Whatever. I was workin'. You know this."

My brow tugs together. She left the apartment at four this morning and it's nearly one a.m. "The whole time?"

Fuck. I'm starting to sound like a jealous boyfriend.

Exasperated, Savannah replies, "Yes, the whole time. Believe it or not, not everybody is a gajillionaire."

Distractedly, with my mind calculating exactly how many hours she's been on the go, I reply, "Billionaire."

Confused, she asks, "What?"

Shoving my hands into the pockets of my gray sweats, I reply, "I'm a billionaire."

Her eyes flare in surprise before she clears her throat and turns away from me. Picking up her bag, she walks to the kitchen, huffing something under her breath.

Like a puppy whose owner has finally returned home, I follow behind her. I need to know why she's intent on burning herself out. "How many jobs do you have?"

Savannah opens the refrigerator, staring at the contents, ignoring me. She pulls out some leftovers from the other night, placing them on the counter. Finally, she looks at me and says, "Not that it's any of your business, but at the moment I have three, although one is a task app thing, so I can have at least two jobs from that a day.

Then on top of that, I have voice lessons, dance lessons and auditions."

Pulling a glass from the cabinet she walks back to the refrigerator, filling it up from the dispenser. When she turns to find me, we stare at each other.

"What are your jobs?"

"Well, I wait tables at a bar called O'Malley's over in Brooklyn until ten, then I cover the bar until closing. I help my friend out at her bakery a couple blocks from the Brooklyn Bridge, in the mornin's." She moves back to the refrigerator, pulling it open and scanning the shelves again. When she turns back, she's holding a jar of pickles. As she opens up the jar and pulls out a spear, she says, "Then there's the task app. I mostly do dog walkin' and school pick ups on that one."

I watch, fascinated, as she puts the tip of the pickle in her mouth, her straight white teeth sinking into it. The juice runs down her plump lips and onto her chin. My cock jerks to life. It takes all of my self-control to not adjust myself in my sweats. Why the fuck am I wearing gray sweats? I pray Savannah doesn't notice.

There's no thought behind my words when I demand, "I want you to cut back on the jobs."

Savannah laughs, choking on the pickle. She uses the back of her hand to wipe up the juice off her chin before moving to the sink to clean up.

When she's done, she turns toward me. I don't see any anger at my uncensored words. Instead, I see a look of determination. "Yeah. That's not gonna happen. I'm close to saving enough to not cramp your style and find my own place." Savannah swallows, briefly closing her eyes before she looks at me again. With a smile on her lips that doesn't quite reach her eyes, she says, "I'll try to be gone by the end of the month."

"You don't need to do that. Please, cut back on the jobs. You're working yourself into an early grave and it's concerning. Nobody needs to be working as much as you are."

Savannah folds her arms over her chest, popping her brow as she replies with more Southern twang than I've heard in a while, "Alright vinegar callin' lemon juice sour." With a sigh, she moves back to the leftovers she'd taken out, turning to put them away as she says, "I know I don't *need* to move out, but I think it'd be for the best. You don't need to worry about me, Noah. Honestly, I'm doin' fine."

When she goes to walk past me, I hold my arm out. She stops inches from me and the intoxicating scent of lavender mixed with the distinct aroma of beer fills my nostrils. "Quit the bar job, Van."

She rolls her eyes, lifting her chin in defiance but also to meet my gaze. "Or what? You'll take me over your knee?" She scoffs at the idea before continuing, "I don't think so. I'm off limits, *remember*."

She is. I need to remember that. Maybe get it tattooed on my body. It seems to be harder and harder each day to keep that at the forefront of my mind.

Brushing past me, Savannah leaves the kitchen, the

sound of her bedroom door closing echoes around the now silent apartment. I need to find a way to get her to quit at least one of those jobs.

The lingering scent of her fills my nostrils. I tip my head back as my cock throbs for attention. Fucking hell. My body feels like it's on fire. An inferno raging inside of me, trying to claw its way out and devour her.

How can I react to Savannah like this from just having stood near her? I'm almost ashamed to admit to myself that I never craved Sutton like this. My relation-ship with Sutton was built on the foundation of a friendship. It's what I've tried and failed to do with Savannah.

Recently, the urge to strip Savannah bare and give into my most basic of instincts has been eating me from the inside out. I know I can't. But it doesn't stop my muscles from tensing when she's near or the way I come alive at the thought of her.

My movements are hurried as I go to my bedroom, flicking off the lights as I go. I move to the bed, sitting on the edge. It's not my intention to pull out my cock and stroke the length of it, but a sharp exhale hisses through my teeth at the first contact.

I couldn't stop even if I wanted to. Closing my eyes, I squeeze the shaft, fighting for control. Ever since Savannah came to stay, I've refrained from touching myself, but there's only so much I can take. I need just a little relief.

An image of Savannah with the pickle in her mouth,

juice coating her lips as she wraps them around it, fills my mind. *Christ.*

It's because I haven't had a release in so long. That's why seeing Savannah eating something as innocuous as a pickle, has me jerking myself off. It's nothing to do with it being *her*.

Whatever you need to tell yourself.

I quiet the voice inside that's taunting me as I lean back. Pushing my sweats and boxers down, they pool around my ankles. Spitting into my palm, I drag my thumb over the head of my dick, gripping the length.

My strokes are slow and steady as I try to hold off from reaching my climax.

Shutting out the world, I close my eyes and sink into the moment. A tingling sensation rolls through me, and my chest tightens as my arousal peaks. My breaths come in short, sharp pants as I try to remain in control.

A rushing in my ears drowns out the outside world, and with each stroke, the volume increases. When another image of Savannah, wearing next to nothing in my kitchen, rolls through my mind, my grip tightens reflexively, strangling my cock. It's like a fucking 4K movie of temptation teasing me, bringing me closer to the precipice.

Even in my imagination, I can smell her lavender scent. I inhale deeply, filling my nostrils with the fragrance. As much as I know I shouldn't, I can't help but imagine it's her hand stroking me as she tells me how she can't wait for me to fill her.

My hips buck into my hand. A ferocity taking me over as I jerk clumsily. "Fuck, angel, you feel so good."

A soft gasp that sounds too damn real has my eyes darting open and my hand freezing. My focus goes to the open door and I'm met with the wide, surprised gaze of Savannah. We stare at each other for a moment, her chest rising and falling in a heaving rhythm that matches my own.

My balls draw up and my body jerks as I bite down on my tongue, unable to stop the thick streams of cum from erupting from my cock.

She's the first one to move; darting away from the door as I fall back onto the bed.

Fuck.

What have I done?

I pull my t-shirt off, wiping up the mess on my stomach with it before I fumble, pulling up my pants. There's a spare t-shirt on the chair in the corner of the room, so I snatch it up, tugging it over my head as I trip over my feet and race after her.

I've seriously fucked up.

TWENTY-SIX

Savannah

NINE YEARS AGO

The sound of *Come & Get It* by Selena Gomez blares out of my headphones as I shimmy my hips down the hallway toward the kitchen. I've had the song on repeat for the last week or so. There's a group of us at college that are learning it for a performance we've been assigned.

I stop on the threshold of the kitchen and roll my body, going over the choreography. It's kinda giving *Mean Girls'* Winter Talent Show vibes and, as much as I love the film, I don't want to be part of a real life version.

When I miss a step, I rewind the song and go over the movements again. It's becoming tedious—listening to a song and going over the same dance moves again and again—but it's all part of being a performer. And this has been my dream for as long as I can remember.

It would help if Jenny stopped changing the steps every five minutes.

My stomach growls, reminding me of why I've ventured downstairs. *Food*.

As I round the counter and take a step toward the refrigerator, there's a loud banging that's definitely not part of the song still blasting in my ears. I pull my earbuds out, certain I'm hearing things. But it sounds again, urgent and thunderous.

I'm home alone and should really ignore it. Right?

Realistically, it's the middle of the day. Who's going to be coming to murder or kidnap me? Putting my earbuds on the counter, I move through the kitchen, into the hallway. My steps are quiet and hesitant as I creep toward the door.

Looking through the window next to the door, my gaze meets Noah's. A pained expression on his face as he clutches at his stomach. As I hurry to open the door, any worry about murderers and kidnappers is replaced with a concern for him.

I pull open the door and he sags against the doorjamb, asking through gritted teeth, "Is Jack home?"

"No, he's running an errand for Mama."

Noah nods, pushing away from the frame. His fingers tighten on the wood as he grimaces. I rush forward, my arms wrapping around his waist as I help him into the house.

"Noah? What's wrong?" I ask, worry evident in my tone.

Breathlessly, he replies, "I need to go to urgent care, Van. Something's wrong."

My chest tightens, and I suck in deep breaths.

No.

No, no, no.

This isn't happening.

Please tell me this isn't happening.

I don't have a car. I've been using Jack's while he's been away at college. And I don't know when he or my parents are going to be home.

Noah collapses onto the couch as I pace in front of him, trying to figure out a plan. Out of the corner of my eye, I sneak glances at him. His normally vibrant skin is pale and coated in a sheen of sweat. A hand rests on his abdomen, his eyes are closed and his brow is tugged together, forming a groove.

I drop to my knees beside him as my eyes burn with unshed tears. All of the feelings I've had for him over the years rush to the surface, threatening to drown me in a panic. Picking up his hand, I hold it in mine, his skin far too warm and slightly clammy.

Noah's eyes flick open at my touch. His gaze is unfocused as he blinks at me. A soft, pained smile pulls at his lips before he whispers, "Angel."

He must be delirious. Whatever is causing him to be this sick is obviously impacting on his reality. I need to be strong for him and figure out a plan to get him the medical help he needs.

Noah grimaces in pain, squeezing my hand hard. I hate seeing him like this. My throat thickens and I swallow around the lump that forms.

"Where does it hurt, Noah?" I question while I smooth away the damp hair on his brow as his eyes flutter closed.

This is *really* bad.

Tears well in my eyes as the enormity of the situation hits me. Silently, I beg him to be okay.

I'm not ready to lose you, Noah Parker.

"Noah, I'm going to get help. Please." My voice breaks on the word and I clear my throat, straightening my spine. "It's going to be okay."

Standing, I frantically pull my phone from my pocket, turning away to protect him from my panic. My hands shake as I dial 911.

It feels like an eternity before the call connects. The ball of tension in the pit of my stomach, twisting, turning and building with each agonizing second.

"911. What is your emergency?"

"Please, my... friend is hurt. I don't know what's wrong. You have to help him."

The operator remains calm as fat, ugly, silent tears stream down my cheeks.

"What is your name?"

"Savannah," I hiccup, trying to calm myself.

"Okay, Savannah, is the patient breathing?"

My stomach drops and I spin on my heel, my eyes roaming over the pained look on Noah's face. Palpable relief coats my words as I find his glassy eyes. "Yes, yes, he is."

Noah's voice is weak as he says, "I don't need an ambulance, Van. I'll be fine waiting for Jack to get back."

I ignore him because he needs help and I'll be damned if we're waiting for Jack to come back. Who knows how long that will take.

"What is the address of the emergency?"

I reel off our address, answering more questions before the operator informs me the ambulance isn't far out. "Can you go and open the door for them, Savannah?"

My eyes roam over Noah's face as I think over the operator's question. I know I need to go and open the door, but I can't leave him. *But he needs their help.*

Noah has always been a strong, lively person, but right now he looks so helpless and it's breaking my heart. Tears roll down my cheeks unchecked.

His voice is barely above a whisper, but Noah pulls me back into the moment, when he asks, "Angel, why are you crying?"

"Please don't die," I wail.

He raises his hand to my face, wiping at the wetness as a weak smile forms on his. "Always so dramatic, Van. I'm not going to die."

I don't believe him.

Sirens sound in the distance. And with one last look at Noah, I stand, racing to the front door, swinging it open just as an ambulance pulls onto the street. Jack's car follows behind and when they pull up outside the house, he jumps from his car, sprinting across the front lawn.

I point the EMTs to Noah, unable to be in there with him while they poke and prod at him.

"Sav, what happened?" Jack asks, his chest rising and falling with his labored breaths.

My voice cracks as I say, "It's..." *I can't even say his name.* If I don't, it might not be true. "It's Noah, Jack," I sob.

His face blanches before he pulls me into a hug. "Shit, Sav."

Jack's hold tightens momentarily before he steps back and darts into the house. With a hoarse voice, I call out to Jack that Noah's in the living room.

I've managed to calm myself by the time the EMTs come out with Noah strapped to a stretcher. A fresh wave of despair crashes into me, but I push it down, refusing to let it consume me.

Jack exits the house and thrusts a jacket at me before striding to his car. "Come on, Sav, we're following them to the hospital."

It's just like Jack to take control of a situation, and I've never been more thankful than at this moment to have him here to do just that. I spring into action as the sound of the ambulance door slamming shut echoes around the cul-de-sac.

The sounds you only find in a hospital filter through the door as I look at Noah, asleep in the hospital bed. It's been a wild twenty-four hours, that's for sure. After some tests, Noah was rushed into surgery to remove his appendix.

Thankfully, it was a success, and now it's just going to be about his recovery. All the feelings I've been trying to keep a lid on bubble and churn inside of me. When I get home, I'll sort through them, but right now I'm not leaving him.

Jack's gone to get some provisions with Noah's mom. She was beside herself when Jack called her. *Much like me.*

I lean back in the hard chair next to the hospital bed. My eyes close as I replay the events from the moment Noah knocked on the door. Every time I shut my eyes, I see the look on his face and feel the panic I felt as I called 911.

A cough sounds from the bed, drawing my attention to Noah. His gaze darts around the room before landing on me.

I give him a tired smile as I say, "Hey, sleepy head."

His voice is hoarse as he replies, "Hey, angel."

Butterflies take flight in my stomach at the endearment. He must still be under the effects of the painkillers.

"How are you feeling?" I ask.

I move toward the bed, helping him to sit up, puffing up his pillow.

"Still in pain, but definitely better than before. Thank you, angel."

My cheeks heat and I look away, suddenly shy. "You're welcome. And you don't need to call me that."

Noah grabs my hand, halting my retreat, his voice suddenly serious. "I know I don't, Van. But you fucking *saved* me. As far as I'm concerned, you're my guardian angel."

We stare at each other, unspoken words passing between us as he holds onto my hand. The contrast from when I held his hand yesterday is another sign that he's going to be okay.

"Oh, honey, you're awake. How are you feeling?"

Noah's mom walks through the door, followed by Jack. Neither of them have noticed our joined hands, so I reluctantly drop Noah's and move to the end of the bed. His words echoing in my mind.

It's not until I'm no longer on high alert over something going wrong that I allow the relief to engulf me. He's going to be okay.

TWENTY-SEVEN

Noah

I make it into the hallway in time to see a flash of dark gingerbread blonde hair dart into her room. "Savannah, wait," I call. She slams her door in response, shutting herself away.

What the hell was I thinking?

When I reach her door, my hands land on either side of the doorjamb. I catch my breath as I try to sort my scattered thoughts. How could I have been so stupid? This is why I haven't touched myself since she came to stay. *Fuck*. I should have covered up the moment I caught her eye.

Looking at it logically, my best friend's little sister just caught me jerking off—in the comfort of my own room.

I shouldn't feel bad about that; she should.

Except for the fact I was fucking picturing her when I was in the heat of the moment. And I called her fucking name. Well, nickname. But she will know it was her I was thinking about.

My head knocks against the wooden door as I tip it forward and murmur, "Van, can you come out so we can talk about this?"

There's a muffled response, but I can't make out her words.

"I can't hear you." Maybe she doesn't want to see me. I mean, who could blame her? She's just caught me in such an intimate position. I feel like I need to make this better for her. "Would it help if I stood so you can't see me? Will you open the door then?"

The lock clicks and I watch, holding my breath, as the doorknob turns. I step back, intent on giving her space. Her cheeks are flushed, and her blue gaze is still wide. A look of uncertainty having replaced the surprise.

Christ. She's scared of me. My stomach drops and a wave of nausea crashes through me. Everything I've tried to do to protect her and my friendship with Jack has gone down the toilet because I couldn't keep my dick down.

A desperation fills my voice as I say, "I'm so sor—"

Savannah holds her hand up, halting my words. I'll get on my knees and beg for her forgiveness if I need to.

She clears her throat, lifting her chin as she maintains eye contact with me. "I said... What if I want it to happen again?"

My brows reach for my hairline and it's like the wind

has been knocked out of me. I've got to be dreaming, because there is no way she just asked that.

"Van?" I question.

Confidence in her proposal has her spine straightening. "No, hear me out. Nobody has to know and we can help each other out. You clearly have needs and, well, so do I."

Just the thought of her with anybody else has spots filling my vision as my chest burns. But I made a promise to Jack and I can't break it.

I can't hide the regret in my tone when I reply, "You shouldn't have seen what you did, and I can only apologize for that. It was a moment of weakness on my part that won't happen again. But *we* can't happen."

Scrubbing my hand through my hair, I assess Savannah's reaction. Or rather, her lack of one. Instead, she blinks up at me, tipping her head to the side as she pulls her bottom lip through her teeth. She's too... serene. Like it's the most normal interaction she's ever had. As if she makes proposals like this on a regular basis. Maybe she does.

Nope. Not going there.

With a shrug, she simply says, "Okay."

I can feel the groove taking up residence on my forehead. I'm missing something. Like this decision is going to bite me in the ass.

We stand in awkward silence, neither of us walking away or saying a word until I can't take it anymore. "Did you need to speak to me?"

She had to have come to my room for a reason. I don't think I was being that loud. Certainly not loud enough for her to hear me from the other side of the apartment.

"Oh." Her mouth forms a perfect O and I imagine what it would look like wrapped around my cock before she brings me back to the moment. "Yes. Ben wanted to know if you wanted to come out tomorrow night. I said I'd check, but that you'd probably be workin'."

I'm distracted by whatever the hell has just happened when I reply, "I'll let you know."

The fact is, she's got my mind so jumbled without even trying that I couldn't tell you what my schedule looks like tomorrow. Which never happens.

She's all mischievous southern charm, when she steps back into her room, closing the door behind her with a sweet as pie 'goodnight'.

I wander back to my room, consumed with guilt but also confusion. Despite the fact that her heaving chest and panting breaths fill my mind whenever I close my eyes, I refuse to give into temptation and claim her. A hot shower does little to ease my mind.

TWENTY-EIGHT

Savannah

*O*h *my.*

I didn't mean to watch him. But when I saw his hand wrapped around his hardness, I couldn't help but keep quiet and imagine it was my hand wrapped around him. *Jeez, he's huge.*

I've fantasized for so long about what he'd look like, how big he'd be.

If he'd break me.

There's no other way to look at it. I've become a sexual deviant and I wouldn't be surprised if Noah told Jack that I was peeking on him in his most vulnerable state.

No. He wouldn't do that, because he knows that Jack might find out what exactly it was I saw.

Him.

Stroking himself.

Thinking about *me.*

I don't think I'll ever get the image out of my mind of him coming undone. My breasts feel heavy and an almost overwhelming urge to touch myself and relieve the coil of tension in my core nearly undoes me.

Goodness gracious, I need help.

I did not mean that. I'm not a pervert. *Yes, I apparently am.*

What I should have done is made it known that I was there; that he needed to make himself decent. *But then I wouldn't have known it was me he was thinking of.*

I need to get out of my own head. Moving toward my bed, I flop back on it, my mind swirling with thoughts. Now, more than ever, I need to move out. How am I supposed to look him in the eyes having seen that?

What I need most though, is to let him go and give up on this silly little crush because it's never going to be more. Although he rejected me again tonight, this time I was ready for it. And it didn't hurt anywhere near as much as that first time.

Dragging myself up, I move around my room, getting ready for bed. Tomorrow night, when Ben and I go out, and Noah isn't there to be a party pooper, I'll find someone to go home with. At this point, anyone will do because the one man I want, I know I can't have.

As I climb under the covers, I pull up the group chat on my phone. I'm so lucky to have found this group of people.

SAVANNAH

@Ben You still okay to be my wingman
tomorrow? No deserting me for some
hot guy…like last time.

His response is almost immediate.

BEN

Count me in. If your boy Noah won't
satisfy you, we will find someone who
will.

SAVANNAH

He's not mine.

No matter how much I wish that was the case.

MEGHAN

Keep her safe, Ben! And no abandoning
her for a 'sweet piece of ass'!

BEN

Come on, Megs. When have you ever
known me to refer to a fine specimen of
a man as a 'sweet piece of ass'? You
know me well enough by now to know
you are all my preciouses.

MEGHAN

First of all, don't call me Megs. Second
of all, you literally said it last week at
brunch and third of all, someone needs
to confiscate your Lord of the Rings
DVDs.

ALEX

Who even uses DVDs anymore?

BEN

Definitely not me. I think Megs is
showing her age.

MEGHAN

I'm younger than you. I was just trying to
reference something you might know,
gramps.

BEN

Somebody hold me back!

ALEX

Pipe down you two. Savannah, why are
you needing a wingman?

I'm not about to embarrass Noah and tell everyone I
caught him tickling his pickle—although, I've never seen
a pickle *that* big—especially when I all but offered myself
up to him afterward. *Only to be rejected.* I go with the
safest option and it's hardly a lie anyway.

SAVANNAH

I just think it's time to get back out there.

ALEX

Okay, well, Ben is going to make sure
that happens.

I'm so upset I can't come!

My 'husband' and I are going to THE
dinner.

SAVANNAH

Have fun.

I can just tell that you two are going to end up together!

ALEX

That would be a nightmare.

Keep me posted on your antics tomorrow. And Ben, make sure she's safe.

BEN

Why does everyone think I'm a liability?

MEGHAN

Because the second a pretty boy comes along, you'll forget all about your mission.

BEN

Just know I'm pouting right now.

I close down the chat, a smile on my face as I relax back into the cushions. Tomorrow night I'll finally get over Noah Parker.

The dress that I bought on my shopping spree with Sutton pops into my mind and a mischievous smile takes over my face. It's the perfect dress for seduction.

Watch out New York. Here I come.

TWENTY-NINE

Savannah

S wiping the lip gloss over my lips, I replace the wand in the tube and step back to admire my reflection. It's a risque dress, that's for sure. But it hints and teases at what's underneath, and I'll be charming the dew right off the honey suckle.

I feel sexy and confident, so how could I not?

My hair is curled and my makeup looks 'expensive', whatever that means. Alex talked me through the steps over FaceTime and I'm actually shocked at how well I did. My skin looks flawless and dewy, with sultry eyes and soft rosy cheeks.

I'm wearing a pair of six-inch stilettos that really tighten everything up. Which is just as well really, because this dress leaves next to nothing to the imagination. It fits even better than it did in the store.

Please, dress, work your magic.

I swipe up my black clutch bag and the fur coat Alex

has kindly lent me, and exit my room. I'm meeting Ben outside Siren, and even if I don't meet someone to go home with tonight, I'll at least have a blast with Ben.

No, that's not the right mindset. Tonight, I *will* find someone to go home with.

Throwing the coat and my clutch onto the back of the couch, I walk into the kitchen in search of something to eat before I leave. I do not need to be a sloppy drunk or wake up with a hangover in the morning.

Rummaging around in the refrigerator, I find a questionable looking block of cheese that will go with the loaf of bread I've been tearing chunks off of from the bakery. Sasha makes the best loaves in the city and I'm not biased at all.

I'm bent over in the refrigerator, looking for anything else that will go with my cheese and bread, when I hear the front door open and close. Footsteps approach, telling me Noah's home before his spicy scent assails my nostrils.

As I straighten, I suck in a breath before turning to put the pickles, mustard, and pastrami on the counter. Noah freezes in the entryway of the kitchen, his gaze roaming over my body in a way that tells me he's not quite in control.

He's probably thinking how I should put more clothes on and that a trash bag would be more appropriate in his mind. *Yeah, not happening, buddy.*

With a serene smile on my face, I move around the kitchen grabbing a plate and cutlery as I say, "Hey, I'm just headin' out with Ben but thought I'd make a sandwich first. You want one?"

Noah blinks, as if just realizing where he is. "Umm, no. I'm good, thanks." He pauses, then asks, "You're going to wear that outside of the apartment?"

My brow pulls into a frown as I look down at myself, searching for whatever it is that he thinks is wrong with what is becoming my favorite dress. When I come up empty, I walk out from behind the island. Standing in front of him as I turn left and then right, looking down at my body and with a cheery tone, I reply, "I did question Sutton when she told me I *had* to get it, but now, well, now I think it's hotter than a hayloft on a Montgomery summer afternoon."

I blink up at him, feigning innocence. Enthralled, I watch as his jaw grinds while he avoids looking at me. He doesn't say anything, and I take that as my cue to leave.

"Ya know what? I can eat later. Have a good evenin', Noah."

My hips sway and I can feel the heat of his gaze on me with every step as I move to the couch and pick up my coat.

He still doesn't say anything, even as I throw it over my arm and walk to the door. It solidifies my plan for tonight. Heck, I might even redownload a few dating apps tomorrow.

With my hand on the door handle, I flick my hair over my shoulder and with a voice that comes out a tad bit too husky for my liking, I turn to him and say, "Have fun workin', Noah."

I open the door and walk to the elevator, leaving it to click shut softly behind me. Just as the elevator doors open, so does the apartment door.

He makes his presence known as his sure strides eat up the space. I step into the car, and turn until I'm facing him. That's when I see he's still in his navy chinos, but has lost the suit jacket and tie, leaving his crisp white shirt collar open. With his sleeves rolled up, I have the perfect view of his veined forearms. *My weakness.*

"I never said I wasn't coming." There's an authoritative note to his voice as he steps into the waiting elevator, turning to face the doors.

I can't hide my surprise when I reply, "Oh, but I figured you'd have work or somethin' else to do?"

Noah shoves his hands into his pant pockets, the fabric stretching tight across his ass. I swallow thickly as I rub my thighs together to relieve the ache building in my core.

I need vodka. Now.

Oblivious to my inner torment, Noah keeps his eyes focused on the doors as we travel down to the lobby. "Well, you were wrong."

Afraid that my arousal might give me away, I lift my shoulder with a shrug, as if it's of no consequence to me if he comes or not. We ride the remainder of our descent in silence as I try to get my voice back.

As the door opens, I turn to Noah and say, "Don't

stop me from hookin' up with someone tonight. You might like to act like you're my brother, but you're not. I don't think even Jack would have the gall to stop me from doin' what I wanna do."

A grunt, that I don't think is his agreement, follows me as I walk across the lobby and out into the cool autumn air. I pray that Noah doesn't ruin my night by doing what he did in Siren all those weeks ago.

THIRTY

Savannah

I think I might smell. And not in a sexy pheramones way.

It's the only reason I can think of that would have any man within a five foot radius completely ignore me. My attempts at finding someone to even flirt with have dwindled as the night has gone on.

And to top it all off, Ben got distracted and deserted me, leaving me with grumpy guts, Noah. He's been such a buzzkill.

When I left the apartment, I was feeling sexy and like I could take my pick of any man I wanted. It's nearly time to go home and every guy I've so much as made eye contact with has grimaced and run in the opposite direction. I'm blaming Noah for being bad luck or something.

A warm body crowds me as I lean over the bar, waiting for a bartender to notice me. "Fancy seeing you here."

Turning in arms that cage me in between his body and the bar, I come face to face with the handsome guy from a while back. *What was his name?* I can remember a whole script and cues for a show, but not the name of a guy I kissed a matter of weeks ago. My brows pull together. He laughs, his white teeth sparkling down at me as he clutches at his chest. "You wound me, cupcake. Jamison, my name is Jamison."

Oh crickets, of course it is.

My error creeps across my cheeks as I let out an embarrassed chuckle. "You'll have to forgive me. I am the worst when it comes to remembering names."

Jamison bends, his eyes level with my own as he swipes something from my cheek. There's still no spark, and I'm distracted on why that could be when he asks, "Any guesses as to why no man in this whole place will come so much as ten feet in proximity to you, despite being a total fucking knockout, cupcake?"

It's like he's been listening to my internal conversation... it's a little creepy.

"Sure," I shout over the music, bending away from him, trying to get a read on him. *Does he think there's more here than there actually is?*

The barman chooses that moment to come and interrupt us. "What can I get you?" they shout over the music.

Darn it, I want to know what Jamison knows. But first, I need a drink.

I order a shot of vodka and a double vodka cranberry, as Jamison moves to stand next to me, leaning against the bar. He shakes his head at the bartender, declining a drink. His gaze is intent on me, and when the barman walks away to make my order, I turn to face him.

There's a knowing smirk on his face and if I wasn't on the receiving end of it, I'd find this whole situation hilarious. We're in a standoff of sorts, neither of us speaks. Why would I when he's the one with something to tell me? If he's just come over here to mess with me, he's picked the wrong woman.

When the barman returns with my drink, I down the shot of vodka before taking a deep pull on the vodka cranberry. I'm seconds away from walking.

As if he can sense it, he looks to my left before he leans in, his hand on my hip as he murmurs, "Your bodyguard has been scaring everyone off. You've had every eye on you since you stepped foot in here, but nobody is going to step up and risk their life for a taste, cupcake."

My bodyguard? It's not going to be Ben. He was on a mission to *help* me 'clear out my cobwebs', as he put it. That just leaves one person.

Noah, freaking, Parker.

Urgh, I'm madder than a wet hen. He doesn't get to tag along on *my* night out and then proceed to scare off any man that might be interested in me. Especially when he's not interested himself.

Throwing the straw from my drink in the garbage can on the other side of the bar, I bring the glass to my lips and tip back the contents, finishing it in one go.

I slam the glass on the counter and say distractedly,

"Thank you, Jamison. Next time, I'll try to remember your name."

I'm on the move before he can reply, but his deep chuckle follows me, mingling with the sound of the music. My eyes are set on Noah, sitting in a booth along the back wall of the club. His stormy gaze is glued behind me on Jamison as his jaw grinds.

Oh, he's angry.

That makes two of us.

When I reach him, an energy flows through me; my fury and a hint of confusion fighting below the surface. The anger wins, because how dare he? Noah stands, his stupid hands going into his stupid pockets. Why is that so hot?

Focus, Savannah.

I come to a stop in front of him and jab my finger into his chest. He looks down at where I've made contact, then back at me. For good measure, I jab him again. This time, he falls back into his seat and I'm thrown off balance. In these stupid heels and with the drink I downed running through my system, I tumble forward, into his lap.

Noah's hand rests on my hip, in the same spot that Jamison's did moments ago. Small sparks zap between us as he makes a circular motion with his thumb. I turn to face him and we're so close that our breaths mingle in the gap between us.

My chest rises and falls as I try to process what is happening to my body. When I look into his dark gaze, I snap back to reality and scramble out of his lap, composing myself before I turn to face him.

Was that heat I saw in his eyes?

It doesn't matter if it was or not. He's already made himself clear. Nothing will ever happen between us—even if that's what his body wants.

Some of the fight has left me, but I'm not letting him off the hook. It's not his place to act like this. "Are you happy with yourself, Noah Parker?"

His brow furrows.

I continue, undeterred, shouting over the music, my words a little slurred. "Don't you dare play dumb with me. I'm so mad at you."

"Van, I don—"

"Don't call me Van." I stamp my foot to punctuate my point. "Only my friends get to call me Van and you *sir*, ain't my friend," I sneer.

With that, I blow out an exasperated breath, then turn and walk away from him.

What is his problem?

He isn't my brother. I only have one and I don't care for another. Especially not one who's gonna stop me from living my life.

I can faintly hear him calling my name over the pounding music, but I ignore him, on a mission to get myself out of here and away from him before I either end up in jail or homeless *again*. I guess, this time I have money for at least a half decent hotel. And Jack won't be able to send Noah a second time.

That's not actually a bad idea.

Maybe I'll get a hotel tonight. The thought of Noah getting a bee in his bonnet over me not coming home tonight almost brightens my mood. Almost.

As I break through the door and into the cool night, I try to get my mind to formulate a plan. I'm not ready to go home. I could go to Passion. That's always a good time and maybe I'll find someone to go home with there. At least Noah won't be around to stop me.

Moving down the sidewalk, away from the club, I dip into the entrance of an alleyway. A gust of wind blows my hair, sending goosebumps scattering over my skin. Shoot, I forgot my coat.

I'm about to turn back when Noah calls, "Van, wait. Please. Let's talk. You shouldn't be out here on your own anyway. It's not safe."

It might be childish, but I ignore him, keeping my back turned. It's best for both of us that I do, otherwise I might say or do something I'll seriously regret. I walk further into the alleyway, away from him. Coming to a stop, I pray that the darkness will envelop me and cloak me from his gaze.

Who am I kidding?

I can't ever seem to hide from him. All the time I've known him, he's *seen* me.

Noah follows me until he's standing so close, yet so far. The heat from his body warms my back, even though I know he's keeping a safe distance from me. We've always been like that. A current of electricity passing through us, as if we might actually combust if we touched.

Noah, touching me? That's almost laughable. He wouldn't dare. He'd be too scared of hurting Jack's feelings. Of breaking a stupid promise he made years ago.

His voice is husky as he pleads, "We live together, Savannah. You can't just ignore me the whole time. Let's be adults about this and go home and talk it through."

I rear back as if his suggestion has physically hit me. Turning to face him, I fold my arms under my chest, drawing his attention to my bust.

Oh.

Don't get distracted. Not now. I have a mission to accomplish.

"I ain't going home. You can. Not that your apartment is my home. In fact, you're not welcome to hangout with me anymore. Not after what you did in there." I point toward the club before continuing, "I'm gonna find a man and ride him 'til he's broken." Moving toward Noah, I run my finger down his solid chest.

Even in my heels I barely reach his chin, so instead of whispering in his ear, I tip my head back and give him my most sultry face, leaning my body into his before I say, "And then I'm going to ride him again. And again."

Just as I step back to walk around him, a growl reverberates in his chest and I think I might have made a fatal error.

Maybe not fatal. But I think I've awoken a beast.

In a flash, Noah's arms band around my waist as he

lifts me to his chest. Instinctively, I wrap my legs around his waist. My dress is pushed up to accommodate his size between my thighs as I hold on for dear life.

Noah moves us deeper into the darkness of the alleyway, out of sight. My back knocks against the wall as he presses me between it and his body. The cool brick scratches my exposed skin, heightening the sensations zapping through me.

Clutching his shoulders, I feel the muscles bunch and move as he adjusts his grip. We've never been in such an intimate position before, and I'm not sure what's going through his mind. My eyes try to read his in the shadows of the alleyway, but I can't see for the life of me.

His breaths are coming in short, sharp puffs, as if he's fighting for control—either that or I'm too heavy.

When he adjusts his grip again, I feel the unmistakable hardness of his cock pressing between my legs. *Is this real?*

I have to be dreaming. There is no way that Noah is letting me feel him in this state.

Noah inches his head forward until he's resting his forehead on mine. It's then that I can finally see his gaze. My hands move along the expanse of his shoulders and down over his straining biceps. I don't know what's happening, but I know I don't want him to put me down.

There's no denying it. I'm aroused, and he hasn't even touched me. Not really. I want him to though... so bad. Fighting the urge to rock my hips against him, I squeeze my thighs around him.

Noah's voice is husky and strained when he says, "I should put you down and walk away."

Please don't.

I have to quiet the needy voice in my head because I'm afraid that if I speak, I'll break the spell he seems to be under.

"God, I should take you home and fucking walk away." His breath mingles with mine in the space between us and his fingers dig into the soft flesh of my thighs. "Angel."

That single word, whispered with a tortured groan tells me of the fight he's trying to win with himself. It's one I hope, with all my might, that he loses. With that one word he's begging me to be the strong one. The one to tell him no, but how can I when it's what I've always wanted? When *he's* what I've always wanted.

My cool fingers grip onto his face, tilting it up so he's forced to look at me. My eyes search his, looking for any sign that he might not want this. All I see is heat, longing and a hint of something I can't quite identify.

I move forward until our mouths are less than an inch away from each other. Breathing him in, I can practically taste him. Sixteen year old me is rejoicing at the fact that I'm about to kiss the man who's had my heart for over ten years.

Any thoughts I might have are cut off when Noah closes the gap between us, taking the lead and kissing me.

Noah freaking Parker is kissing me.

With his mouth.

How is this even happening?

Okay, sixteen year old me needs to calm down and let me enjoy the moment.

His lips are soft as they move over mine. It's a stark contrast to the roughness of his beard. In this moment, I'm certain that I could kiss this man for an eternity. When Noah opens his mouth, I allow him entry and the first touch of his tongue on mine is like coming home.

It's like he's putting all the care he has for me into this kiss. He's consuming me and I'm consuming him right back. He's happy to feed me his soul as he devours mine.

Noah's moans fill my ears, urging me on as I roll my hips into him, a desperation I've never felt taking over as I try to relieve the ache building inside of me.

Never in my life have I wanted to be taken against a wall more.

He breaks the kiss and I suck in lungfuls of air, tipping my head back against the brick as I look up at the dark sky above. Noah's mouth moves down the exposed column of my throat, dropping kisses and nips in a trail to my chest.

I wish we were somewhere more private, so we could be naked and really explore each other, but I'm worried that if I suggest we go home, he'll stop. If we move, he could come out of whatever fog he's in that's allowing him to indulge in *me*.

No. I'm just going to enjoy this moment before it ends.

We're staying and if it means our first time together is against a wall in a dirty alleyway, then so be it. At least we'll have had a first time.

Noah's hips buck against my pantie clad pussy and I release a moan that draws his attention back to my face.

Our gazes clash, and time stands still. The music that was a dull thump is suddenly silenced and it's as if we're the only two people in the world. My chest heaves with every breath I take. I'm certain my panties are ruined.

"Noah," I plead because he's stopped and I don't want him to.

He lifts a hand, smoothing away a strand of my hair and tucking it behind my ear. "Angel, I'm going to take you home and then you're going to do what you said you would do to someone else when you were mad at me."

Oh.

My eyes widen as Noah sets me down and I remember my words from earlier.

He doesn't want this to stop?

Noah chuckles, "No, I don't want to stop."

I smooth down my dress before lifting my chin. Injecting as much nonchalance into my tone as I can, I reply, "Oh, I said that out loud?"

He pulls on my hand, and I fall into him. His arm bands around my waist and he looks down at me. "Yeah, you did, angel."

Neither of us looks away, the heat building between us until a car horn blares, breaking through the night air.

Licking his lips, Noah drops his gaze to my mouth before he grunts, "Let's get you home." I watch the flame of desire spread through his eyes as he continues, "I'm hungry."

I think I might die.

THIRTY-ONE
Noah

I drag Savannah to the entrance of the alleyway, a desperation to get her home and do things with her I never imagined possible fuels me.

The sound of her heels clicking on the cement at a hurried pace trails behind me. With that one kiss, I'm drunk on her. The all consuming need to have her spurs me on, blocking out any rational thoughts I might have.

There's a giggle in her voice when she breathlessly calls, "Noah, I'll break an ankle if you don't slow down."

I don't want to slow down. Ever since she wrapped her legs around my waist and I felt the heat between her thighs, I've been in a heady rush to claim her. But I don't want her to get hurt, either. Protecting Savannah has always been my goal.

Stopping in my tracks, I turn to face her. The movement is so sudden that she doesn't have a chance to stop and the forward momentum has her stumbling into my chest.

She lands against me with an adorable squeak, looking up at me with a startled gaze. Her eyelashes flutter as a cloud of worry darkens her beautiful eyes. "Have you changed your mind?"

My fingers brush into the soft strands of her hair as I tip her face further back. "Not a *fucking* chance, angel."

I watch as the tension releases in her body and a calm washes over her. Her voice is thick with arousal as she asks, "Then why did you stop?"

Without a word, I bend down and place a hand behind her knees, the other supporting her shoulders as I swoop her up. A startled gasp leaves her lips, and she wraps her arms around my shoulders, looking down at my now moving feet. The space between us and the car closes with my urgent strides.

Her voice trembles slightly. "Noah, I'm going to need you to talk to me. I need to know where your head is."

Fuck, she wants to know where my head is?

It's fucking gone.

I want nothing more than to be buried so deep inside her that we become one. And I'm terrified that I'll never be able to get enough of her.

It's why I always stayed away.

Not just because of the promise I made to Jack, but because she would be it for me. She's fucking beautiful, both in and out. Every time I was alone with her as she grew up, I was drawn to her, I just didn't know what it meant. I still am, and when she leaves, my thoughts are still consumed by her.

Christ, if I tell her all of that, she'll no doubt run from me.

Living with her these past few months, as she's walked around my apartment like she fucking belongs there has been torture. It's enough to make even the strongest of men falter.

Shaking my head, I bring myself back into the moment. I don't need to be thinking about anything happening past tonight. We'll both enjoy each other for this one night and then whatever happens, happens.

Standing next to the car, I set Savannah back on her feet. Her body rubs against mine and I grit my teeth to hold back my moan. I take a step forward and she takes one back until she comes up against the car. My body presses into hers and I dip my head, my lips ghosting the shell of her ear.

Hands on her waist, my thumb rubs over the sheer material just under her right breast. "I'm going to take you home, Savannah. You're going to take this dress off, but leave the heels on and bend over the back of the couch as I eat your dripping wet pussy. I'm going to devour every inch, angel, and I can't fucking wait."

Her eyes darken, and I watch as her chest heaves with each breath. A desperation that matches my own fills her sweet southern voice as she says, "Then what the heck are we waitin' for?"

I reach around her and open the door of the car. A growl reverberates in my chest as I command, "Get in the car, Savannah."

She bites her plump bottom lip and my cock jerks in the confines of my pants. My mind is filled with images of her with her mouth wrapped around me, saliva running down her chin as she looks up at me with wide eyes.

Fuck.

I don't think one time will be enough.

Following behind her, I step into the car, widening my legs to relieve the pressure on my dick. Savannah shuffles into the middle seat, her hand resting on my thigh. Instinctively, I lift my arm and she tucks further into my side.

It should scare me how natural it feels to have her in my arms. Or how it was second nature as my lips moved across hers, and my tongue dipped into her mouth as I took my fill. But it's not scary. I feel electric, like I could conquer the world two times over.

Rupert navigates the car with his expert precision, but I've never been more regretful of not having a limo with a divider.

The car pulls up outside my apartment building, and my hand finds the doorknob before we've come to a stop. I say goodnight to Rupert and step from the car, waiting on the sidewalk, holding my hand out for Savannah.

She takes it before we walk across the lobby. Her

voice is soft and almost hesitant when she asks, "You've gone quiet. Are you getting up in your head?"

I watch the movement of her throat as she swallows when I turn to look down at her. My lips form into a smirk that no doubt tells of the thoughts racing through my mind. "I was just wondering if you'd be able to take all of me or if you'll be begging me to stop as you tell me how full you feel."

"Oh." A beautiful blush steals across her cheeks and she fans herself with her hand as she looks away and says, "Well, aren't you just full of filthy little surprises?"

The doors of the elevator open, the ding cutting off what I was going to say—that she hasn't seen anything yet.

I wait until we're inside and on the move to our floor before I speak, my eyes focused on the numbers above the door as they increase. "Just like you need me to communicate with you, I need you to do the same. If I'm too much, you need to tell me."

Savannah steps in front of me, drawing my focus to her. She bites that damn bottom lip again as she looks up at me from under her lashes.

Her hand moves down my front until it's resting on the buckle of my belt. "Noah, I don't think you could ever be too much for me."

When her hand cups my throbbing cock, I can't help the hiss that leaves my lips. It echoes around the elevator car. My fists clench at my sides as I wage a battle with myself to not touch her. If I do, we won't make it to the apartment.

"Savannah," I warn, because I only have so much self-control.

"Noah," she mocks, a mischievous smile curling her lips as she enjoys every second of the torment she's inflicting.

I'm trying to sort through the fog clouding my mind, looking for a punishment I can issue, when she removes her hand and steps from the elevator.

I hadn't even realized we'd reached our floor.

What the hell is she doing to me?

Standing under the glaring light in the hallway, she looks like a fucking dream and I can't wait to claim her. For her to be as addicted to me as I am to her.

When the doors go to close—because of course I haven't moved—I slap my hands on either side, forcing them open.

My breaths are labored as I try to gain control of the fire burning bright within me. "Angel?"

Her nipples are puckered, and it's not until now, as my eyes hungrily roam over her body, that I realize she doesn't have the coat she left with.

With a throaty voice conveying her desire and an innocence I don't quite believe, she replies, "Yes, Noah?"

"Run."

Her head tilts to the side, and she takes a step back. I'm not sure she even realizes she's done it but I can see a sudden uncertainty flit through her eyes at my demand.

"Run. Because if I catch you, I'll bend you over the first thing I can find and fuck you until you scream my name. If you get away, I'll take it nice and slow. Maybe."

I really hope I catch her.

When I take a step forward, she takes two back. Her hips sway in a hypnotic rhythm as she walks backward toward the door. With her gaze half on me, she rummages through her bag looking for the keys.

I can't be certain I even locked up. I was too desperate to get out, making sure nobody touched what's mine.

My mind reels at the thought.

She is mine.

Savannah always has been, even if I can only have this one night.

I watch as she pulls the keys from her bag, trying to find the lock, but they fall to the floor with a clatter. Still standing by the elevator doors, I watch as she bends, the fabric of her dress pulling taut across her behind.

She's fucking playing with me.

When the keys fall to the floor for the third time and she looks over her shoulder before bending to pick them up, I move. My strides are casual but purposeful. Like a lion on the prowl, stalking its prey.

A shiver wracks her body as I approach. It doesn't take me long to reach her. She's still standing in front of the door, the pretext of opening it long gone.

My hands land on her hips at the same time that my lips find her hair. "Were you pretending to run, angel?"

Her voice is a throaty whisper as she replies, "I don't want you to chase me because I want you to do the first thing you said."

She's going to kill me.

I buck my hips into her, pressing my hard cock into the softness of her ass. Savannah's head tips back, resting on my chest. Her eyes are closed as she moans, grinding back and forth.

I'm not cumming in my pants like a teenager with no self control.

With a voice that sounds foreign to my ears, I demand, "Open the fucking door, Savannah."

She springs into action. Unlocking it on the first try, she pushes it open and takes a step forward. My arms band around her waist, halting her movement before I lift her, pressing her back into my chest. She lets out a yelp of surprise at the action, but relaxes back into me.

I cross the threshold, kicking the door shut behind me. The last thing I want is for our neighbors to see what I have planned for her.

Setting Savannah on her feet behind the couch. My hand lands on the nape of her neck and I turn her so she's facing the back of it. I apply a light pressure and she folds over it. Running my hand down her back, I gently slap her ass, testing her limits.

"Noah," she pleads as her ass wiggles back searching for me.

My name on her lips, with all of her need for me plain to hear; it's the best *fucking* sound in the world.

I don't speak, afraid that if I do, I'll end up telling her everything I want to do. I've had years to think of all the things I'd do to her. *My angel.*

Shaking my head, I pull myself back into the present, to the goddess bent over my couch. "If it's too much, you have to tell me to stop because if you don't, I won't, Savannah. Tell me you understand," I demand, my hand smoothing over the delightful curve of her ass again.

I can't get enough of her.

She nods and I bring my hand back, the sound of the slap reverberating around the living room as it mingles with her gasp. "Speak to me. With words."

Savannah's breathless as she replies, "Yes, I understand."

Satisfied that she understands my demand, I find the zipper on the dress, hesitating before I tug it down. There's no going back after this. Hell, there was no going back the second she wrapped her legs around my waist. She's mine for as long as I can have her, and for tonight at least, I won't stop until we're both too exhausted.

Savannah straightens and helps me remove her dress. She returns to her position, bent over the couch without a word.

Her ass cheeks are slightly spread from her position. I run my finger through the crack, following the line of her G-string. A shudder runs down her back as she presses into my hand. She moans into the cushions, wriggling her hips as she tries to relieve herself.

Kicking her legs out, I stand behind her, my mind sparking images of me taking her from behind.

I know what I said would happen if I caught her, but I don't even know where to start. I'm like a man who's been starved for years but has finally been offered a seat at the buffet.

"Noah," she purrs, her voice dripping with seduction as she pushes back, rubbing over my covered cock. "Please don't go back on what you said. I'm dripping wet for you. Only for you."

Like a caveman, I grunt and growl, ripping the flimsy material covering paradise off her. Throwing them over my shoulder, I look down.

Before we do anything else, I just need a small taste.

Dropping to my knees on the soft carpet, my hands grip the front of her thighs as I hold her steady.

She wasn't lying. Sweet nectar glistens all over her pussy, coating her thighs.

As I lean close, I inhale the scent of her, one I want to memorize for any lonely nights that might come. My tongue swipes out, flicking over her clit.

She tastes like nirvana, and I can't be certain that I haven't just died and gone to heaven.

What have I been missing out on all these years?

I know that if I'd had a taste when she'd offered herself to me, I never would have been able to give her up. I'd have become addicted to her. I'm certain I will now.

In that sense, she's the most dangerous woman I

know. I'm about to dive off the cliff into the rocky waters below and I couldn't be happier about it. My desire consumes me as I lick, nip, and suck on her pussy.

As her orgasm builds, murmurs and moans spill from her lips. "Oh God, I'm so close."

My hand comes down hard on her ass cheek and she screams out at the sharp contact. "That's not my name, angel."

I can imagine the look on her face as she tries to be defiant even while her legs tremble. Panting, Savannah replies, "It should be. I've never felt like this before."

Fuck if that doesn't make me feel ten feet tall. Pulling back, I run my thumb over her clit as I try to keep the cocky grin off of my face. When it's nice and wet, I replace it with my mouth and move my thumb up to her puckered entrance.

With a light pressure on her ass, I add a finger to her pussy, the walls clenching around me. *She's so reactive.*

I lean back, my eyes on the way my hands are commanding her most intimate parts. My breath skates over her as I say, "One day, I'm going to fuck you in your ass as your pussy rides my fingers."

Am I?

My words set her off, and she clenches around me as her back arches and she claws at the couch. She rides out her orgasm on my fingers, but with my steady pace and her hips hungrily bucking, it doesn't take long for her to climb again.

Savannah collapses onto the couch, her body going

limp. She turns her head to the side, looking back at me as I rise from my knees, still fully clothed.

Roaming my hand over the expanse of her naked back and down over her ass, I say, "I wish I could take a picture of you looking like this."

Biting her bottom lip, she smirks and replies, "So do it."

Her absolute faith in me is a testament to our relationship. The thought rocks me to my core.

What we've just done has crossed the line, but I don't feel how I thought I would about it.

I feel alive and greedy for more.

Like a statue, I'm fixed to the spot, my gaze trained on Savannah's perfect ass and pussy. I never thought I'd get to see her like this. Let alone have her taste lingering on my tongue. It doesn't stop me from wanting to dive in again and again. Savannah pushes up, standing and taking away my view.

Turning to face me, I get my first view of her front, with her flat, toned stomach, perky breasts, and a small tuft of hair covering her pussy. She's like a siren, calling to me.

I'm helpless.

"Noah, sit on the couch," she cajoles.

She's trying to take control and I find that I'm not entirely adverse to it. I snake a hand around her waist, tugging her into me. As I dip my head, she looks up at me and our lips connect in a soft kiss.

Suddenly I don't want to go fast and hard, I want to

savor every moment. This is our first time together and that shouldn't be rushed.

"No," Savannah commands, pushing against my chest.

Immediately, I step back, my hands dropping from her. That one word has me both regretful and sad. My mouth goes dry at the same time as my stomach twists in knots.

"No, you aren't about to get into your own head. I can practically hear the cogs working, Noah. Get undressed and sit on the couch and let *me* taste *you*. It's only fair."

My brows shoot to my hairline. I wasn't expecting her to say that, but I'm grateful she doesn't want to stop.

Unbuttoning two buttons, I grab a hold of the back of my shirt and pull it over my head. I can feel her hungry gaze roaming over my body. A soft gasp leaves her lips when I toss my shirt to the side.

I go to the gym, and I know that right now, after my most recent bulk, I'm bigger than she's ever seen me, but she's not shocked at that.

No, her gaze is on the tattoo on my ribs, under my right pec.

It's all out on the table now.

Savannah steps forward, her fingers hesitate to touch, but when she looks up, I give her a nod, telling her it's okay.

It's her tattoo after all.

Angel wings now mark my skin, with the date she saved my life in Roman numerals above them and 'my angel' underneath. Her hands are cool to the touch as she runs them over my marked skin.

Barely above a whisper, she murmurs, "I didn't see this when I ran into you that— How long have you had this?"

She's going to ask questions I don't want to answer. Not yet. "Van," I warn.

Her eyes lift to mine, a million questions behind them before with one final touch she steps back. For a moment, her gaze darts to the scar on my lower abdomen before she looks up and says, "Right. Let's get to screwing. Where do you want me?"

Savannah turns, but I band my arm around her waist, tugging her into me before she can circle the couch. I'm not going to let her diminish what this is. Even if I don't know what *this* is myself.

I bury my nose in her hair, inhaling her scent. "Angel, one day I'll tell you all about it, but right now, I just want to enjoy this moment."

Wiggling her ass, Savannah drops her head back onto my shoulder giving me a perfect view of her front. My eyes flit around her body with a hunger my mind doesn't know how to filter. Lifting my left hand, I palm her right breast, rolling the tight bud of her nipple between my fingers.

"Talk to me," I urge, I need to know what she wants.

She moans, "The weather was nice to—"

Her words are cut off as my hand slaps at her breast. Her eyes flair in surprise, darting to mine.

Growling, I command, "Don't test me, angel. Tell me what you want, how you want me to fill you, *where* you want me to fill you."

Savannah picks up my right hand, moving it down with her left until my fingers move through the soft tufts of hair above her pussy, sliding through the soaking wet folds. "Here," she rasps.

Moving her right hand to the space between us, she squeezes my cock through my pants. Black dots fill my vision at the feel of her hands on me, even with the material of my slacks between us.

"I want this." She rubs her hand over my rock hard cock. "Here." Her fingers move with mine as I flick her clit. "Be as rough or gentle as you need to be, Noah. I can take it."

Dipping my head, I capture Savannah's mouth with mine as she turns to press her body against mine. My hands grab onto the soft globes of her ass cheeks. Lifting her, she wraps her legs around my waist. Our tongues dance as the urgency that had consumed us earlier returns.

I'm vaguely aware of the soft thud of her shoes hitting the carpeted floor.

Moving my hand between her legs, I dip a finger into her tight channel. Fuck, she's going to need stretching. She moans into my mouth and I walk us to the couch. We practically fall onto it when I sit down.

Straddling my lap, Savannah breaks the kiss and reaches between us to unbuckle my pants. I lift my hips as she pulls it through the loops before dropping it on the floor. Her fingers fumble when she gets to work on the button and zipper.

This is it.

It's too late to stop this, and even if I could, I wouldn't.

My head drops to the back of the couch and I moan as she pulls me free, stroking the length of my cock. Of their own volition, my hips thrust up into her hand.

Not wanting to miss a second more, my heavy eyes look down at her petite hand stroking me. I watch, transfixed, when Savannah rubs her thumb over the head, the pre-cum that had gathered now coating her thumb. She brings it to her mouth and I'm unable to look away as she sucks it clean.

My hands dive into her hair and I drag her face toward mine, my tongue forcing entry into her mouth. It tastes like *her* mixed with a saltiness that is all me.

She's still stroking me, bringing me closer and closer to the edge. Moving my hands between her legs, I push a finger inside her. My pace is steady, matching that of my thumb as it rubs over her clit.

Breaking our kiss, I rest my head on her shoulder, trying in vain to get myself under control. If I don't, it's very likely that I'll only last two fucking pumps.

Gripping Savannah's wrist in my hand, I pull it behind her back and away from my sensitive cock. The action causes her to rest her other hand on my knee or risk falling back. With her perky breasts exposed to me, I suck on one of the tight buds as I add a second finger to her pussy.

"Noah, that feels so good. Please don't stop," she breathes.

As if I could.

Her juices run down my fingers and into my palm, but I still don't stop. I want her to come on my fingers. Again. Tonight, I'll have one on my tongue, two on my fingers and the rest on my cock.

Savannah's thighs push against my own as she tries to fight off the inevitable. The tremors rack through her body and I sit back as I watch the show. Watching her come undone is my new favorite thing and even though I might only experience it for tonight, I know I'll remember it for eternity.

With her chest rising and falling at a rapid pace, her hips lift as she tries to wriggle away from my hand. Adding a third finger, I don't let her get away from me. She's going to take my fingers and then she's going to take my cock.

"Noah, please, it's too much."

A dark chuckle reverberates through my chest as I reply, "You're strong, angel. You can take it."

Her cries get louder as she gasps out, "I can't. I'm not strong enough. It's too much."

She's so close. The little spasms gripping my fingers tell me she is. Even though she's telling me she can't take any more, the fact that she's the one fucking my fingers says it all. I don't think she realizes her hips are moving, not my hand. Her body trembles as she reaches her peak.

"Noah," she cries out, her nails digging into the flesh of my thigh as she tumbles over the edge into ecstasy.

Collapsing forward onto me, she chuckles, "Wow. I've—Just wow."

Removing my fingers from her pussy, I lick them clean, conscious that she's going to need a minute.

She tastes like the best kind of dessert.

THIRTY-TWO

Savannah

hat is happening?

I've got to be dreaming. Never in my wildest dreams did I think Noah and I would ever actually do this. Of course, I hoped one day it would happen, but I never thought it really would.

Sex has never been a thrilling event for me, but I've also never had someone make me feel the way Noah does by just existing.

When he bent me over the couch, I thought he was going to take me, hard and fast, like he promised. I was a little disappointed that he didn't. At least until the first swipe of his tongue, with his beard adding even more friction, nearly had me evaporating on the spot.

Noah Parker, my teenage crush, has tasted me.

Not even tasted. He devoured me.

My body is limp and languid as I watch him lick my orgasm off his fingers. *Why is that literally the hottest thing*

I've ever seen? Just watching him clean himself up has my body coming alive.

"Noah," I purr, needing him to fill me.

His hard cock sits between us, dripping pre-cum onto his stomach. I'm slightly terrified of his size but I'm equally excited to feel him stretching me wide.

Moving to the side, I help Noah remove his pants until he's as naked as I am. His body is magnificent. Each muscle is perfectly carved and protruding on a body that I know he's worked so hard on. There's a lot of power in this man. But right now he has nothing but heat for *me* in his eyes.

Even watching him put on a condom is sexy.

I want to capture this moment, to memorialize it so I can look back at something when it's over.

Climbing back onto his lap, I wrap my hand around his length. Stroking up and down as I try to convince myself that he'll fit. He's huge and I'm not truly convinced that he won't split me in half. Noah lifts his hand and tucks my hair behind my ear before he cups my cheek. "We'll go slow. If it hurts or it's too much, we can stop, okay?"

I'm not going to stop. Not until he's buried to the hilt. I've wanted him for too long.

Suck it up, buttercup, and all that.

Great pep talk, Savannah.

Lifting my hips, I position him at my entrance. His eyes are glued to what's happening between my legs. If the way his fingers are pressing into the skin of my thighs is anything to go by, he wants this as much as I do.

I hiss as his length presses into me. The stretch burns despite how wet I am. I've never experienced anything like I have with him tonight, I'm soaked. Resting my hands on his shoulders I ease down, inch by glorious inch.

There's no doubt about it. I'll still feel him inside me tomorrow, and maybe even the day after.

When he's buried to the hilt, I close my eyes, giving us both a moment to adjust to this new found intimacy.

"Savannah?" Noah questions. Opening my eyes, I look into his. They're filled with a sincerity and longing I haven't seen from him in such a long time. "Thank you."

My brows tug together. *Why is he thanking me?* This isn't pity sex or me doing him a favor. This is… I don't know what this is.

I don't reply, because how can I? What do I say? Thank you for giving me the most orgasms I've ever had in one night? Thank you for forgetting about the promise you made to my brother all those years ago? Or maybe, you're welcome?

No, if I say anything, I risk pulling him out of the moment, and that's the last thing I want to happen. Instead, I roll my hips, testing out the movement with him filling me. Starting slow, with gentle shallow movements, I find a steady rhythm.

The only sounds filling the apartment are our

labored breaths and the sounds of our bodies moving together.

Noah leans forward, capturing my nipple in his mouth. The way his beard grazes over my sensitive flesh heightens my sensations.

I just know I'll end up with marks tomorrow.

His big hands run up my rib cage, stopping just under my breasts as he feasts on me. My hands trace over Noah's shoulders, up his neck and into the short strands of his hair.

When I tug, he pops off of my nipple, his head tipping back so he can look at me. We maintain eye contact as my movements increase. It's far too intimate but I can't look away and neither can he.

This isn't just fucking, it feels like so much more.

A desire that I'm sure mirrors my own, fills his gaze.

We'll never be the same after this. Intrinsically, we'll be two different people moving through the world.

There's nothing we can do to stop it.

I dip my head to capture his lips. If I'm not careful, I might read too much into the things his eyes are telling me. I might fall even more in love with him than I already am.

Oh no.

"Angel, look at me." His voice is soft and cajoling as he demands my focus.

This is too much and not enough at the same time. I thought after years of telling myself it would never happen that I could do this without any real feelings involved. That I'd be able to take my fill and walk away. But the second he looked at me with care and tenderness, all of my hard work went out the window.

Mentally steeling myself, I open my eyes. I can't avoid him when he's inside me.

"There she is. Don't shut me out again, okay?"

Nodding my head, I resume my movements, except this time I lean back and offer up my chest to him. Anything to not have that bubble of intimacy blanket us again. This new angle has my clit touching his pelvic bone with every movement.

As my pace increases, his hand moves between us, and he rubs his thumb over my clit. A tension builds inside of me and I struggle to maintain my focus on moving my body. My clit pulses beneath his thumb as tingles travel the expanse of my spine. Whimpers spill from my lips as I give myself up to the feelings coursing through my body.

My breaths come out in short, sharp pants as I race toward my climax. When I tumble over the edge, my walls clench around him as my whole body is wracked with tremors. It feels like it lasts an eternity before I'm left a limp and weak mess.

Noah gives me no time to regain my strength. Instead, he lifts me up and flips me onto my back, still buried deep. As he hovers above me, his eyes roam over my body and he growls before his hips start moving in hurried, jerky thrusts.

"Fuck, angel, you feel so good. I'm going to cum."

He pulls out, ripping the condom off as he spills himself over my stomach with a roar. Ribbons upon ribbons of white cum splatter across my stomach and I barely resist the urge to reach out and taste it. I move to the side as he collapses next to me, his heavy body half on me and half on the couch.

Noah kisses my shoulder, muttering into my flesh, "I'll get up in a second and we can get in the shower. I just need a minute."

"It's okay, I can clean myself up." I go to move, but his strong arm pins me to the couch.

"No, I made the mess, I'll clean it up. I just need a second. And anyway, I need to get cleaned up too."

Clearly, he's not going to let me up to clean off, so I'll do it right here.

Using my index finger, I drag it through the cum on my stomach, swiping up as much as I can before I pop it in my mouth. Savoring the salty taste, I close my eyes and moan.

I feel Noah tense next to me. When I turn my face to him, opening my heavy eyes, I say, "I just wanted a taste. You got to sample me but I never got to try you."

His voice is thick and filled with desire when he replies, "The night isn't over, Van. You'll get to 'sample' me all you want, just as soon as I've recovered."

I like knowing that he's as affected by what we've just experienced as I am. That even though he's so strong and virile, I've still managed to make him weak.

Stifling a yawn, I say, "That might have to wait, big

guy. I've had more orgasms tonight than I have in my whole life and I'm exhausted."

Noah bounces up, suddenly filled with energy. Watching him skeptically, I can't help but notice that even though he's just come, he's still hard.

My eyes widen as I say, "You need to tell that thing to calm down. I can't go again."

He chuckles, as if what I've said is funny, I'm being deadly serious. I do like that there's a lightness to him that wasn't there before. Holding out a hand for me, he waits, confident that I'll take a hold of it.

Swinging my legs off the couch, I take his hand, preparing to stand. But Noah has other ideas as he yanks me to my feet. I fall into him, covering him in his own release.

"Noah," I admonish. "Now you're a mess too. I'll go shower down the hall. You want to watch something before bed?" I ask, distractedly looking at his cum covered stomach.

He doesn't say anything and so I look up to find him smiling down at me. "You're showering *with* me, and then you'll be sleeping next to me."

"But—"

Noah's finger silences me. "It wasn't a question, Savannah." Spinning me in the direction of his room, he taps me on the ass, urging me forward.

Have I orgasmed into some sort of twilight zone?

In a trance, I walk to Noah's room. It's not until I step over the threshold that I come to a stop. My eyes land on the trinkets dotted on the chest of drawers, moving to the cushions on the bed and throw on the chair in the corner. Images of Noah and Sutton run rampant through my mind. What did they do in here? I mean, obviously they had sex, but was it recently? Is he going to compare us?

No, Noah wouldn't do that. I might be his first hook up since they broke up, but I've known him for nearly half my life.

I'm his rebound.

The thought roots itself in my mind, twisting and turning until what we've done suddenly feels ugly and dark. I don't know what we were thinking.

What was I thinking?

He's just ended a long term relationship with an amazing woman. There's no way, no matter how much I want it to be, that this will be anything more than sex for him.

I need to be alone.

Suddenly feeling deflated, I turn to go to my own room. I find Noah blocking the door, a look of concern on his handsome face at my abrupt change in energy. As if sensing where my mind has gone, he takes my hand and without a word, walks us out of the room and down the corridor.

We walk into the main bathroom. Noah flicks on the overhead light, moving across the room to switch on the shower. My eyes catch on my reflection in the mirror. The makeup I'd worked so hard on perfecting is smudged and my hair is a mess. Faint red marks show on my pale skin from where Noah's beard has rubbed against me.

Noah comes to stand behind me, his hands land on my waist as he tugs me back into him. Our height difference is almost comical; I barely reach his pecs. Tracing his fingers over the red marks, I feel his chest puff out behind me.

"Are you happy with your work?" I tease.

He tweaks my nipple, and I groan at the sensation. "I'm fucking ecstatic with it."

Running his hand up my chest, Noah lightly grips my throat before moving further up and forcing my head back. He dips down and captures my mouth with his own, forcing it open as his tongue demands entry.

Behind me, I feel his hard cock pressing into my back before he breaks the kiss, only pulling away slightly. His thumb rubs a soft circle on my jaw as he looks deep into my eyes. So much is said without actually being said in this moment.

His possession of me is clear in how he has me held captive, not just with his hand, but his gaze too. I wonder if he feels it too. If he can see how much I want to claim him as mine, just like he has me.

My heart races at the thought. At the risk of saying something I shouldn't, I break eye contact, moving away from him before I step into the walk-in shower and close the door. The water rains down on me, washing his cum away. I watch, fascinated, as it gets washed away down the drain.

Meghan would say I'm dickmatized, and I couldn't really argue with her on that. I am. I'm not sure how I'll get over him now.

The cold air from the shower door opening draws my attention to Noah. With his size, he takes up over half the shower. His hands cup my face as he walks me back until the water showers down over his back. "Where have you gone?"

Forcing a wide smile on my face, I answer, "I was just thinkin' how, other than you cockblocking me, I've had a great night."

Noah doesn't laugh like I expect him to, instead his gaze assesses me, looking deep into my soul. "Now give me the truth."

Rolling my eyes, I say, "You don't wanna hear the truth, Noah."

"Try me."

"Fine." I move out of his hold, back under the water as I grab the body wash and squeeze some onto my loofah. "I was thinkin' how, after just one night, I've been hypnotized by your dick. And I'm not sure I'll be able to look at you the same way without rememberin' what it feels like to have your hands or mouth on my body and your cock fillin' me up. I didn't get any further than that before you interrupted my thoughts, but I do know I need to find my own place, so I don't beg you to devour me again and again like you did tonight."

Like that time I all but begged you eight years ago.

THIRTY-THREE

Savannah

EIGHT YEARS AGO

J ack and Noah return today for the summer. I came back a week ago and, am over the moon to see them. A lot has changed. Not just in Montgomery but with me too. Well, there's one big thing that hasn't.

I'm still a virgin.

That's going to change this summer though. I'm nineteen now and if my plan works, Noah will be the one to take it. There's no way he can see me as a kid sister anymore.

Twisting left then right, I admire my toned figure in the mirror before I get dressed. The guys at college have actually noticed me. Although that's kind of stopped. Ever since Bobby Wright, the star quarterback, asked me out.

Me.

Plain old Savannah O'Riley.

Of course, I said yes.

I went on one date with him and when he tried to kiss me in his car, I punched him in the throat. It was just a reflex from having grown up with Jack. He kicked me out of his car after sputtering and trying to catch his breath. I did feel bad, but he could have warned a girl or even asked for consent.

Of course, Mama is happy that I've returned. She's been alone since I left for college. My dad died suddenly of a heart attack nearly two years ago. Even now, her grief and pain are palpable. And she won't hear it when I mention her going on a date or moving on.

My throat clogs and unshed tears burn the back of my eyes at the thought of my dad. I miss him almost as much as Mama does. Some days are harder than others, but it will get better. At least that's what my therapist said.

To celebrate my return, we went shopping. We were at the mall for hours and when we got home, I had to take a nap. Shopping is not for me. But with all that said, I've found the perfect outfit for seduction.

With one last look at myself, I give a determined nod before I swipe up my short sleeve mint green floral mini dress. Stepping into it, I tug at the zipper, pulling the fabric tight across my body. It fits like a glove and I can't wait to watch his jaw drop.

Throwing my hair into a ponytail, I swipe some lipgloss across my lips. Voices from downstairs travels through my closed bedroom door, telling me the boys have arrived. With one last look at my reflection, I smirk to myself as I bounce on my heels.

At the sound of my name being called, I walk out of my room and bound down the stairs and into the kitchen.

Everyone is seated around the table. Jack is the first to acknowledge me when I enter the room. He stands and walks toward me. My eyes search out Noah as he talks to Mama. He looks good. His broad shoulders fill out his white t-shirt and a light dusting of stubble coats his jaw.

I wonder what that will feel like when he's kissing me.

A warmth grows and spreads out from my core as I stare at him. When he doesn't acknowledge my presence, the feeling wilts and crumples until there's nothing but coldness in its wake.

I don't know why I had some idea of a grand reunion. That maybe he'd be so surprised at seeing me he'd pull me close and give me my first kiss and ask me to be his and only his.

Goodness, what am I, sixteen?

No, I'm a grown woman now and just because he hasn't so much as looked in my direction, it doesn't mean my plan won't still work.

"Sav, what've you done to your face?"

Rolling my eyes, I pull Jack into a hug, a smile on my face. Before I went to college, makeup wasn't really something I did, but I've enjoyed experimenting. I'll never be able to do the fancier looks, but I know I look good, so I only take his words as brotherly teasing.

"It's good to see you too, Jack."

When I pull away, I smooth my hands down the front of my dress as I peek around Jack, trying to get another look at Noah. Still, there is no acknowledgement of my presence.

"Do you want some sweet tea, boys?" Mama asks as she stands from the table.

Noah's deep voice sends a thrill down my spine, straight into my core when he replies, "That would be great. Thanks, Sadie."

As Mama prepares the drinks, I sidle my way over to the table, taking a seat. "Hi Noah, how's college?"

There's a little bit of shock and a whole lot of heat filling his gaze when he looks at me. His eyes roam over my body and I squirm in my seat, a weird sensation building between my legs.

Finally.

That's exactly what I wanted to see from him. My plan will work. There's no denying he wants me.

Jack clears his throat, drawing Noah's attention away from me. Never in my nineteen years have I, until this very moment, wished that I was an only child.

"Hey, Van." His eyes make another sweep over my body before he sits straighter in his chair, cutting himself off. "College is good. How are classes going?"

"Good. You know how it is, parties and stuff."

Jack slaps my ponytail, cutting the tension that

seems to have taken over the room. "Come on, Noah. Let's go get unpacked."

Pushing back his chair, Noah gives me one last look and an apologetic smile before he follows Jack across the room.

They're just on the threshold when Mama asks me, "What time are you leaving, honey? Do you have time for something to eat?"

There's a party tonight that one of the guys I know from high school is throwing at his house. I'm certain it'll be the first of many this summer and I can't wait. It'll be good to have a break and really let my hair down from all the pressure that comes with college.

Apparently there's also going to be skinny dipping and lots of drinking. My best friend Cecila said it's going to be a 'fuck fest' but I'm not so sure about that.

With a quick look at my phone, I reply, "In a hour an' a half." I lift my chin, being sure to keep my back to Jack and Noah who've taken it upon themselves to listen into a private conversation. "And I'll grab somethin' to eat there."

She turns to me, a look of concern on her face as she says, "Okay, but make sure it's a meal, not snacks."

My cheeks heat from the embarrassment at being coddled."Of course."

I stand from the table, suddenly needing to not be under Mamas assessing gaze. She probably knows I won't eat a proper meal. Mamas know this kind of stuff.

Jack and Noah make way when I reach them at the kitchen doorway.

"What party are you going to, Sav?"

With a cheeky smile, I look over my shoulder, my eyes connecting with Noah. "A nude one."

Bounding up the stairs, I walk into my room, dropping back onto my bed. I think that went well. Based on the look he had in his eyes when he finally looked at me, I think I can safely say my plan has got off to a good start. I'm daydreaming about what's to come, finally making Noah mine, when there's a soft knock on my door.

"Come in."

I lift onto my elbows, looking at the door. Mama doesn't usually knock, despite the amount of times I've had conversations with her about it. Which means it's either Jack or Noah.

My stomach flips, hoping Noah's come to see me. Anticipation has my stomach twisting in knots. In slow motion, the handle turns and Noah walks in. My heart rate kicks up as my eyes roam over his face and body.

His gaze goes to the hem of my dress, which is dangerously high on my thighs. I cross my feet at the ankles, as I tug on the material. "Is everythin' okay?" I ask.

His only answer is a grunt, as if words are too much for him. *Has he come to seduce me?* Well, I'll be... I could scrap my plan. I was sure he'd shoo me off like a fly buzzing 'round the church picnic. But maybe he wants me too?

I know he made a promise to Jack, but they've been friends long enough that Jack won't throw that away because Noah starts dating me. In fact, I'm sure Jack would love it.

"O—kay." I drag out the word when he still doesn't speak. "If it is, why are you in here?"

Scooting down the bed, I sit on the end. My hands clench the cotton of my sheets, as I wait for him to speak.

He doesn't say anything for such a long time that I worry he's having a stroke or something. But aside from his jaw grinding and an occasional flaring of his nostrils, everything seems to be fine. My heart races with every second that passes.

Finally, he breaks the silence, his voice gruff and... sexy. "Where's the party?"

"Huh?"

His voice is almost pained as he demands, "The party, Savannah."

He wants to know where the party is? Why? It's going to be full of people my age. My head tilts to the side as I try to process his question.

Like a light switch flicking on, it dawns on me that Jack has sent Noah in here. He wants to know so he can go get free booze, make sure I don't get into any trouble, and probably hook up with someone.

Does Noah want to hook up with some random chick?

My stomach drops at the thought and a desperation fuels me as I push away from the bed and stalk toward him. Maybe it's born from a need to prove to Noah I'm not a kid anymore or to send a message to Jack, but I let that desperation push me forward until I'm standing in front of him.

There's a flare of surprise in his gaze at my movement. But he doesn't back away and that's more telling than anything else he could have done.

My hand lands on his stomach as I press my chest to his and stand en pointe so I can whisper in his ear. "You can tell Jack, the party isn't for y'all. And it would be *very* awkward for him to watch his little sister skinny dip *and* hook up with guys."

When I go to step back, Noah grabs a hold of my wrist, tugging me back into him. I land with a huff against his chest. My heart races at the intensity in his gaze and I'm certain he can feel it. There's no mistaking the threat in his voice when he says, "I'll kill any *boy* that lays a fucking hand on you, angel."

The words should scare me, but instead a jolt of electricity passes through me and my breath hitches. I can feel the heat emanating from him and the cool air from his breath on my earlobe.

"Where's the party, angel?" The command in his voice reverberates in my head and my brain malfunctions. It's the only reason I can give for telling him the address of the party. I don't realize what's happened until the soft click of my door closing brings me back to the moment.

I'm as mad as a mule chewing bumblebees.

Tonight I'm going to make them both regret crashing the party.

Walking to my wardrobe, I rummage through the box of swimsuits that sits on the floor under my clothes.

My hand digs out the stretchy material of a white one. It's a two-piece that consists of a push up bikini top and high cut bottoms. Gleefully, I clutch the scraps of material to my chest before darting out of my closet to put it on under my dress.

I have exactly two hours until Cecila is going to pick me up. I might need Mama's help to perfect my hair and makeup for tonight.

With my swimsuit on, I throw on an oversized navy sweater that falls to mid-thigh before I swing open my bedroom door and race downstairs. I'll put my dress back on when I'm ready. I'd hate to get anything on it.

I find my mom in the kitchen, stirring a pot of dumplin's. "Mama, I need your help."

She drops the wooden spoon into the boiling water with a plop. Turning to me, her face lights up as she asks, "What is it, baby?"

"Can you do my hair and makeup?"

Switching off the stove, she walks toward me, taking a hold of my hand and dragging me back upstairs.

When I left the house, I was disappointed that I didn't get to see Noah... I mean Jack. So I could tell him to not bother coming. But I'm determined to have a good time tonight and if Noah turns up, it might actually help me with my plan.

I know he wants me. There was no way he could hide the heat in his eyes when we were alone in my bedroom. That and the threat to anyone touching me.

I take a large swig of my vodka and lemonade, needing to cool down. Even though it's late in the evening, it's still hot and humid out. A pool party is the perfect way to cool down though.

Rhys Wilkins, the guy whose party it is, has the coolest parents. He said that they told him they'd rather he drink at home than in the woods or somewhere equally dangerous. The only caveat is that when you arrive, you have to hand over your keys and don't get them back until the next day.

Cecila and I move through the house to the pool area. It's magical. I'd never get fed up of looking at it if I lived here. There's a grotto behind the waterfall that streams into the pool. It's very *Playboy* mansion-esque.

Loungers are evenly spaced around the pool and Edison lights are strung around the garden, lighting up the space but giving it an intimate feeling. Right at the back of the garden there's a pool house, but Rhys says it's off limits. No doubt people will end up back there hooking up anyway.

Nobody's in the pool just yet, but with how the

night's going, it won't be long until someone makes the first move. The backyard has been made into a makeshift dance floor, and outdoor speakers blast out a song I don't know the name of.

With my eyes closed, I swing my hips to the beat, getting lost in the rhythm. I probably look stupid as my hands roam over my body, but I don't care. Once upon a time, I would have and it would have stopped me from having fun, but since starting college I've realized how little others' opinions of me matter. It's done wonders for my confidence.

Feeling a gaze on me, I open my eyes and get sucker punched as a familiar set of green mixed with brown eyes stare back at me.

He came.

Neither of us looks away. At least not until Stacy Schnider wraps her arms around Noah's neck. He doesn't push her away.

My stomach drops at the sight as he breaks eye contact with me and smiles down at her.

No. This isn't happening.

Kicking off my shoes in the middle of the dance floor, I move on autopilot as I unzip my dress and then pull it over my head. Shoving the wad of material at Cecila, I spin on my heel and sashay my hips to the pool. "Who's ready for skinny dippin'?" I call over my shoulder, vaguely aware that Noah is stalking toward me.

My question is met by cheers and hollers as others remove their clothes. I untie my top, dropping it on the floor by the edge of the pool before I dive into the cool water.

Eek, I hope that looked as sexy as I was going for.

The sounds of other bodies hitting the water vibrate throughout the pool.

I break through the surface and tread water as I laugh at the fun everyone is having. There's splashing and people making out, as well as a couple of cheerleaders on the shoulders of some jocks.

The smile falls from my lips when I meet the unimpressed face of Noah.

In hindsight, I suppose it's a good thing Jack wasn't around to see me bare my chest to the party. To be fair, I told them not to come. Swimming to the edge, I fold my arms onto the side of the pool, kicking my legs as I look up at Noah.

Feigned innocence coats my words as I ask, "You not joinin' us?"

"Get out of the pool, Savannah."

Ignoring his command, because he doesn't get to tell me what to do, I push under the water before breaking back through the surface. "Sorry, I just wanted to clear out my ears. I could have sworn it sounded like you were telling me what to do."

It's his turn to ignore me as he bends to pick up my bikini top. He hands it to me before folding his arms over his impressive chest. "Be in the pool house in five minutes or there'll be hell to pay, Savannah."

Trying to keep the smug smile off of my face, I snap

the top into place before giving him a pointed look. With a nod of his head and one last look, he stalks off toward the back of the garden.

Cecila races over to me, a grin on her face. "Oh my, Van. Is it actually gonna happen?"

"I think so," I murmur, suddenly nervous for what's to come.

Pulling myself from the pool, I take the towel that Cecila is holding out for me, roughly drying my hair before dabbing it over my body. "Do I look okay?"

Cecila swipes under my eyes and flattens down a strand of hair before stepping back and saying, "You look hot. Go get 'im, Van."

With a shimmy of my shoulders, I drop the towel on a lounger before I squeeze Cecila's hands and race toward the back of the garden.

The noise from the party dies down with every step I take, and the butterflies that took flight in my stomach the moment he told me to meet him at the pool house, flutter wildly.

A light shines next to the front door, guiding my way. On the other side, the guy who has my heart is going to have my body, mind and soul. Finally. It's been a long time coming.

My hand rests on the doorknob as I will myself to relax. I just jumped into a pool in front of nearly thirty people, without my top on and *this* makes me nervous.

Sucking in a deep breath, I unlock the door and step into the room. My eyes find him in an instant, leaning against the back of the couch. When I close the door behind me, we're engulfed in darkness. It takes a minute for my eyes to adjust before I can safely walk toward him. In here, it's just the two of us.

"You wanted to see me?" I say, my voice a throaty murmur.

In a stark contrast, his is pained when he says, "You need to stop, Van."

My brow tugs into a frown as my head rears back. Stop what exactly? I'm staring at him mutely when I realize I haven't actually voiced my question. "What exactly do I need to stop, Noah? Having fun?"

"Yes," he roars as he stands and starts to pace. "Fucking hell, yes, if it means you being half naked around other people. You need to *fucking* stop."

I can honestly say I don't know what is going through my mind when I reach behind me and unclasp my top, pulling the straps down my arms. It falls to the floor at my feet and I don't miss the way his eyes dart to my chest before he turns away and curses under his breath.

"Can I be half naked around you?" I ask, my voice thick with lust.

Cautiously, I move forward until I'm standing in front of him. He shouldn't let the promise he made to Jack keep us apart. I love him and I have since the moment I met him.

His voice is filled with torment when he says, "No."

Smoothing my hands over the expanse of his chest

and down his arms, I ask coyly, "Even if I want to give you all of me?" I pray he understands what I'm saying. What I'm willing to give to him.

Noah cups my face, smoothing his thumbs over the apples of my cheeks. My eyes widen at the realization that he might kiss me. His gaze dips to my mouth before lifting to meet mine again.

This is it.

Heat pools between my legs at his touch and what's to come.

Closing his eyes, Noah's hands fall from my face as he takes a step back. Suddenly I'm cold and a ball of dread settles in the pit of my stomach.

"I'm sorry, angel. You're like a sister to me. I can't do that with you."

I reel at his statement. My arms coming up to cover myself as a heat so different to the one I felt moments ago washes through my body. This one is embarrassment and humiliation mixed together, dragging me down.

Desperate to not feel this way, I mutter, "You don't mean that." An urgency takes over as I continue, "I've seen the way you look at me, Noah. The hunger in your eyes."

Sighing, he rubs the back of his neck as he says, "You don't know shit, Van. I have a girlfriend. And even if I didn't, I wouldn't hook up with a kid."

It's like my world has imploded. My only saving grace is that he doesn't stick around to watch me crumble. Noah turns on his heel and leaves me to surrender to the pain coursing through my body.

From this moment on, I vow to never beg him or another man for affection. My guard is up.

Two weeks later, I lose my virginity to Alfie Devereux in the back of his parent's car. I feel nothing but a sense of loss deep in my heart.

I don't see Noah again for the rest of summer.

THIRTY-FOUR
Noah

Savannah's back is to me as she scrubs soap all over her body. The body that's now burned into my memory forever. My hands slide around her waist and I pull her back into me, dipping to whisper in her ear, "You won't scare me off, angel. Now I've had a taste of you, I'm fucking addicted."

Savannah stills before she composes herself and steps out of my embrace under the water. I watch, enthralled as it washes away the suds. Her nipples pebble under my scrutiny, and in the confines of the shower, I hear the barely audible hitch in her breath.

"Van, don't look at me like that."

Her tongue darts out and swipes over her lips. Her voice is husky when she asks, "Like what?"

I look away, closing my eyes as I try to gain some sort of control over my raging arousal. "Like you're ready for me again."

Dainty hands touch my stomach, my muscles tensing and contracting under her fingers. My gaze finds hers, the need clear. An overwhelming urge to know that she won't think this is a mistake tomorrow rushes through me.

Cupping her cheeks, I bend my knees searching her eyes as I ask, "Do you think what we did was a mistake?" I don't realize how desperate I sound until my words hang in the air around us.

Her mouth drops open before she closes it and grips onto my wrists with her hands. "How could you even think that?"

I don't answer. Because how could I? Everything she's done up until this moment has screamed at me that she's enjoyed every second of what's happened since I touched her in that alleyway.

At my continued silence, Savannah's voice is soft, almost cajoling when she says, "Noah. Why would you think that I thought us having sex was a mistake?"

A heavy breath leaves me. I need to answer her, even if it bares all of my insecurities. "I just needed to know that you feel as overwhelmed as I do by all of this. That you want this as much as I do."

Shaking her head with a huff of a laugh, Savannah replies, "What part of *'I need to move out so I don't beg you to do this again'*, makes you think I didn't want any of this?"

Sheepishly, I duck my head because I'm clearly a

fucking idiot. My chest swells as her words sink in. She wants to do this. My dream girl wants *me*.

With my confidence rebuilt, I wrap an arm around her waist, tugging her into me as I murmur into her hair, "For the record, I won't ever deny you if you beg me. Scratch that, I might, but only if it's to make it so much better for you."

When I release her, her dark blue eyes are swirling with arousal, the ring of gold around her iris more prominent.

Savannah opens the door and steps from the shower. Her gaze on me as she grabs a towel and pats herself dry. When she's done, she puts it back on the towel bar and walks from the bathroom. Her eyes seek me out over her shoulder on the threshold, promises alight in them.

Fuck. She's a temptress and I'm not immune to her pull.

I switch off the shower and step out into the now cool air of the bathroom. Using her towel, I dry myself before switching off the bathroom light and following her to her bedroom.

Savannah slips under the covers as I reach the doorway. Although she keeps one side of the sheet pulled back and her invitation is clear, I still need her to tell me what she wants.

She flutters her eyelashes, her gaze dropping to my painfully hard dick. My hand rubs over my chest and down my stomach, wrapping around my cock as I stroke myself. I watch as her eyes follow the movement and it's an effort to keep the smile off my face.

Distractedly, her eyes still on the movement of my hand, she asks, "Are you coming to bed in here or are you going back to your room?"

Leaning against the doorjamb, I don't stop. "If I sleep in here, I'm not sure I'll be able to keep my hands to myself."

Savannah drags her teeth over her bottom lip and her eyes get heavy as she watches me. "Noah?"

"Yeah, angel?"

"Get in the bed."

The command in her tone has me pushing away from the jamb. *Who am I to deny her?*

I stalk toward the bed, my cock painfully hard. When I reach the edge of the mattress, I don't climb in, instead I let her get her fill as her eyes roam all over my body. My heartbeat pounds in my ears as I silently beg for her to touch me.

"I just meant for us to sleep tonight," Savannah mutters teasingly.

My voice is thick with desire when I reply, "Then why are you naked?"

Her eyes finally lift to mine and she blinks, momentarily confused, before she replies, "I always sleep naked. Why are you naked?"

Chuckling, because I'm not sure she fully comprehends the question she's asked, I say, "We just got out of the shower. I'm hardly going to sleep in a towel."

Switching off the lamp on the bedside table, I climb

under the covers, settling them over us before I direct Savannah to turn onto her side with her back to me.

Giving into my body's most basic of desires isn't going to happen right now. If I do, I'm not sure I'll ever be able to quit her. I curl around her as if it's the most natural thing in the world.

Maybe it is.

Christ. I'm in too deep already.

Dropping a kiss into her hair, I tighten my hold on her. Closing my eyes, I settle into the bed, whispering, "Goodnight, angel."

Savannah tries to wriggle out of my hold but my grip holds her still.

Confusion fills her voice as she demands, "What do you mean 'goodnight, angel'?"

Playing dumb, I inject humor into my tone as I reply, "Well, let's see, how can I break this down for you?" I can't help the grin that nearly splits my face in half. "Goodnight is what people say when they are about to go to sleep. It's a way of saying goodbye, I gue—"

Savannah swats at me, her hand making contact with my thigh under the cover.

Moving my lower body back, out of hitting distance, I exclaim, "Hey, what was that for?"

"Stop bein' a smartass and tell me why you're goin' to sleep."

She really needs to be more specific, but I'm loving being able to mess with her. "Because it's night time?"

Her voice is stern, or at least trying to be when she says, "Noah."

"Okay, okay. We're going to sleep now, because I'm very aware—and not to sound conceited—of how big I am and I want to make sure you can still walk tomorrow."

"Oh." Savannah turns around, her features soft and relaxed before she continues, "Can I touch you?"

There's no hesitation when I reply, "Of course."

I should have asked her where she meant because the moment her hand wraps around my cock, I hiss at the contact. Throwing my head back, I try to control the urge to buck into her hand.

Her voice is almost shy as she asks, "Does that feel good?"

My gaze seeks out hers in the moonlight as I cup her face, "Fuck, angel, it's so fucking good. Too fucking good."

A small smile slips across her lips and I can't resist the need that builds inside of me demanding that I capture them. She has the softest lips I've ever touched. They're like velvet and pillowy like a cloud.

What starts out as a testing kiss, soon escalates to more. My tongue demands entry that she gives freely with a lust filled sigh.

Pulling away, she strokes my cock once more before her heavy eyes seek mine out and she says, "Noah, I wanna taste you."

Savannah's hand moves to my hip, pushing me onto

my back. She throws back the covers and I spread my legs, making room for her as she settles between them on her stomach.

I watch, mesmerized, as her hand wraps around me again and her mouth descends onto my cock. I'm not sure I'm ready for this.

The wet, warm heat of her mouth is nearly my undoing. My hands dive into her hair, holding it back as her head bobs up and down. Her tongue swirls around the tip before her lips wrap around my length and I hit the back of her throat, once and then twice.

It's nearly impossible for me to hold back. To let her set the pace and take as much as she wants. She repeats the motion, swirling her tongue, engulfing me in her mouth and then a double tap down her throat.

Sitting up on her knees, Savannah pops off my cock, a line of saliva caught on her lips, connected to me. She sucks in deep, sustaining breaths as her hungry, wide eyes bounce around my face and down over my body, before resting on where her hand holds my cock.

Flicking her thumb over the head, she strokes my length, as the hand not wrapped around me finds her pussy. The sight of her touching herself as she strokes me has my cock twitching and weeping for release.

I don't think I'll last long.

Especially when she moans at the contact of her fingers. I close my eyes as my mind runs rampant, thinking about just how wet she'll be. I want to taste and touch her so bad.

A tortured groan slips past my lips, and Savannah's eyes open, capturing mine.

My hips buck up into her hand as the tension builds in my spine. God, everything she does has me aroused.

"Are you close, Noah?" she teases, her voice sultry as it breaks through the quiet.

Am I close?

Fuck, I'm one foot over the edge.

Barely able to form a coherent sentence, I grit my teeth as I rein myself back and reply, "Yes."

Her hand moves from her pussy, and I look at the light sheen coating her fingers. Automatically, I sit up, grabbing at her hand and bringing it to my lips. Her heady scent fills my nostrils as I inhale. A wave of dizziness makes my grip momentarily tighten.

I take each finger into my mouth, swirling my tongue around the digits as I look into her eyes. Her hand stalls on my cock before she releases me.

Fuck. "I don't have any condoms."

Her eyes are on my mouth, when she replies, "We don't need one."

My brows tug together. I know I'm clean but we should still use protection.

"I mean, you can touch me and I'll touch you. Like this." She takes my hand, widening her legs as she guides me to her pussy. *Just as wet as I knew she would be.*

She wraps her hand around my cock, stroking my length. I rest my forehead on her shoulder and groan, "I won't last long, Van."

She's barely audible when she whispers, "That's okay. I don't think I will either."

I pull back, not wanting to shield her from the reactions she pulls from me. My thumb flicks over her clit as I push my index finger inside of her. I keep a steady pace, my eyes bouncing to the paradise between her legs and the beauty that is her face.

Licking her palm, Savannah wraps her hand back around my cock. Her strokes match my rhythm and our combined pants fill the space between us.

When I'm certain she can take more, I add another finger. Tremors wrack her body, telling me she's close. Her chin drops to her chest as mewls of satisfaction roll off her tongue. "Noah, I'm so close. I'm going to come."

The pressure I put on her clit is unrelenting, pushing her toward the edge. My own pleasure forgotten as I want her to come undone on my hand first. Her body tenses and contracts around me.

The image of reaching her release and her grip tightening on my cock has my balls drawing up and spurts of cum flying onto my stomach. My heart races as I try to catch my breath.

Euphoria crashes into me, leaving my body feeling light and free. I never thought I would get to experience something like this with her. I'm both amazed and terrified at the reality. Amazed because it's Savannah, and she's everything I ever dreamed of. But terrified because of how complicated this makes things.

Savannah's limbs visibly relax and I drag her down

with me onto the mattress, careful to keep her away from my mess.

Her voice is sleepy as she yawns. "Do you think it'll always be like that?"

I fucking hope so. It's never been like that with anyone else, that's for sure.

"I think so," I murmur into her hair.

When I can finally move, I go to the bathroom, grabbing a towel. She doesn't hide from me as I clean her up and her eyes are still hungry as I move onto cleaning myself.

She's going to be the reason I end up in an early grave.

I'll be fucked to death. It doesn't actually sound like such a bad way to go.

Discarding the towel in the hamper, I return to the bed and climb under the covers behind her.

She doesn't say anything when I tug her back into my arms.

That night I have the best sleep I've had in years. It's deep and unbroken. The only thing I can attribute it to is having Savannah in my arms.

THIRTY-FIVE

Savannah

A giddiness overtakes me as I unlock the apartment door and rush through. *I can't believe I got the part.* The first person I wanted to tell when I got the call was Noah, but I wasn't sure if he'd be free to take my call. And I figured, this isn't something you share in a phone call.

I throw my keys in the bowl on the table by the door and kick off my snow boots. It's Christmas season in New York and I love it. Lights line the streets and snow falls nearly every day. It's almost magical.

Dropping my bag on the floor, I shrug out of my jacket, hanging it in the closet by the door. It's not until I turn to get my bag that my eye catches the tree that Noah and I put up last weekend all lit up. It looks beautiful. And with the snow falling outside as a backdrop, it's like something out of an old movie.

When I pick up my bag, my happiness dims slightly

as the lease for an apartment I found in Brooklyn peaks out at me. Tomorrow, I'm due to sign it and pick up the keys. It's the thing I've been saving for these past few months, but there's none of the excitement I was hoping to feel with getting my own place.

How can I sign the lease when—if I take the part—I'll be going out of town for at least three months?

That'll be three months without Noah.

For the past two, we've become closer than I could have ever imagined. Each night he's made my body come alive with an intimacy I thought only ever happened in romance books. And then I've had the best sleep, falling into a deep slumber cocooned in his arms. I'm not sure how I'll cope for so long without him. He's an addiction that I don't want to quit.

I guess I can't have it all.

Resigned, I bend to pick up my bag. A crash in the kitchen makes me snap up, my spine ramrod straight. *Is Mary still here? No, it's too late, she'll have finished cleaning up hours ago.*

With my bag forgotten, I take a step forward. Clearly, my feet have decided that it would be best to confront the intruder. My head is screaming at me to leave the apartment.

Noah steps into the living room and my shoulders sag with relief at not having to fight for my life. His eyes twinkle as a smile breaks out on his face. "I thought I heard the door. I'm making dinner. Are you hungry?"

My brows pull together in confusion because he

should be at work. I can count on one hand how many times Noah has been home before me and not cooped up in his office. "Why are you here?"

He chuckles as he scrubs a hand over his beard and replies, "I live here, angel. Did you forget? Because I'll happily make my presence known to you."

Heat sparks in his eyes as a darkness overtakes his handsome face. His tongue darts out, leaving a glistening trail over his lips. The Noah I knew before we started hooking up never would have said something like that.

Shaking off my arousal, I hold up my hand as I walk toward him. "Woah, slow down, cowboy. I meant, I thought you would be back late. I'm starving for actual food. And I have news. What's for dinner?"

I go to walk past him into the kitchen, but his hand on my waist stops me. He tugs me into him, capturing my lips with his own. "I wanted to see you. What's the news?"

Smiling against his mouth, I reply, "Food first."

He pulls back, his gaze searching mine. My stomach gurgles, easing some of the tension. I'm nervous to tell him, because part of me is worried he'll tell me to go and then where does that leave us?

I walk into the kitchen, the smell of spaghetti and garlic bread filling my nostrils. Noah moves about with ease, plating up two servings as I watch the movement of his body. His arms flex and his muscles ripple under the tight fabric of his t-shirt. When he's done, he carries the food over to the table, throwing me a wink as he passes. He's lit two candles, adding to the intimacy.

My voice comes out almost wistful. "You know, a girl could get used to this kinda treatment."

Noah pulls back a chair and inclines his head. I really don't need to be asked twice. Sidling over to the table, I take the offered seat and inhale the tomato-y aroma from the plate in front of me. It looks so good.

He's marriage material, that's for sure.

The thought catches me off guard. I gobble the delicious pasta down like I'm a pig with a full trough, distracting myself from the spiral that will inevitably come.

Moans spill from my lips as I devour the food in front of me. Reaching out, I pick up a slice of garlic bread, dipping it in the sauce. When the flavors explode on my tongue, I wiggle in my seat, unable to sit still.

With a heated gaze, Noah watches me, his untouched plate sitting in front of him. His voice is thick with lust when he asks, "Are you enjoying that?"

Nodding, I finish my mouthful before replying, "Yes. Thank you."

Resting his fork on the edge of his plate, Noah picks up his wine glass, bringing it to his lips. The motion of his throat bobbing as he takes a sip momentarily distracts me from my food.

Why is his throat so sexy?
It's thick and strong...
Goodness, what is wrong with me?

Humor laces his words, as he asks, "What's your news?"

Right. Stop being a perv, Van.

"Oh. Well, I got a part for a small show."

A wide grin splits across his face and he puts his glass down. Leaning across the table, he gives me his full attention. "Shit, Van. That's amazing. When do you start?"

Twisting my mouth, I look down at my plate, suddenly not so hungry. With too much precision, I place my fork on the edge, buying myself some time before I lift my gaze to his. "I think I'm gonna turn it down."

Noah's brows tug together as he asks, "Why? Isn't this what you want to do? Won't it help you get closer to being on Broadway?"

Right now, I hate that he knows what my dreams are, because I know Noah and he'll push me to achieve them. No matter what.

My gaze moves to look out the window at the snow blanketing the city. It brings me a sense of peace before I turn to him. "I have responsibilities, including signing a lease tomorrow for my own apartment. And I'll need to keep up with the jobs I have to pay for that. There'll be other roles, I'm certain."

Confusion fills Noah's voice and his brows tug together forming a groove when he asks, "What do you mean you're signing a lease tomorrow?"

He's got to see how odd this is. Us living together.

And sleeping together. Especially when we aren't anything more than a hookup. At least I think we aren't.

"Don't you think it's a bit weird living with your booty call? I mean, even when I move out, we can still hook—"

My words are cut off when Noah pushes back his chair, standing above me. He puffs out his chest before he bends, resting his splayed hands on the table. His face is inches from me and I squirm in my seat. Anger mixed with lust swirls in his hazel gaze.

With an oddly calm voice that portrays none of the angry fire raging in his eyes, he says, "Savannah, you're not a fucking booty call and if you refer to yourself like that again, I'll make it so you can't sit on your 'booty' for a *fucking* week. You are my girlfriend. End of story."

Amusement fills my face at the same time as my chest flutters with excitement. Folding my arms over my chest, I tilt my head as I ask, "Do I get a say in that?"

Noah huffs out a laugh as he collapses into his chair. Scrubbing his hand over the back of his neck, he replies, "Well, of course you do."

"Okay. Because I have standards for my boyfriends."

He cocks a brow. "Really?"

"Will, not included. But my point is, you know you haven't actually taken me on a date, right?

Noah's eyes widen and his brows lift, reaching for his hairline. He looks away from me, and I watch as he tries to find a date when we've gone out. "That can't be right."

Crossing my legs, I pick up my glass, taking a sip

before I reply, "It is right. We've had lots of sex and eaten in together a whole bunch but we haven't stepped foot outside of this apartment to go on a date."

Clearing his throat, he sits up in his seat. "Okay. Well that's gonna change." Almost sheepishly, Noah asks, "I don't know if maybe you want to come to the holiday party at Parker and Anderson next Friday? As my date."

I can't help the smirk that pulls at my lips, because despite my cool facade, Noah *freaking* Parker just asked me on a date. Heck, he called me his *girlfriend*. "I would love that."

"Great. That's settled." He fights against his grin before it breaks free. Lifting out of his chair, he leans across the table and captures my lips with his. When he pulls away slightly, he whispers, "It's fucking fantastic, angel."

Playfully rolling my eyes, I push at his shoulder, unable to keep the smile from my face. I feel like a teenager. I'm giddy all over again but for a whole other reason.

Taking his seat, Noah stares at me, his gaze going serious as he says, "If I asked you to do something for me, no questions asked, would you?"

I'd do almost anything for him so my answer is almost immediate. "Of course."

"Do you promise?"

Where is he going with this?

My mind immediately goes to something sexual

before I check myself. He'd be playful about that. Not cryptic like he's being now. This is something serious.

I nod at the same time as I say, "If it's something illegal though, I reserve the right to politely decline."

Noah chuckles. "It's not illegal."

Holding out his pinky finger, I huff out a laugh before linking mine with his. His eyes light up, and a flutter twitches in my stomach. I have a feeling I shouldn't have agreed to this. He tugs our joined fingers toward his lips, kissing my finger before urging me to do the same.

As soon as my lips leave his finger, he says, "Now that we've agreed. What I'm asking you to do, which you can't say no to, is quit all the jobs that don't involve you doing your passion and take the part."

My eyes go wide at his demand. He's one fry short of a Happy Meal if he thinks I'd do that. That's the only rational explanation for his demand.

Laughter bubbles up and spills from my lips. "Right. And then I'll truly be a starved artist. A homeless one, to boot."

"We've already solved your housing situation. You're my girlfriend and we live together." He shrugs like it's not a big deal.

"Noah, I can't just live here," I plead, begging for him to understand. "And anyway I have bills to pay."

"You already live here—"

"Temporarily," I correct, cutting him off.

Turning his seat to face me, he moves his hand between my legs and grips my chair, tugging me around the table toward him. I don't try to stop him. Even if I wanted to, I couldn't. My eyes are glued to the veins popping on his forearm as it rests between my legs.

"I don't think I've been clear enough. You." He points toward me. "Are my." He points to himself. "Girlfriend. This is our home and there's no point in you moving out to only move back in a couple of months.

"I'll cover any bills you have because I want you to fulfill your dreams, angel. And being realistic about it, that's not going to happen anytime soon if you're burying yourself in work that has nothing to do with what you want to accomplish. I'm giving you the chance to do it, and I don't want anything in return."

"I ca—"

He cuts me off with a kiss. It starts out testing, before growing deeper and more urgent. Our mouths are still connected when I stand, placing my hands on his shoulders as I straddle his lap. We nip, suck, and lick at each others mouths.

Noah grabs handfuls of my ass cheeks as I roll my hips into his hardness, my need for him clear. Sparks build between us and I know that just like every time we come together it will be a colorful explosion of light and *love*.

Pulling away, Noah carries me to the living room where he unceremoniously dumps me on the couch. A squeal leaves my lips and I tip my head to the side as I look up at him.

"Hey," I sulk.

Pulling his bottom lip into his mouth, he scrubs his hand over his beard, tugging on the hairs. It's like he's trying to decide what to do.

Or committing me to memory.

"I like you like this," he grunts.

I look down at my body, confused by what he could mean. I'm fully clothed. "Like what?"

When he looks away, I watch his chest rise and fall as he composes himself. His voice is a growl, filled with a hunger that matches my own. "Flustered. Turned on. Needy. And ready for me to fuck you."

Oh.

He bends down, his hand cupping me through the fabric of my leggings. I squirm under the light pressure, rocking my hips into his palm.

His voice is dark and laden with lust when he says, "Just like I thought. Your greedy little pussy is soaking wet and practically begging for me. Isn't she, angel?"

My body trembles as I nod, desperate for him to give me more.

With a shake of his head and a knowing smirk on his lips, Noah releases me and strides across the room. My mind reels at the abrupt change. I sit up on my elbows, watching him as he moves to the front door and retrieves my bag. He makes quick work of the space between us, falling back onto the couch by my feet.

I can't keep the frown from my face when he lifts my legs and rests my feet in his lap. "Are we not going to have sex?"

Snickering, Noah replies, "You have something to do first."

With my purse open, he holds it toward me so I can find whatever it is he thinks I have to do. The only things in there are my lip gloss, lip balm, bank card, the lease and my phone.

I pull out my lip balm, holding it up to him. "Was this your way of telling me that my lips are chapped?"

It's his turn to roll his eyes. Inclining his head toward my bag, he asks, "Do you mind?"

"Go for it. I'd love to know what you think is more important than this." With a raised brow, I wave my hand down my body.

"Absolutely nothing is more important than you, angel," he mutters.

He pulls out the lease, tsking at me before he throws it on the table. Within seconds, he pulls out my phone, holding it out to me.

Blindly I take it, saying, "Who am I calling?"

With a smile that tells me I'm not winning this one, he replies, "You have some jobs to quit. I'm not touching you until you've done it."

Wiggling my toes, I look down at them pointedly and taunt, "You're not doing a very good job not touching."

Noah follows my eyes down to where his hands are gently massaging my aching feet. The moment he realizes, he shoots up from the couch. "Christ, Van. Just quit the jobs so I can bury myself in you."

I can't hold back the chuckle as I reply, "So romantic, Noah."

With a grin on my face, I bring up the task app and close down my account. There isn't any hesitation or worry as I go about quitting the jobs I've held down for years.

Next is a text to Sasha telling her I'm sorry for the short notice, but I can't come back because of the role. The final message is to Mindy, my boss at the bar. Her response is almost immediate and simply says, 'Congratulations'.

Sliding my phone onto the coffee table, I look at him and say, "It's done."

Holding his hand out, Noah helps me to sit up and straddle his lap as he takes a seat on the couch. "And you'll take the part?"

And be away from you for three months, if not more?

My fingers fiddle with the fabric of his black t-shirt before I reply, "I don't know. It's gonna mean I go away for a while."

Noah's hands rub over my thighs and I'm not entirely sure he knows he's doing it. But either way, it's soothing and eases the ache settling in my chest.

"How long?"

I swallow, unsure if he'll still be as excited about it when I tell him. My eyes seek him out as I say, "Three months, maybe more."

His eyes widen as he looks away momentarily. "Wow. That's a long time."

Neither of us speaks for a moment, the reality of what this would mean cloaking us in a cloud of sadness. I open my mouth to speak at the same time as Noah does.

"It's okay, angel. I'll come out and see you every chance I get, and we can call or video chat. We'll make it work."

I love this man.

Leaning forward, I capture his lips with mine, afraid that if I speak, I'll tell him just that. Instead, I tell him with my body how much I'll miss him and how deeply I care for him.

THIRTY-SIX

Noah

My throat feels thick. Like I'm being slowly suffocated by my own body and no matter how much I gasp for air, I can't get enough. Running a finger around the collar of my shirt does nothing to ease the feeling of being strangled.

Jack is a silent partner in the firm, although he still hasn't quite grasped the idea of the silent part and likes to come into the office on occasion. Which means he knows half the people in this room.

Was this a bad idea?

Christ, who am I kidding? Of course it was a bad idea. How can you not remember a fucking knockout like Van?

She's looking like a sexy Mrs. Klaus tonight in her tight red dress and silver strappy shoes with fur around the ankles. Her lips are coated in a red lipstick. She had to fix it before we left the apartment, because I couldn't help myself.

A pain hits me in the chest, twisting and tightening with each breath I drag in.

I feel guilty.

For wanting her. For betraying Jack. For hurting one of them when this inevitably comes to light.

Right now, Savannah's talking to a group of guys that work in our IT department. Instead of a feeling of pride at her being mine, I'm stuck with the panic at being outed and not prepared for the possibility of my thirteen year friendship coming to an end.

Savannah lifts her head, her eyes searching for me.

When she finds me, a soft smile lights up her face before her brows pull together with concern. She turns to excuse herself from the group, and I watch the gentle sway of her hips as she walks toward me.

It's the strangest feeling, wanting to be seen by someone at the same time as wanting to hide from them. The weight of it all feels like it's crushing me.

I was fine asking her to come with me, but as the week has gone on, having her here has plagued my mind. Every waking thought is filled with what if's. What if Jack finds out before I can tell him? What if Savannah tells someone she's with me? What if I told her I couldn't do this?

I throw back my drink, placing the empty glass on the table beside me. There's one thing I know for certain. I won't give her up. I can't. She has my heart and has for thirteen years.

"Here you are, man." Teddy claps me on the shoulder, his gray eyes alight with mischief.

The smile I give him feels fraudulent on my lips. He's dressed in his signature black suit and shirt, looking like he's going to a funeral.

Hell. He just might.

When Jack finds out I've been fucking his sister, he's going to kill me. And I can't blame him.

"Hey, Teddy, how are you?" Savannah asks, coming to a stop in front of us.

Hunger fills her gaze when she turns to me. My body relaxes as I inhale her signature scent and I stuff my hands in my pockets to keep from touching her. As conflicted as I am about the betrayal of my promise to Jack, one thing is clear, I still want her. As much as, if not more than, my next breath.

"Hi, Van. You look delectable this evening," Teddy praises pulling me back into the party.

My neck snaps to him, as a wave of fury races through me. If I could kill a man with one look, he would be dead.

Savannah rests her hand on my arm, sensing my mood. "Thank you, Teddy, but I'd appreciate it if you kept those thoughts to yourself."

Saved by my angel, Anderson.

My fingers clench in my pocket, as my anger ebbs.

Teddy inclines his head, oblivious to how close he's skating to the edge, chuckling. "As you wish. How are you?"

A smile spreads across Savannah's lips, the whiteness of her teeth a stark contrast to the red of her lips. "I'm just fine and dandy. How a—"

"Noah, it's a wonderful turn out," Patrick Olsen interrupts, his granddaughter, Evie, on his arm. "Teddy," he greets tersely.

I thought I could keep them apart but I've been so distracted with my own spiraling panic that keeping an eye out for Patrick was the last thing on my mind. Taking his outstretched hand, I greet him distractedly.

The last thing I need is for shit to hit the fan between Teddy and Patrick. Teddy needs to let it go. Could *I do that with Savannah if I had to?*

My response is an immediate–*no*. But in reality, would I have a choice?

The last time Teddy saw Evie was when she broke things off with him. He came in for the final takeover meeting and barely said two words the entire time, instead boring a hole into the side of Patrick's head with his searing gaze. Fury and heartache rolling off him in waves.

Teddy knocks back his whiskey, his eyes on Evie as a tension builds, swirling around us all like a hurricane. "Mr. Olsen. Evie." He inclines his head to them before continuing, "Please, excuse me."

Turning on his heel, Teddy walks through the room, his back ramrod straight. I make a mental note to check in with him later.

"And who is this, Noah?" Patrick asks, as if Savannah

isn't perfectly capable of introducing herself. His inability to move into the present century is part of the reason his business was taken over by the firm.

Distractedly, I reply, "Mr. Olsen, this is Savannah. Jack's little sister."

Out of the corner of my eye, I see Savannah's body tense before she forces herself to relax. Pasting a smile on her face, she holds out her hand. "It's a pleasure to meet you."

Patrick lifts Van's hand to his lips, pressing a kiss to the back of it. He holds on a fraction too long, and I stiffen, giving him a stern glare. The silence building between us before he releases her hand and pulls Evie forward, presenting her to Savannah.

"This is my granddaughter, Evie. Why don't you be a dear and give her a tour while the men talk business?"

His inability to treat women as equals is part of the reason we'll be offering him a more than generous severance package come Monday. When we took over, we had no choice but to keep him at the helm, but with our handpicked team in place, now is the right time.

If he doesn't accept our offer, we'll terminate our agreement. Teddy doesn't know, and I'm not entirely sure how he'll feel about it when he finds out. My stomach twists, and a pain settles in it.

Savannah tips her head to the side at Patrick's request. A fire burns bright in her gaze before she catches herself, shutting down in front of my eyes. "I would love to, but I was just telling Noah here, how I don't feel too good, so I'm headin' home."

Confusion pulls my brows together. She didn't say anything. God, I've been so wrapped up in worrying about being caught that I haven't even noticed she's not well. Resting my hand on her lower back, I lean into Savannah. My voice is low as I talk into her hair. "I'll call Rupert and meet you out front in five. I've just got to say goodbye."

When I pull back, her usually vibrant eyes are cold and hard. My stomach sinks when she takes a step back and my hand drops to my side. I watch as she retreats into herself, shutting me out.

"I don't need you." Her message is clear, even though she continues, "To come with me."

With that, she wishes Evie and Patrick a good night before walking away. My mind reels from the interaction. I don't understand what I've done wro—

Shit.

How could I be so stupid? I was too in my own head about Jack finding out, and I completely disregarded her feelings. We never discussed how I should introduce her to people. But of all the options at my disposal, introducing her as Jack's sister was probably the worst I could have gone with.

I should have taken her out to dinner as our first date.

I've really fucked this up.

My chest tightens, and I instinctively rub my palm over the center as I stare after her.

Patrick is half walking away to speak to Nick from finance when he calls, "I will speak to you later, Noah."

Holding my hand out to him, I reply, "I'm actually heading out. I have an important meeting in the morning."

He eyes me suspiciously, clearly not believing my lie, before he clasps my hand and gives it a firm shake.

"I will speak to you soon then."

With that, he walks away, leaving me to my misery, watching longingly in the direction Savannah left in.

I need to make it right with her. But I wouldn't be surprised if she wanted nothing to do with me, especially after I all but demanded she be my girlfriend a week ago. My stomach feels heavy with the guilt of sending her so many mixed messages.

A quiet voice next to me cuts through my berating thoughts. "You should go after her. It's clear she's more to you than your friend's little sister. I saw the way you looked at each other from across the room. The way your eyes have tracked her all night, even if you thought you were being subtle about it. When you love someone, you shouldn't ever let them go."

Regret coats Evie's words, and I get a glimpse into the sorrow she's carrying with her. "It'll be the biggest regret of your life. And it'll break your heart with every day that passes as you watch her crumble in front of you."

Evie squeezes my forearm before walking away in the direction that Teddy left.

Was that a pep talk for her or for me?

But more importantly, do I love Savannah?

I know that I care deeply about her but is it love?

Despite having told Savannah that I needed to say goodbye to people, my feet carry me toward the exit. A desperate need to see my girl and right my wrongs spurring me on.

All of the lights are off when I enter the apartment. It feels cold and lonely. The whole ride home, my body felt cold as my thoughts spiraled, going over all the worst case scenarios. I listen for a moment, waiting for any sounds to tell me where she might be.

Please be here, angel.

Wishful thinking has me walking toward the main bedroom. A month ago, we brought new sheets and I had a new mattress delivered so that she felt comfortable sleeping in the room I used to share with Sutton. We've spent every night since wrapped around each other, alternating between sleeping and making love.

Even as my steps eat up the space, a weight settles in my stomach. *She won't be in there.* She's shutting me out. If she's in the apartment, she'll be as far from this room as she can get. *In her old room.*

The door to the main bedroom is open, the room shrouded in darkness, but I still see her. My body relaxes, surprise and hope burning through me at her being here. She's hugging her legs to her chest as she sits in the chair by the window looking out over the city.

A sadness similar to the one I've carried with me since she left the party cloaks her. It's like a darkness is seeping in, consuming her, where there should only be light.

Still a glimmer of hope at her being in *our* room, ignites inside of me as I stand on the threshold, my eyes drinking her in. She's changed into a pair of sweats and a slouchy sweater that hangs off one shoulder. Her face is free of makeup and her dark gingerbread blonde hair is piled on top of her head in a messy bun. If it's even possible, she looks even more beautiful than she did at the party.

She doesn't turn to me when she speaks. Her voice is flat and void of any emotion. "You didn't have to leave early. I'm just going to bed."

My mouth goes dry and my pulse kicks up another notch at the invisible walls she's built around herself. "I wanted to be with you, angel. Can we talk about this?"

I don't miss the flinch at the use of her nickname. A desperation to make this better fuels me and I cross the room in a hurried stride, dropping to my knees in front of her. My hands rub the smooth skin of her thighs, seeking comfort from her. Anything to tell me that I haven't fucked everything up over a handful of misspoken words.

Her voice is quiet and lost when she says, "I think it's probably a good thing that I'm going out of town on Sunday. We both need some space to figure out what exactly it is we want. What happened tonight hurt me, Noah."

Guilt consumes me and I drop my chin to my chest, unable to look at her. "Christ, I know, angel. I'm so sorry. I've..." I swallow thickly, lifting my eyes to hers as I silently beg her to understand. "I've really been struggling with guilt at betraying Jack. I never wanted to hurt you. It was the last thing on my mind. I panicked and the words that I've said a million times to describe you just came out."

She stands abruptly, forcing me to back up.

Pacing at the end of the bed, she turns to face me. "I don't want to say anything that I might regret, Noah. But you need to hear this. It should never have been a promise that you made. And it certainly shouldn't have a hold over you like it does. I'm not a kid anymore and neither are you. We're two consenting adults who have feelings for each other."

I walk toward her, cupping her face. She has to understand. I need her to see what a big deal this is.

Looking into her eyes, I beg, "I hear you. But I'm afraid. He's seen so much of me and he's stood by my side through it all. It almost feels like I'm chucking it all in his face while stabbing him in the back. You have to understand, it's the longest friendship I've ever had, Van. I'm afraid to lose him. I don't want to lose you either. And I'm very aware of the fact that I can't have it all."

"But you can. Don't you see that? Jack would understand. Thirteen years is a long time to hold you to a promise."

I rest my forehead on hers, closing my eyes. My words a whispered plea, "Angel, I just need more time."

When I open my eyes, I find Savannah's closed, a sad smile on her face. Her hands reach up to hold my wrists before she pulls them away and steps out of my reach. The sense of loss engulfs me, pulling me deeper into despair.

"And I could do with some space. I'm going to sleep in my room tonight. Like I said, it seems the timing of my workshop was just right."

She steps forward and presses a soft kiss to my cheek before walking out of the room. I want to scream at her that this is her room. That her place is with *me*. But my words are stuck in my throat, refusing to come out. Instead, I watch as she walks away from me.

THIRTY-SEVEN

Savannah

I t was a mistake to come tonight. I've been visiting Jack this weekend and, for the most part, I've managed to avoid seeing Noah. Jack sprung it on me last minute that he's throwing a party tonight, and I thought it would be the perfect opportunity to show Noah what he's missing out on. And although I feel sexy and confident, my stomach still twists at the sight of him.

If I'd listened to my gut when it told me to not go out tonight, I wouldn't be staring at Noah as he dusts kisses over the neck of the girl he came with.

She's real pretty too.

Soft features, dark hair and a slender body. She's everything I'm not.

Maybe this is what I needed. To see him with someone else. To really hammer home that he meant what he said last year. That I'm not his type. I made a mistake thinking he would ever be interested in a girl like me. Sorry, a *kid* like me.

Ever since the pool house incident last year, Noah and I have grown distant. I've avoided him whenever we've been at the same thing, which has been on less than a handful of occasions. I don't plan on changing that now. Especially when, thinking back on the incident, embarrassment, anger, and shame are the only things I feel.

Well, screw you, Noah Parker.

I look darn good and I'm not going to mope around after a guy who's too stupid to see what a catch I am.

Spinning on my heel, my drink splashes out over the rim of my cup when I collide with a solid, very male, body.

My hands dart out, brushing at the liquid as it seeps into his t-shirt. It's only when a deep chuckle vibrates the stomach under my hand that I realize I'm basically feeling up a stranger. It's a very flat and defined stomach.

"You know, if you wanted to touch me, you didn't need to spill a drink on me, gorgeous. For a pretty girl like you, well, you can touch me anywhere you like."

An idea forms and my hand reaches out and under his shirt before I can stop myself. I look up into his light brown eyes from under my lashes. He's a good looking guy, a straight nose and full lips snag my attention. With a height that reminds me of Noah and an athletic build that tells me he looks after himself, if I wasn't set on using him for a one night stand, he'd be a catch. "I can touch you here?"

His hand reaches out and lands on my hip, squeezing as he flexes his fingers. "Yes," he grunts.

Moving my hand lower, I rest it on the buckle of his belt as I press my chest into his. Whispering, I ask, "How about here?"

An arm wraps around my bicep and I'm tugged away from the stranger. A sultry smirk covers my lips as I look at his confused expression. Tingles erupt from the contact, traveling through my body until I feel energized and aroused.

I know exactly who's grabbed hold of me.

I will myself to feel nothing.

It's all in my head.

None of it is real.

Noah opens the door to Jack's bedroom, all but throwing me inside. My eyes scan the dark room, grateful that Jack isn't in here. When I think about it, it's kinda surprising that he isn't, given he's been making out with the same girl for the last hour. *Eww, not an image I need to bring to mind ever again.*

Noah's voice holds a warning as he says, "Angel."

An involuntary jerk wracks through my body. I hate that nickname. And the fact that he's using it, rubbing salt in my wounds, makes me hate him more.

Do I mean that?

Folding my arms over my chest, I turn to face him, coming up short at his proximity. The space between us is practically nonexistent and I fight against the rising tide of arousal that being near him always seems to crest when he's near.

I should take a step back. Move to the other side of the room. Yes. If my feet would just move, that's exactly what I'd do. Pulling in short sharp breaths through my mouth, my brain tells my body to move. Nothing happens.

His voice is tortured, as if he too feels whatever is happening right now. My name a plea on his lips, "Savannah."

When I tip my head back to look at him, his gaze drops to my mouth. *I think he might kiss me.*

Noah lifts his hand, smoothing his fingers down my cheek. "I just wanted to tell you to be careful. These aren't like the guys you're used to hanging out with."

A groove forms between my brows as his words register. There he goes, dousing me in a metaphorical bucket of ice cold water. Pain settles in my chest and I sink into the feeling. I allow it to consume me and fuel my anger.

My anger at him for saying what he said a year ago. For making me feel like I wasn't good enough and that everything that had passed between us was just my imagination. Anger that he thinks he has any say in who I talk to, flirt with, or even have sex with.

Pulling in a breath, I blow it out slowly, soothing myself so I don't scream at him. My words come out calm and calculated as I say, "Despite what you might think, Noah, you aren't my brother or my father. I'm twenty years old. I can fuck whoever I want. And I don't appreciate you draggin' me away from someone who was darn right willin' to satisfy my needs when you have no intention of doing so."

When he doesn't answer, I tilt my head and look him up and down. Still nothing. He just looks angry.

"Have a good night, Noah. I know I certainly will." I throw a wink at him as I go to move past him toward the door.

His arm darts out and his hand lands on my hip, stopping my movement. Goosebumps form on my skin from his touch. His voice is a low growl when he says, "This is the sort of shit that pisses me off about you, Savannah."

I take a step back, folding my arms over my chest. "And what might that be?"

"I'm trying to look out for you and you're throwing it back in my face."

Fury clouds my vision and I poke him in the chest. Undeterred by the party happening on the other side of the door, I shout, "I don't need you to look out for me. Or try to be my friend."

Noah grabs a hold of my wrist, holding it above my head as he backs me up. The air leaves me in a rush as I hit the wall. My startled gaze lifts to his.

Dipping down, he rests his forehead on mine, "Fucking hell, angel, I don't want to be your friend. I want—"

He's cut off when the bedroom door swings open. I've never seen Noah move as fast as he does when he realizes it's Jack on the threshold.

I can't get a read on Jack's expression, the light behind him obscures his face. His voice gruff, almost chastising as he asks, "What's going on in here?"

Leaning against the wall, I try to catch my breath. My mind is stuck on what might have happened had Jack not stormed in.

Noah scrubs his hand over the back of his neck, sheepishly he replies, "I was just warning Van about O'Donnell."

Skepticism coats Jack's words as he says, "Right. You definitely weren't doing anything else with my sister."

Not bothering to wait for whatever excuse Noah will give, I push away from the wall and walk from the room to find O'Donnell, determined to have fun.

And maybe spite Noah.

THIRTY-EIGHT

Savannah

I *'m homesick.*

It's been thirty one days since I last saw Noah Parker and I miss him like I miss my mama's chicken 'n dumplin's. But I miss him more.

He's been a distraction of the best but worst kind. This is the first time in my life that I haven't been able to throw myself into a workshop and give it my all. I haven't been sleeping, my body feels like it's been repeatedly run over by a truck, and worst of all, I haven't been eating properly. Nothing seems to make sense without him.

Of course, we've been texting and calling where we can, but it just isn't the same. And it hasn't been as often as I would like due to my unrelenting schedule. Each time we do talk, he seems just as sad as I am about the distance that's grown between us.

Or maybe I'm just projecting.

The second I sat on that bus and watched as it pulled away, I knew I wanted to come back to him. It was like I was leaving a piece of my heart behind and I haven't been whole since I left. I'm desperately confused. He told me a week before the holiday party that I was his girlfriend, then he introduces me as Jack's sister. This is just like him. Always hot and then cold. He's been like this the entire time I've known him. The promise he made to Jack can't be something he allows to come between us. I need him to be all in.

Who am I kidding? It already has come between us.

I resent Jack for making him promise that.

My eyes burn with unshed tears as my heart aches with a longing that might never be fulfilled. I don't know what I'm gonna do if he wants to keep us a secret, something to only be celebrated behind closed doors.

He's the love of my life, my soulmate, and I'll be a broken shell drifting through the world if I have to walk away for good.

I wish I'd never asked for the space, because I can't even take a guess as to what he might be thinking. At least if I was home with him, we could have talked.

Right, because that's worked so well for us in the past.

Since I left, there have been a couple of times on the phone that he's gone to say something. Hope has bloomed in my chest, only to be crushed by his muttered 'it doesn't matter' as he shuts down on me.

I don't like how it feels as if he's pulling away. Especially when I'm not there to keep him from spiraling into a pit of self hatred. But I also can't blame him, because I did the exact same thing after the holiday party.

All of this just brings me back to one thing: I miss him so much.

This workshop has been unlike anything I've ever experienced before. There have been many days when I've wanted to up and quit, exhausted from months of working myself to the bone and unable to feel any excitement for the show. But I've pushed through, knowing that this could be make or break for my career and the time apart is what we need. Even if it's not what I want.

Roise, my roommate, interrupts my heavy thoughts. "Come on, Van, we're going to be late."

Rosie is a unique character. She's quirky in a way that only comes from someone who's been in the business for years. Where I'm short with curves in most of the right places, she's tall and lithe. When I first met her, she seemed stuck up, but she's really relaxed these past four weeks. But that might have been more to do with the fact that she was getting tired of listening to me jabberin' on.

Glancing at my phone, I leap from my chair, realizing we have less than fifteen minutes to get to rehearsal. Rosie lets the door swing shut behind her as I swipe up my bag and grab my jacket from the back of my chair. Patting my pockets for my room key, I race after her when my hand lands on it in my back pocket.

Gabriel, our choreographer, hates it when we're late. The other week he made us all practice pirouettes ten times over until we could barely stand still. All because one person was late. I jog after Rosie as she heads in the direction of the elevator, not putting it past her to leave without me.

The hotel the production company put us up in is nice. There's nothing fancy about it, but it has everything you could possibly need within a short distance or down in the lobby. It's certainly better than the one I was staying at all those months ago when Noah...

Every thought seems to lead me back to him.

I can't keep carrying on like this.

Shaking my head, I turn to Rosie, needing a distraction as we step into the elevator. "Do you think Gabriel will be in a better mood today?"

She pops an eyebrow at me. "Honey, the moon would fall from the sky before Gabriel's mood improves."

Chuckling, I reply, "Ain't that the truth."

I lean against the wall, my mind going back to Noah as I wonder what he's up to. *Probably working*.

He's thrown himself into his work again, and I'm really worried about him. I've seen how gaunt he's looks on the rare occasions we've video chatted. Teddy's been providing me updates, but I just know that he's not giving me the full picture. I should call Jack and ask him to check in with him.

No, I can't do that. He might ask questions I can't answer.

Maybe I can go home in a couple of weeks. I can see for myself if he's taking care of himself. No, that won't work. I don't have time for a trip. Maybe I should stop worrying about him and trust that he's an adult who knows how to look after himself.

I follow Rosie out of the elevator and through the lobby of the hotel, determined to stop thinking about Noah Parker. At least for five minutes.

THIRTY-NINE

Noah

I t's been the most hellish three months of my life. I haven't been eating or sleeping properly. My mind won't focus on work, and I've dropped the ball on so many things that I wouldn't be surprised if Teddy and Jack got together and ousted me.

I'm like a fucking lovesick puppy.

For the first time in my life, work hasn't been a priority for me.

The contrast isn't lost on me. That when Sutton and I broke up, I was able to carry on like normal, that the breakup was barely a blip on my radar. With Savannah, it's like my world has imploded.

All of this is why I left the meeting I was in. I couldn't concentrate. I didn't say a word. I just stood up and walked out. Hired a helicopter and flew the hour it took to get from Manhattan to Albany. It's why I'm now sitting in the back of a theatre, watching as she blows me away.

I just need to see her, then I'll leave. Being in the same room as her is enough for a blanket of calm to cover me. I relax back into the uncomfortable seat, sinking down low so as not to be seen.

As much as I want to make my presence known, I know that if we're going to work this out, I need to give her the space she asked for. Even though I fucking miss her and want to tell her how I feel. That I choose her. Nothing else matters. Just her.

I've done nothing but wrestle with this decision for months. Each day, I've flipped between claiming her as mine and keeping my promise to Jack.

An image of Jack comes to mind but I push it away along with the guilt. I can't keep going on like this, but I'm still afraid. Losing him as a friend is going to be like losing a brother. But I know I'll get through it, because I'll have her. And maybe Jack will come around eventually. *He'll be my brother-in-law one day, so he has to. Right?*

Either way, the betrayal is done and I can't take it back. Not that I would, because that would mean not having had her. I need to own my actions and step up to the plate for her, instead of cowering away like I have been.

The curtain closes and I stand with everyone else, applauding the performance. This run through is supposed to be closed to the public, but after making a six figure offer to the producer, I've been allowed to sit in and observe. Of course he was hesitant, but I wasn't going to let anyone or anything get in the way of seeing her. And it's not really my style to stalk her from a parked car.

When the curtain opens again, she bends at the waist before straightening. I swear it's like her gaze finds mine and the soft smile on her lips is only for me. My breath stalls in my throat. In my mind, I know it's impossible for her to see me, but it doesn't stop me from believing that she knows I'm here. That she wants to see me too.

I stay rooted to the spot as she disappears from my view again. At least ten minutes pass before I can get my body to move. My feet carry me from the center of the back row, out of the building and across the parking lot. All the while, a rushing sounds in my ears as I drown in my loneliness.

"Noah."

My heart races, and when I turn around, I see my angel. Her face breaks out into a smile and her hair flows in the breeze as she races toward me. With a halo of light behind her, she really does look like an angel. She leaps into my arms, wrapping her legs around my waist as her lips seek mine out.

Banding my arms around her, I hold her tight, allowing her to set the pace. Her tongue seeks entry into my mouth and I give it willingly. The strokes are gentle, as if she's savoring the taste. Hope erupts in my chest as a warmth floods my body. It's going to be okay. We're going to be okay. All my fears are slayed just holding her in my arms.

She pulls back, her fingers playing with the hair at the nape of my neck. Her voice is throaty when she says, "I missed you."

Fuck, if those three little words don't tell me so much yet, so little.

"I missed you too, angel."

I love you, angel.

With one hand, she strokes the side of my face before leaning in for another kiss. This one is chaste and like she couldn't help herself. It's the most natural thing for me to hold her in my arms like this. For our mouths to touch and my heart to race in her presence.

This doesn't feel wrong.

It's so fucking right.

She whispers against my mouth, breathless and needy, "Take me home."

I pull back, my gaze searching hers as hope blossoms in my chest. The need to take her back to New York, to lock us away in my apartment and lose myself in her for days is overwhelming.

"To a hotel, Noah. I can't leave."

Of course.

My stomach drops, and a weight settles heavy in my chest at the realization. Nodding, I slide her down my body, taking hold of her hand as I walk her to the car I arrived in. I wasn't planning on staying, so I don't have a room booked, but I won't let something as insignificant as that stop me from spending time with her.

Opening the door for her, I watch as she slides in and scoots across the seats, making room for me. I instruct the driver to take us to a hotel. Any five star hotel.

Relaxing into the seat, I hold her hand, rubbing small circles on the back as we cruise through the streets. My breaths are slow and easy and a looseness takes over my limbs. I'm content to just sit in her company, taking comfort in her touch.

It doesn't take long before we pull up outside the hotel, and when we're checked in, I take hold of her hand again, leading the way to the room.

On autopilot, I go through the motions of letting us into the room, my stomach twisting and churning with a nervousness I haven't felt in years. I take my time closing the door, knowing that a lot rests on this moment. When I'm ready, I turn, facing Savannah as she stares out of the window.

Where do I even start?

This should be easy, right? To convey the feelings I've had for her for years.

And yet, putting it into words seems like the hardest thing I've ever had to do.

Clearing my throat, I step forward. "Thank you for coming out to find me. I'd like it if we could ta—"

My words are cut off when Savannah spins to face me, pulling her t-shirt over her head in one swift movement. I'm frozen to the spot as her hands go to the waist-band of her leggings and she pushes them down her legs. When she's in nothing but her underwear, she walks toward me.

Her fingers make quick work of the buttons on my shirt, pushing the fabric off my shoulders with my jacket. She dusts kisses over the expanse of my chest, her words a plea as she demands, "Make me forget all the time we've been apart. Remind me what your hands feel like on my body, Noah. We can talk when I come home. Give me all of you, one last time."

My hand dives into her hair, pulling on the strands so her head is tipped back. A growl leaves my lips, vibrating deep in my chest at her words. Frustration, anger, desperation and hurt all fight to be heard when I say, "One last time, Savannah? I won't lay a hand on you if you tell me this is the end. There is no 'one last time' with us. Tell me you understand that? This isn't some-thing I can walk away from. Fuck, I need you like I need air to breathe."

Savannah whimpers, her fingers flexing on my waist. Her need for me is clear in her eyes, and with her whis-pered words of 'I understand', my mouth crashes onto hers.

Bending, my hands find the back of her legs, lifting her into my arms. Her thighs wrap around my waist and she clings on as I climb onto the bed.

Hovering above her, my hand skates down her

stomach and into her panties. *Just one touch and I'll be able to focus.* At the first swipe of her clit, a hiss escapes through her clenched teeth before she moans, arching into my touch.

Moving to the edge of the bed, I pull her panties down, greedily taking in her wet, pink pussy. Liquid pools at the entrance and I lick my lips, anticipation building inside of me. My hand finds my belt buckle, undoing it and pulling it through the loops. The entire time, my eyes are on her.

On my woman.

And the body nobody else will ever get to see, touch, or taste.

Mine.

I want to shout it from the rooftops and pound my chest for the world to see.

Heat pools in the pit of my stomach as I rush to undress. I'm naked before she can say my name, my approach to her one of desperate need. My hands skate up her legs, spreading them wide before I dip down and run my tongue through her slit. She tastes like candy; sweet and decadent.

Unashamedly, I devour her. Sucking on her clit as I push one finger inside her wet heat. Her body trembles and I know she's missed this as much as I have. Replacing my tongue with my thumb, and I rub small circles over her clit as I sit up to look down at her. She's writhing under my touch, coming alive as she tries like crazy to keep her eyes from closing.

Fuck, if I don't feel the same.

The need to take in every second while giving myself up to it.

My cock bobs against my stomach. Aching for relief that I'm trying to hold off from seeking. My hand wraps around my length, squeezing it almost painfully. Savannah's eyes follow the movement, and I can't help stroking myself for her.

Releasing my cock, I rest my hand on her stomach, applying a light pressure. Her eyes close and she squirms under my touch. My other hand is still working her, a steady pace with a relentless force pushing her toward her release.

My name is a breathless plea on her lips that I ignore. Instead, I add another finger, stretching her out as she leaks all over my fingers.

Angling them just right, I rub over her G-spot. The first swipe has her hands fisting the sheets. She looks perfect as she comes undone. Taking a mental picture, I continue with the pressure on her stomach.

She contracts around me, her eyes closed as her mouth drops open. Her expression almost pained. Little mewls spill from her lips as she claws at my forearm. Her body thrashes around on the bed, like the impending ecstasy is too intense for her to handle.

I feel powerful and elated that I get to see her like this. That my hands and body have her so on the edge of losing control.

Her orgasm is an eruption that I watch with satisfaction. My cock twitches painfully, begging for attention that I deny.

When I'm certain she's spent, I remove my hand, licking it clean.

Dazed and slightly confused, she searches for me. Her gaze lands on me, awe lightens her eyes, the gold like a ring of fire.

I don't give her time to recover. My need for her fuels my movements as I fist my cock. My thumb swipes at the pre-cum beading on the head, using it to lubricate myself. Leaning over her, I capture her lips as I slide home.

A hiss escapes from my lips and I rest my forehead against hers, closing my eyes as she spasms around me.

I gasp as I fight against the rising tide inside of me. "Fuck. I forgot the condom. I'm so sorry, angel."

Delicate fingers smooth over the lines that have formed on my face. When I open my eyes, I find nothing but affection gazing back at me. So much being said in her dark gaze. I don't want to be wrong about what I see there. My arms tingle with a hopefulness that slowly spreads from head to toe.

"It's okay. I'm on the pill and I..." She swallows thickly before continuing, "I trust you. I want to feel you inside of me. All of you."

Lifting up, she kisses me, moving her hips as she urges me on. Why does this feel like so much more than anything I've ever experienced before? Neither of us can stop this. Can stop *us*.

I start slow and steady, but when I feel her walls gripping me every time I bottom out, I can't control my hips. My thrusts are almost punishingly jerky as I chase out my completion.

My words come out hoarse, needing to make sure I haven't misunderstood her when I say, "I'm going to cum."

I go to move out of her, but her fingers dig into my ass cheeks, pulling me close. My eyes seek hers out, asking for permission even as I explode inside of her. Savannah's eyes flutter closed, her back arching as she comes, milking the last of my cum from me.

I love you.

Broken, I close my eyes, holding inside of her for a moment. When I open them, she's looking up at me, as the last spasms of her orgasm wrack through her body.

Certain that she's finished, I pull out and collapse onto the bed next to her. Our labored breaths are the only sounds filling the room. She's staring up at the ceiling, but when her hand reaches out to clasp mine, she turns to me with glassy eyes.

My brow furrows, confused at the lost look in her gaze. When I go to open my mouth, she lifts her finger, silencing me. Savannah buries herself into my side and I take the comfort I get from that simple act. My body relaxes and my eyes flutter closed as I succumb to the fatigue I've fought for the last three months.

In the morning, I'll force her to talk to me. For us to figure this out.

What just happened meant more than either of us might be ready for. But if we face it head on together, I know it'll be a journey of beauty and love. One where we can take on the world.

FORTY

Noah

A month ago, I woke up alone in a hotel room in Albany, New York. Savannah had skipped out in the night, leaving a note asking me to give her one more month and then we can figure us out. I thought something indescribable had happened between us, but she's been distant since that night, saying she needs to concentrate on her work.

I don't like how her distance makes me feel, like on her list of priorities I don't come first. For a moment, a wave of guilt descends upon me and I can't help but feel like this is just karma biting me on the ass for how I treated Sutton all those months. No matter how valid and time consuming work is, making someone feel like this, with a sense of rejection, is never justifiable.

The first time I've seen Van in person since that night was as she walked down the aisle earlier today. This morning, her bus was running late, so she went straight to Alex's to get ready. It's part of her bridesmaid duties, apparently.

Her light green dress floats around her, highlighting the warmer colors in her hair as it tumbles down her back in bouncy curls. For a second, as she walked down the aisle, I imagined what she'd look like walking down it in a different dress. Would I be her groom or would I be watching on as she pledged her love to another man?

The image of her smiling at another man, making her way to him in a wedding dress, winded me and no matter how hard I try to banish it from my mind, it keeps coming back. Haunting me and reminding me of the promise I made.

Christ. I so desperately want to have it all, but I know I can't.

Jack won't forgive me for this.

All the way through the ceremony, I watched her as it felt like my air supply was being cut off. I just don't know how to make this work. How do I have it all? How can I choose between the two of them?

My best friend and the girl I love.

In a daze, I met up with Savannah and traveled with her to the reception. We agreed to put the conversation we both know is coming on hold, to be there for Alex and Sebastian.

Savannah's showing Meghan and Ben steps to a dance routine. She's having fun, her head tipping back exposing the smooth column of her throat as she laughs loudly when she finds something especially funny.

Finishing my drink, I watch her freely. Her gaze lands on me and she sashays her way toward me with a drunken smile on her face. When she goes to sit in my lap, I stand. She doesn't hide her confusion at my sudden movement but she does brush it off. "Are you gonna come dance?"

I hold up my glass as I shove my freehand into my suit pants. "Just heading to the bar. You want anything?"

Her mouth forms a perfect 'O' before she closes it and shakes her head. She looks over her shoulder, pointing to Meghan and Ben. "No, thanks. I'm gonna go back to dancing." She walks away and I head to the bar.

I'm not stood at the bar for more than five minutes when she sidles up next to me. I turn to face her, asking, "You okay?"

"Yeah. Just changed my mind about that drink."

She reaches out to take my hand, but I move it away, my eyes on Sutton across the room as she talks to Meghan.

Hurt fills Savannah's beautiful blue gaze as she looks up at me. "Why won't you let me touch you?"

"It's not you, angel. It's me."

Savannah straightens, a knowing look on her face. "It's not you either. It's that stupid promise." A defeated sigh leaves her lips before she continues, "I can't believe I thought the time apart would help you see that what we have matters. I've been such a fool, putting my trust and heart in your hands, just for you to throw it back in my face. Again."

Her pace is quick as she storms from the room. Waves of angry energy roll off her as I follow.

Why can't I get it right when it comes to her?

She breaks out into the corridor. The door doesn't have time to close before I push through. Thankfully, the space is deserted.

My words come out as a growl, demanding that she listen to me. "Savannah, stop."

She halts, her back still to me before she whirls around. Fight is alight in her eyes as she shouts, "No, Noah, you stop! I'm tired of all o' *this*. Just leave me alone."

My anger turns to a plea, desperation taking over every ounce of my body. I need her to understand. She can't leave me. "You don't understand. I made him a promise."

I love her.

But I can't lose Jack either.

I watch as her shoulders slump and she looks down at her feet. There's nothing but sadness coating her words. A sadness I don't want there because it means she's shutting me out. "A promise you made thirteen years ago. Things change Noah, and that's okay."

At a loss for words, I can only look at her as she gives me a heartbreaking smile before she turns and walks away from me. Again.

"Savannah."

She doesn't stop this time.

Shit. I know I should follow her, but I've left my

phone and her coat at the table. Maybe in the time it takes me to get home, I'll have figured out how to tell her how I feel.

Returning to the ballroom, I weave my way through the tables. My path is intercepted by Sutton as she comes to a stop in front of me.

"Hi Noah, you're looking... I'd say good, but you look tired."

This is the last thing I need right now.

Exasperated, I say, "Hi Sutton. Thanks, you look great too."

I'm not really looking at her, my focus on getting out of here so I can find Savannah. I go to step around Sutton, but she follows my movement.

She doesn't speak until I look her in the eye and when I do, all I find is contentment. Sutton looks happy, like the weight of the world isn't crushing her.

Unlike me.

"I'm happy for the two of you, Noah. But you're really going to mess it up if you don't go after her. She deserves the world."

I look away, her words like a punch to the gut. Of course, I know what she's saying is the truth, but I might have fucked it up already.

My anger wins out and I turn to Sutton with malice I don't mean. "No offense, Sutton, but please stay out of this. You don't know shit. Whatever you think you saw, you're wrong."

Folding her arms over her chest, she doesn't back

down. Instead, she lifts a brow and replies, "I'd have to be blind to have mistaken what I saw. Don't treat me like a fool, Noah. I just need to tell you this one thing and then I want you to go and get her and figure it out. When we were together, you always struggled to verbalize your affection. You were great at showing me how you felt, but what Savannah needs from you is for those words to match the actions. If you can do that, then you can have it all."

She doesn't wait for me to respond, instead she turns on her heel and walks away.

I move toward the table, snatching up the items before leaving without so much as a goodbye to anyone. Determination guiding me as I race home.

Christ, I hope she's there.

FORTY-ONE

Savannah

I rush through the apartment door, throwing my clutch on the floor as I kick off my heels. Tears fill my eyes, but I refuse to let them fall. Noah might not realize it, but he's made his choice and I want to hate him for it but I can't.

I'll always love him because I always have. After everything we've been through and the hurtful words we've said to each other, it never faded or went away. All I can hope for now is that over time it'll get easier to not feel like he consumes me.

Moving into the living room, I pace in front of the windows. Panic settles in, taking root inside of me as it demands control. My body feels like it's on fire and the dress that once felt loose and airy, now feels tight and restrictive.

I had so much hope at the start of the day. Hope that he'd tell me he loved me enough to tell Jack.

Sucking in deep breaths, I pull back my shoulders refusing to give in. What I need is a plan. Something to tick off as I go through the motions of sorting out the end of a relationship that never really was.

First and foremost, I need to get out of this dress and take a shower. Maybe then I'll be able to think clearly. I know for certain that I can't stay here tonight. Maybe Jack's place is finished and I can stay there. If not, I'll check in to a hotel and then tomorrow, I'll set him free.

Free of the choice he thinks he has to make. In reality, he could have had it all but I don't think he'll ever see that. Jack would've understood. He wouldn't have stood in the way of us. But I'm not going to force Noah's hand by going behind his back and telling Jack myself.

On autopilot, I move through the apartment and shower in the bathroom I used before I moved into his room. I'm disconnected and the actions of showering and getting changed pass by in a blur.

I'm looking out of the window, committing the view to memory one last time when Noah walks through the door, his bow tie hanging loosely around his neck. The sight of him nearly brings me to my knees. He looks just as broken as I feel.

I follow his eyes to the bags by the front door. Rupert must have brought them up while we were at the ceremony. I hadn't even noticed them.

Wide eyes come to me, panic filling them as he races across the room. Dropping to his knees in front of me,

Noah grabs onto my hips as he buries his face in my chest.

"Please don't leave me, angel."

I swallow around the lump in my throat, my chest aching for him even as my mind screams at me to step away. Instinctively, my fingers dive into his hair as I rest my other hand on his shoulders. My fingers flex over the material of his tuxedo jacket.

One last touch and I will.

My voice sounds foreign to my own ears, like all the longing and pain of the last thirteen years is threatening to choke me. "Noah."

I release him, taking a step back, hoping the space will make my jumbled thoughts clearer. He stands and suddenly the man who was so sure and strong, looks lost and hurt. I thought I'd have more time to prepare my heart.

My throat hurts, every word painful as I push it past my lips. "I'm done with not being enough for you to break a promise you made thirteen years ago, Noah. I'm setting you free and taking back my heart. Honestly, I thought we would be in a better place, but today showed me how much of a hold Jack has over you.

"And what gets me the most is that he doesn't even know it. I refuse to let my love for you make me miserable because we have to remain behind closed doors. What we have, sorry, had, was beautiful and deserved to be seen in the daylight not locked away in the darkness. Love shouldn't be treated like it's something shameful. It should be embraced and put on a pedestal for the world to see."

A single tear rolls down my cheek, but I dash it away, sucking in a breath as I step toward him. He needs to see how much I mean my next words because once I say them, I won't say them again. Not to him. Not for anyone.

Perhaps it's selfish of me, but I can't help dusting my lips over his one last time. I pull back. I need to get this off my chest. Searching his face, I say, "I love you, Noah. You'll always be the greatest love of my life, but this has to be goodbye. We can call this a blip, a mistake, a glitch, whatever you want. Just know that I won't tell Jack, and your secret is safe with me."

Noah reels back as if I've hit him. Turning away from me, he runs his fingers through his hair, tugging on the strands. When he turns back to me, his voice is tortured as he demands, "Say it again."

My brows tug together, confused at why he'd want me to relive my heartbreak again. Lifting my chin, I look him in the eyes as I whisper, "This is goodbye, Noah."

He exhales a huff of a laugh as he smiles at me. "Angel, don't fucking test me. Say. It. Again."

"I'm not in the mood for your games. This is hard enough as it is."

"Angel." It's a warning but I don't understand what for. He isn't a vindictive person, so why would he— Everything clicks into place and hope crashes into me.

"Ah, there she goes. You got it, angel. Now, say it again."

"I love you."

A smile stretches across Noah's face as he softly says, "Angel, I'm all in. I have been for such a long time. My tattoo?"

I nod, wondering where he's going but eager to hear him out.

"It's *your* tattoo."

My breath hitches at his words. Of course, I had some idea, but I didn't want to allow myself to believe it was true.

Noah continues, "It's a constant reminder of the day you saved my fucking life. The day I knew I loved you. I tried so hard to fight us, to move on and find someone else to fill your shoes. But it always came back to *you* being the one.

"I'm sorry I was distant, I just didn't want Jack to find out about us the wrong way. We'll make it work, I promise you that, angel. I'll get on the first flight to England tomorrow and tell Jack everything. I don't care that I might lose his friendship because I'll have you."

My eyes widen at his admission. I shouldn't have insisted that we wait until after the wedding to talk through everything. *Is he really all in? Has all of this anguish and pain been for nothing? More importantly, what if he changes his mind when he's in front of Jack?* Wrapping my arms around my waist, I try to contain the rising tide of elation, love and hope. I don't want him to hurt me again. I can't let him.

"This," Noah calls, drawing my focus back to him as he holds his arms wide. "Is me begging you to stay, Van. Telling you that I choose you because you choose me. Christ, Savannah, you're all I've ever wanted and now that I have you, I don't want to lose you. I can't."

I don't hold back. I run toward him, jumping into his arms as I rain kisses on his face, murmuring, 'I love you' over and over again. Noah snakes his arms around my body, squeezing me close to him. Burying my face in his neck, I breathe in his musky scent. My heart is full and happy.

"What the hell is going on?" Jack demands.

I slide down Noah's body, my cheeks heated at having been caught by my brother, of all people. *What is he even doing here? Did Noah leave the door open?* My mind tries to put the pieces together but it's no use.

Noah maneuvers me behind him, out of Jack's sight. I know it's a protective gesture, he's not hiding me.

"I can explain, Jack."

Peeking around Noah, I wave my fingers at him. "Hey, Jack."

"Hi, Sav."

He doesn't look as mad as I thought he would. I step to the side, sliding my hand down Noah's arm as I take hold of his hand, offering my support. He may have just told me he *wanted* to come clean to Jack, but it's a bit different when he's had no time to prepare for this moment.

"I'm sorry, but I'm also not. It was never my intention for you to find out like this, but Savannah and I have been seeing each other for a while now and, man, I love her."

He loves me.

My eyes widen and I look down at the floor, hiding my face with my hair as a grin breaks out across my lips.

"How could you do this to Sutton? I thought you were a better man than this, Noah. Sav." At the sound of my name, I lift my head. Jack's brows are pulled tight as he points between Noah and I. "I think this is a mistake."

Frustration laces Noah's words when he replies, "If you'd wanted to talk about anything other than business the past eight months, you would know that Sutton and I broke up more than six months ago, Jack. The fact you think I'd do that to Savannah or Sutton..." His words trail off as he looks away. Clearing his throat, Noah stands tall, continuing, "I really am sorry for breaking the promise I made to you, Jack. But we were inevitable. I can't stay away from her anymore than—"

Jack cuts Noah off, his brow furrowed as he asks, "You and Sutton broke up?"

Exasperated, Noah replies, "Yes."

Jack nods, processing what he's said. Scratching at his chin, he tilts his head, confusion lacing his words as he asks, "What promise?"

"You told me to stay away from Savannah, that I

wasn't allowed to hurt her. I promised that you didn't have to worry about that with me. I should never have promised that to you."

Taking a step forward, Jack moves further into the living room and I watch as he recalls the conversation from thirteen years ago. "No. I made you promise to look out for her and make sure she doesn't get hurt. *By you.* Man, I thought you liked her and were going to ask her out." Jack laughs, but it dies down as he looks between me and Noah.

Pain laces Noah's words as he says, "You told me, on many occasions, that she was off limits, Jack. You warned me away."

Jack's brows tug together, concern pinching his features. "I was giving you shit, Noah. Teasing you about your feelings for her. Jesus, your crush was plain as day."

Noah takes a step back, as if he can't quite believe it. He collapses onto the couch, his face pale as he squeezes his eyes shut.

We've wasted so much time.

Jack grimaces as he says, "I'm going to leave you two to do whatever it is you need to do. I just wanted to come over and say I was back in town. Maybe we can all go to dinner next week."

Distractedly, I nod waving Jack off as he leaves. His words play through my mind over and over again like a recording. Today has been a lot.

"Are you okay?" I ask, taking a seat next to Noah.

He tugs me onto his lap, burying his nose in my neck

as I straddle him. His voice is barely audible when he mutters, "Yes. Never fucking better, angel."

I pull back, cupping his face. A smile pulls at my lips as I echo his earlier command, "Say it again."

He doesn't tease me. He knows what I need to hear. A seriousness taking over his face as he tucks a strand of hair behind my ear. "I love you, angel. Always have and always will."

I let his words sink in, luxuriating in his declaration.

He's mine.

My hand swats at his chest and he covers the spot I hit. "What was that for?"

Folding my arms over my chest, I pout. "You told my brother you loved me before you even said it to me. And I told you a whole bun—"

I squeal, as Noah flips me onto my back, his body hovering over me on the couch. I'm momentarily distracted by the veins that pop in his forearms as he holds himself up.

He bucks into me, bringing my attention to his face. My moans come freely as I grip his hips, begging for more. There's no denying the heat in his gaze, or the hardness pressing between my legs.

"Noah," I plead.

His voice is thick with lust as he promises. "I'll spend the rest of my life making these lost years up to you, angel. Any way you like. You own me. You have for a very long time."

My hands roam over his shoulders and under his

tuxedo jacket, pushing it off. Noah lifts up, pulling it all the way off and chucking it onto the floor before he claims my mouth. The kiss is searing and demanding. My mouth opens, welcoming his tongue inside.

When I can't take anymore, I break the kiss, throwing my head back as we grind together. He takes the opportunity to suck on the sensitive skin on my neck.

His teeth graze my earlobe and he whispers, "I'm not going to make love to you on the couch, angel."

He pulls away, resting his forehead on mine as our panting breaths mingle in the space between our mouths. I feel electrified. Tingles cover me from head to toe as my need for him builds with each passing second.

Standing from the couch, Noah towers over me. Biting down on my bottom lip, I barely contain my moans as my eyes land on the bulge in his pants. Squeezing my legs together, I try to ease the ache there.

Pulling me from the couch, he turns me in the direction of the bedroom, smacking my ass he demands, "Bedroom. Now, angel."

I feel sexy and courageous as I throw teasing looks at him over my shoulder while I undress. It's an effort to walk, my body on fire under his heated gaze.

When I reach the bedroom, I'm naked and aching for him. Noah's arms wrap around me from behind and I tilt my head to the side to give him better access to my neck as he licks and nips at me. His warm, naked body presses into me. Somewhere along the way he must have lost his clothes too. I can't help but be a little disappointed that I didn't get to see him stripping for me.

I guess I've got the rest of my life to see that.

Noah's hand moves up my body until his palm is holding my right breast. He rolls the nipple between his thumb and forefinger, the bud tight and almost painful. His voice is gruff as he demands, "Bed."

I don't need to be told three times. Moving toward the bed, I crawl into the middle, aware of Noah's eyes on me as I do. Laying on my back, I wait for him, watching as he stalks toward me. The muscles of his body thick and powerful. And all mine.

Grabbing onto my ankles, he pulls me to the edge, lifting my legs to rest on his chest. His hands smooth up and down them as he looks down at me.

The first swipe of his finger through my folds has my back arching. He dips the tip of his finger inside, twisting it before he pulls out.

"Noah, please don't tease me. Not right now."

His voice is dark and dangerous when he asks, "Do you need me, angel?"

How can he not tell? I can practically feel the liquid dripping out of me. "Yes"

With two fingers, he enters me, stretching my core as he mutters, "I think telling you I loved you might have got you ready for me already, angel."

My body contracts around him, confirming his assessment and earning me a dark, sinful chuckle.

Desire laces his words as he says, "I need you now,

Van. I'm going to spend the rest of my life taking you however you want, but not now. Get into the middle of the bed."

Not one to deny him anything, I crawl up the bed, laying on my back as he climbs over me. He dusts kisses over my sensitive skin until he captures my lips. Settling between my legs, he wastes no time in lifting one and hooking it over his hip.

When he slides in, my body stretches around him, welcoming him *home*. We rock together, maintaining eye contact. It's far more intimate than anything I've ever experienced before. More intimate than that night a month ago in Albany, when I ran, scared that he'd come to break my heart.

I nearly told him then that I loved him, but I wasn't ready to let him go.

His voice is breathless as he murmurs to me, "Angel, where have you gone?"

I don't want to talk, we have plenty of time for that. Right now I want to welcome in everything that he makes me feel. I want to enjoy all that he is as he collides with me and we erupt into a beautiful kaleidoscope of colors.

Reaching up, I capture his lips with mine. Moans of pleasure falling from my lips as I chant, "I love you."

Adoration shines bright in his eyes, his words coming out choked as we near our completion. "I love you too, angel. Forever and always."

This is the start of our forever, with nothing coming between us but our love for each other.

ONE YEAR LATER

Savannah

Applause erupts as the curtain falls and I can't hold back the smile that makes its way onto my lips.

I did it.

Not only did I make it through the performance without messing up, but I've achieved my dream. I stay on the stage, lining up with my co-stars as we prepare to bow to the audience. When the curtain rises again, I search the audience for Noah.

Instantly, I find him. He's sitting in the front row with Jack, Mama, Alex, Sebastian, Meghan, Cooper, Ben and Sutton. My nearest and dearest.

Who would have thought when I made my Broadway debut that I'd be supported by so many people that have come to mean so much to me? I certainly didn't.

Noah winks at me, and even over the sound of the collective audience, I can hear him loud and clear as he claps and hollers for me.

I love this man.

Ever since that night a year ago where all the pain and love of the past thirteen years came to a grand finale, our love has thrived and grown stronger each day. Noah's been the most supportive boyfriend a girl could ask for. For that reason, along with my hard work, I credit his unwavering support for being the reason I'm standing on this stage today.

With one final bow, the curtain descends. But not before my gaze seeks him out one last time and I nod toward the door that leads to the backstage. His feet are in motion before I can take even one step. The laughter that falls from my lips is carefree and filled with a goofy love for my man.

He bursts through the door, his eyes crazed as he seeks me out. I'm two steps above him when he wraps an arm around my waist and tugs me toward him. Thankfully my co-stars left the stage on the opposite side. My hands land on his shoulders as I try to balance myself. I cling to him, unfazed by the crew moving about around us.

His words are rushed and filled with excitement. "Angel, you were amazing. The best show I've ever seen. God, I love you."

Chuckling, I cup his face and brush my lips over his. "Hi. I love you too."

I thought I was supposed to be the one high off the adrenaline. Tonight has been amazing but there's one thing that's going to top it. I just have to be a little more patient and get through the cast party.

I slide down his body and Noah hands me a bouquet of Marguerite daisies. I remember the day he first brought me flowers since we became an official couple. He'd stopped on the way home at a flower stall after he'd spotted my favorite ones from the car.

Sheepishly, much like now, he'd thrust them at me and shrugged as he asked me if they were still my favorite. Given the fact that nobody had bought me flowers in a long time, I threw myself at him. Ripping his clothes from his body as I said thank you, repeatedly. Since that day, he's bought me flowers every week and I've thanked him in my own unique way each time.

He smooths a strand of my hair back. "You can thank me later, angel."

I press my chest to his, wrapping my arms around his neck. His hand skates down my back and he grabs a handful of my ass.

My words come out husky and charged with my need for him as I reply, "Oh, I plan to."

A throat clears behind Noah and we turn to find Jack standing on the threshold looking less than impressed. "Do you think you could maybe not do this right now? Some of us would like to get to the party."

Biting my lip to keep my grin at bay, I say as sweetly

as I can, "Of course. I'll go get changed and then we can head out."

Jack nods, closing the door behind him. An inherent need to see my brother happy has me asking, "How have Sutton and him been?"

I told Noah about the conversation I had all those months ago with Sutton. He wasn't mad or jealous, and although it wasn't my intention, it solidified his love for me even more.

I'm under strict instructions to not meddle, and let Sutton and Jack find their own way to each other. But clearly my man doesn't know me as well as he thinks he does. I already have five ideas on how I can get them on a date. He did make a good point about that possibly being the reason that Jack left town.

Noah shrugs, pulling me into his side as we walk to my dressing room. "About as well as you would expect. She's ignoring him, while he looks at her like she's a balloon he accidentally released into the sky."

I'm sure they'll figure it out. *With a little help*.

"Don't even think about it, angel."

I hate that he can read me so well. But I also love it so much.

There's been one thing he hasn't been able to get a read on though. Or maybe he has, and he just doesn't want to ruin my surprise.

When it's just us at home, I'm going to take the ring I have stuffed in the spare room closet and ask him to marry me.

Noah

I've wrestled with this decision for weeks, not wanting to take the shine away from her special day. It's why I'm still going to wait. Even as the ring box burns a hole in my suit jacket pocket.

She was captivating to watch up on that stage. And I want her to bask in the praise and attention from everyone for that. For what she's achieved with her hard work and skill. Not because I put a ring on her finger. It's the least that she deserves.

I can wait.

Maybe if I repeat it to myself over and over again it'll be true.

The fact of the matter is that I want to make her my wife. I want to fill her with my babies. I want to give her everything her heart has ever desired. But most of all, I want her to know that she has my heart and my soul *forever*. She always has, and I was a fool to think that I'd ever be able to keep it from her.

I waited in her dressing room as she got changed, the flowers arriving thick and fast. The only ones she kept going back to were mine. I don't think she even realized she was doing it. It would be a sniff here or a feel of a petal there, but she gravitated towards them as she moved about the room. It was a beautiful sight to see, making my heart burst with love for her.

After mingling with the cast and crew for a couple of hours, we came home to eat some 'proper food', as Savannah called it. We celebrated her and the success we all know will come for her. I'm in awe at how lucky I am. To think I nearly lost her, that she was ready to say goodbye to me because I thought I'd promised something I never did.

We've been home for an hour now. Savannah ran off to the spare bedroom twenty minutes ago, and although I'm pretending to read a book on business strategy, my mind is wandering.

The ring box sits in the drawer of my bedside table, just in case the mood strikes me in the middle of the night. It's not beyond the realms of possibility, especially as on many occasions, I've been tempted to slip it onto her finger to see if she notices when she wakes.

Savannah clears her throat, standing on the threshold as she leans against the doorjamb with her hands hidden behind her back. She's naked and I don't have to be asked twice to give her my undivided attention. I throw the book on the bedside table, the dull thud of it hitting the carpet the only thing telling me I missed.

"Come here," I command, my cock stirring to life under the covers.

She shakes her head. "If I asked you to do something for me, no questions asked, would you?"

The question is the same one I asked her nearly a year and a half ago.

My response is immediate, because I'd do anything for her, even if it meant breaking the law or giving up my own life. "Of course."

Nodding, she continues, her voice trembling as she says, "Okay, just remember, you can't say no."

With a smirk on my lips and my cock fighting against the confines of my boxers, I reply, "Okay."

As if I would ever say no to her.

She pulls her hands from behind her back and takes a step forward. I don't know where to look. My eyes roam over the glory that is all her. That is until they rest on a familiar looking box.

"Angel," I warn.

Her voice is soft and tentative. "You can't say no."

"Fuck, I'm not going to. Never to you, but—" I reach over and pull out my own box from the bedside table.

Her jaw drops and her eyes go glassy as they flick between me and the box in my hand.

"I won't take this away from you, angel. I just need you to know that my question is the same."

She doesn't say a word, instead she sprints toward me, falling into my arms. Kisses rain down on my face as she chants 'yes'.

My chest vibrates with a barely contained chuckle as I say, "I didn't even ask you."

She pulls away, her gaze searching mine. "But you were going to?"

"Fuck yes. Just not tonight. I wanted it to be about the show and your success."

Tilting her head, she replies, "I wanted it to be about us. Will you marry me, Noah?"

I smooth the hair from her face, running my thumb over her lips as I nod. "Yes. Always, yes. Will you marry me?"

She takes the platinum ring from her box and slips it onto my finger. Lifting her head, she murmurs, "Yes. A thousand times, yes."

Opening the ring box, I reveal the *Harry Winston* three carat cushion-cut sapphire ring with long, tapered diamonds on either side. Her gasp tells me she approves. I slip it onto her finger, kissing the back of her hand as I look at the ring that looks so natural on her delicate finger.

She is mine, and I am hers.

Everything we have been through has led us right where we need to be. I can't wait to take on whatever the future holds for us.

The End.

Want to find out what happens with Jack and Sutton? Sign up to my newsletter here (subscribepage.io/4kdNEJ) to get the ebook of their story for FREE.

Afterword

Thank you so much for reading Savannah & Noah's story. If you loved it, be sure to leave a review.

Be sure to sign up to my newsletter here (subscribepage.io/4kdNEJ) and get monthly updates on my books, enter giveaways and hear about some other awesome authors.

You can find the rest of the books in the Breaking the Rules series here.

Acknowledgments

A huge thank you, first and foremost, to Allie Bliss, my editor who has been with me since book one and who I hope will be with me through to the end of my author journey. I love working with you and that you pull me up on everything I need to be pulled up on.

Thank you to Sarah from Word Emporium for your thorough work with proofreading Don't Make Promises. I can't wait to work with you again.

Thank you to Jasmine, my PA, you've come in and really supported me with everything. You're a star and this is just the beginning of our journey! Sorry for being such a pain!!!

My beta readers also deserve a mention for all of the fantastic feedback and hyping that they have given me since I sent them over Savannah and Noah's story. I hope they stick around for what's to come.

Everything happens for a reason. That is why TL Swan and her Cygnets gets a special shoutout. Without the amazing writers in the group, I wouldn't be putting out my third book in less than a year. In fact, I probably wouldn't have put out my first. Thank you, Tee, for all of the guidance and being there to support us all on this amazing journey.

As always a special shoutout to my street team, thank you all for taking a chance with me and shouting about my books! Every single one of you means so much to me and I hope that you stick around for rest of this crazy ride.

Finally, a massive thank you to my boyfriend Ryan and our doggo Mia. For not minding that I've been very anti-social in hiding away in the office to get this book finished. And for putting up with my stressed self.

About the Author

KA James is an author of contemporary romance. She lives near London, UK with her partner and their Bichon Frisé, called Mia. Before starting her author journey, KA was an avid reader of romance books and truly believes the spicier the book, the better.

Outside of writing, KA has worked in HR for eleven years but has truly found her passion with writing and getting lost in a world that plays out like a movie in her mind. After all, getting lost in the land of make believe, where it's much spicier is way more fun.

 KA is always in the process of writing the next book, but hopes that you enjoyed reading her third book and following Savannah and Noah's story. Be sure to follow along on one or more social media channels to be kept in the loop.

Printed in Great Britain
by Amazon